8 LIVES OF A
CENTURY-OLD
TRICKSTER

8 LIVES OF A CENTURY-OLD TRICKSTER

MIRINAE LEE

virago

VIRAGO

First published in Great Britain in 2023 by Virago

1 3 5 7 9 10 8 6 4 2

A CIP catalogue record for this book
is available from the British Library.

Hardback ISBN 978-0-349-01674-0
Trade paperback ISBN 978-0-349-01675-7

Typeset in Sabon by M Rules
Printed and bound in Great Britain by
Clays Ltd, Elcograf S.p.A.

Papers used by Virago are from well-managed forests
and other responsible sources.

Virago
An imprint of
Little, Brown Book Group
Carmelite House
50 Victoria Embankment
London EC4Y 0DZ

An Hachette UK Company
www.hachette.co.uk

www.virago.co.uk

To my husband,
my muse, and the greatest hero in my book

Contents

Prologue

The idea came to me while I was going through my divorce.

I was forty-seven and overweight. I had no child who would occupy my lone, silent days. I wasn't one of those independent modern women who decided not to have babies early on. I wanted to have one but my husband couldn't – due to his oligospermia, he told me. I wanted to try IVF treatment but he refused, saying the whole process felt too *demeaning* to him. I was furious later when I learned that he had already signed up to a famous fertility clinic in Gangnam with that new girl, twelve years his junior, a month before our divorce was finalized. For weeks I had the occasional dream of hammering him to death. In reality, of course, I possessed neither the courage nor the penchant for violence to do it. Yet I did imagine myself bursting into his office in Gwanghwamun, like an angry *ajumma* in Korean Morning Drama might do to attack her cheating husband, hands busy filling the air with leaflets that detail his treacherous deeds, all the while shouting the list of his sins in front of his coworkers, who would ostracize him for what he'd done. Of course I never executed this fantasy: submitting to such a hysterical course of action would be too *demeaning* to my dignity. Entertaining the thought of it, though, was quite thrilling.

I was desperately seeking a change in my life. I signed up for a gym and worked out for an hour three days a week. Although I began to lose weight and feel healthier, the physical change alone wasn't enough for me. Ever since I was little I've been a pensive being, fond of reading and thinking and scribbling things down in my Moleskine. I needed more than just a fitter body. I needed a change that would engage my mind as well.

I was waiting for an appointment with my therapist and flipping through a women's magazine when I saw the article. It was the story of a hospice doctor in Singapore, who helped his dying patients organize their funerals and write their obituaries before their death. Contrary to common belief, the doctor explained, many of his terminally ill patients weren't that afraid of death: they were more concerned about the aftermath, the posthumous grief and turmoil that their loved ones were to endure. His new program was met with a surprising degree of enthusiasm. Lots of patients reported they felt mentally and physically better after they had participated in the arrangements for their passing. It gave them a sense of control and reassurance, and an invaluable opportunity to derive their own meaning from their short journeys on earth.

I showed this article to Director Haam, my boss, and told her I wanted to launch a similar program for our patients. I couldn't really complain about my job at the Golden Sunset: the salary was pretty decent, the company guaranteed plenty of paid holidays, and my schedule and tasks were never taxing. What I mostly did was a mild version of accounting, but my official title was personal assistant to the director. Director Haam was a nice woman in her early fifties, a double-divorcee raising her three kids with two different family names. She didn't seem to possess much passion for her job at the Golden Sunset; she told me she'd chosen it mainly for its stability, which she needed badly as a single mother of three children.

Director Haam tapped her desk nervously with her blood-red nails before she declared the Golden Sunset had no funding for custom-made funeral preparations. I told her the obituary-writing program alone would be sufficient to make a change. Though reluctant, she gave me permission to start it after I promised her that it wouldn't affect my performance of my primary duties, and that I would work extra hours if necessary. Before leaving the office, she threw me a worried look, as if she were thinking, *I've been there, too.* But instead she said: "Give me a call if you need a drinking buddy from time to time." As I listened to the clicks of her heels fade away, I wondered if divorce would be any easier the second time around.

The obituary-writing program first helped me on a practical level. It diverted my attention from divorce. My thoughts, which until now had raced back to my husband and our fallen marriage again and again like a faithful dog, began to dwell on the lives of others.

"I'm here to help you write your obituary," I told the elderly, in the most calming voice I could muster. "You can tell me a brief version of your life story, things that have made you happy, things that you're proud of, and things you regret. How you want to be remembered by others, those who love you and care about you." After taking a few deep breaths, most people began to open up quite naturally. Awareness of your limited time can bring a surprising degree of honesty to your speech, by shutting off the inconsequential background noises that would normally obfuscate your life. To the small number of people who had difficulty starting their stories, I offered a simple prompt that always worked: "Pick three words – noun, adjective, verb, anything – that could define you or best describe your life." Three is the magical number that people tend to fall for. A single word seems impossibly limiting, while two may feel unpalatable, as if they imply a double life. But three suggests a perfect balance, as in triumvirate and trilogy and trinity. People feel comfortable with it – neither too little nor too much.

Looking ahead to the end of their lives, people feel the urge to leave their footprints on this world, no matter how small they may be. And writing their obituaries confirms that their lives mattered – to them, and to the people for whom they had happily sacrificed their dreams. In the minds of youth, an obituary is a sad and solemn thing, but old folks understand that it means, among other things, a privilege. Old folks, who are used to flipping through the pages of a newspaper, know that an official obituary is reserved for the deaths of household names. Even the famous ones must fight constantly for ever-so-cramped space; most should be content with just a couple of lines, while a very lucky few get an entire paragraph. A whole page is, of course, impossible, unless you're a high-profile politician, such as an ex-president, or an internationally influential warlord. At the Golden Sunset, however, every death merits an entire page. That was the central idea of my project: Don't we all deserve a full obituary of our lives? I wanted to believe that every death and life, even the most obscure and inconvenient ones, have important stories to tell. And I was there to lend my ears and pen to the final whistles of the tumbleweeds.

It was the second day of the Lunar New Year holiday when I met Ms Mook for the first time. I had volunteered to work since I wasn't ready to face my first big family gathering after the divorce. I knew the kinds of questions I would get from my uncles and aunts, and especially my cousins, all of whom were still happily married with kids. I wasn't ready for others to pick at my scabs yet.

A public nursing home might be the loneliest place on earth on a big national holiday. More than a third of the residents at Golden Sunset had no immediate families. A small number of fortunate people, those still in decent health and in touch with caring relatives, were invited out for a day or two. After the lucky few left the facility, a harrowing silence took over. The kind of quiet that put even the jumpiest dementia patients into a coma-like gloom.

That evening, in the lonely silence of my office, I received a call from the head caretaker of Section A. It houses nearly half of the senior citizens of Golden Sunset who have been diagnosed with Alzheimer's disease. Normally I didn't have much business with that half of the facility because only the mentally competent and coherent can participate in the obituary-writing process. That day, however, many staff members were on leave so I was to help with whatever task was at hand.

I was asked to stand guard in front of a double room. Grandma Song Jae-soon had disappeared again, the head caretaker told me. My job was to wait and notify the other staff immediately if the runaway returned to her room while they searched every nook and cranny of Golden Sunset for her. I wedged the door open with the small folding chair I'd brought from my office and sat down on it. Walkie-talkie in hand, I looked up and down the corridor, hoping for a sign of Grandma Song Jae-soon.

Then I saw a figure standing inside the room, her back leaning against the wall. A slender woman, covered with white from head to toe. I let out a muffled cry. "Don't worry, I'm not a ghost," murmured the figure, and laughed off-key. "You saw me earlier, remember?"

Her name was Mook Miran and she was a roommate of Grandma Song. I had indeed seen her when I visited her room. She'd been in her bed, slowly coming around from her late nap. I didn't recognize her: she was quite tall standing up, but lying down she was indistinguishable from other silent and small-framed elderly bodies. "You're the *obituary woman*, aren't you?" She grinned, and color rushed to her face.

Mook Miran was a strange-looking woman with an equally strange name – it was my first time meeting a Korean with the last name *Mook*. She had big frizzy hair, which was entirely and evenly white, and it hung around her head like a halo. Her limbs were long and thin like a snow crab's. Under the fluorescent light I felt I could read her body like a map. Veins showed through her translucent skin, like crisscrossed mountain paths, mostly mauve and pale blue. The bleaching light also drew a pair of butterfly-like shadows under her high cheekbones.

"Yes, I'm the obituary woman," I answered, still in awe of her.

"I've seen you out there in the cosmos garden, talking with the old ones," said Ms Mook.

She called the other patients *the old ones*, as though she was different. And yet with her sharp eyes, and her memory of me, I wondered what she was doing in Section A.

"You should write my obituary," she said, revealing a chipped front tooth.

I hid my bewilderment and told her we could have our talk right now if she didn't mind, while we waited for the return of her roommate. I was surprised by the clarity of her mind, but I was still wary of her: I assumed that if the administration had decided to put her in the section for patients with Alzheimer's, they must have had a good reason for it.

"Do you remember why you're here in Section A?" I started,

a little ruthless because I wanted to know if this was going to be worth my while. I didn't want to come back to her the next week and be greeted with a flummoxed face shouting, *Who the hell are you?*

Ms Mook said she had been in the regular section at first but they'd moved her here about six months ago, for a reason she never fully understood. "I would say my mind works normally, but it's up to them to decide, isn't it?" she whispered. Her cheeks twitched.

Still suspicious, I asked her the big first question. "Which three words would you choose to sum up your life?"

She walked back to her bed and sat down on it. Then she turned her head slowly toward a wall and stared at it. Her face was blank – as flat and pale as the whitewashed wall behind her. Mouth slack, eyes ashen. She's blacking out, I thought, anticipating the inevitable: soon she would bring her gaze back to me and ask me who I was, what I was doing there.

Instead I heard a snort. "You genuinely believe a person can sum up her life in just three words?" she murmured, eyes still fixed on the wall.

Her question caught me off guard but I feigned calm. After a moment of silence, I asked her how many words she would prefer.

"What would *your* three words be? Have you thought about that?"

Again she asked *her* question, ignoring mine.

I felt strangely tense. I felt as though Grandma Mook and I were suddenly engaging in a war of questions, and the one who answered first would be the loser. I summoned a wan smile, the gentle curving of eyes and lips with no teeth showing, the kind I usually wore to disarm incredulous grandpas. I was doing this partly because I couldn't answer her last question. I had no idea what my three words would be. I'd never given it a thought, although I asked it of others all the time. And no one had asked me before.

"Ms Mook, do you want me to talk to the administration for you?" I asked her, holding on to my work smile, like a shield. I told her I could talk to the staff about her accommodation if she thought she was in the wrong place. I said all the elderly residents I had helped with their obituaries were in the regular section. I knew this wasn't a question she could easily ignore.

"That's not necessary," she said casually, defying my assumption again. "I'm fine here in Section A. And there's not much difference in the end, is there? In neither section are we allowed to walk out of the facility alone. Besides, although people in Section A get one hour less for the daily garden stroll, each room here has fewer people and thus more space. Before, in the regular section, I shared a room with three other old women. Here, only one. So, more privacy."

"But don't you find it difficult to room with Grandma Song?"

I'd heard this wasn't the first time Ms Song Jae-soon had pulled off a stunt like this. The head caretaker told me her condition was getting worse rapidly – she had, on occasion, smeared feces on the wall.

I heard another snort – a gentler one this time.

"I volunteered to room with her," said Ms Mook. Another answer I wasn't expecting to hear.

"Why?"

"If you have some context from a person's life, you can handle her better. Even if that person happens to be an Alzheimer's patient." She turned her head toward me to look me in the eye. "Did you know that both of Song's parents were killed during the Japanese occupation?" she asked me.

I shook my head, wondering where this was leading. I clenched my jaw, the way I did unconsciously when I felt impatient.

Ms Mook said Grandma Song's family had been rich landowners for generations. But overnight the Japanese had taken almost everything they owned – under a false pretext, for sure. "Such things happened all the time back then," she added flatly. "Luckily her parents were warned by one of their neighbors, just a minute before the Japanese police burst in and ransacked the place. They didn't have time to hide big objects, just small things."

Ms Mook looked up at me, as if expecting me to take over and finish her statement. Clueless, I stared back at her.

"Grandma Song, with her little sisters, had to swallow as many jewels and rings as possible, as fast as they could. The police took all the valuables they could find and killed the parents on the spot, in front of the children. But Song had to move on, you know. No time to weep. She was the head of the family now. She had to spend the next few days rummaging through her own excrement as well as her little siblings' to find the jewels. Their whole fortune now."

Ms Mook sounded different. Her speech was now slow and halting. Her face was flushed, and a purple vein jumped in her thin neck.

She said Song Jae-soon at Golden Sunset, with Alzheimer's playing her time backward, seemed stuck in this period of her childhood – the death of her parents and trying to support her little sisters. Ms Mook once noticed, when she saw Song engaging in fecal smearing again, that she mumbled names such as Jade, Pearl, and Ruby. The nursing assistants thought those were the nicknames of Song's younger sisters. Ms Mook knew they were wrong.

"She wasn't simply toying with her stool the way others with dementia do. She was going through her excrement to find the jewels. In her mind, in her receding memory, Grandma Song is again the thirteen-year-old girl struggling to survive."

Ms Mook stood up and walked to the wooden dresser in the back of the room. She squatted and opened carefully the silicon child-safety lock on the bottom drawer. Then she took out a round rusty Fruity Drops can. She put it into my hand and gestured for me to open it.

Inside lay a dozen glitzy pieces of plastic jewelry.

"Those are toys for little kids. Too big to swallow," said Ms Mook, picking up the heaviest piece that was shaped like an oval diamond. It shone gaudy pink, the image of Sailor Moon embossed on it. It was as big as an eyeball. "I put these in Grandma Song's hands when I see her getting ready to examine her number two. I tell her we've already found the jewels. Then she's happy, and stops immediately what she's doing. No need to use force then. No needles and no drama."

Speechless, I stared at the Sailor Moon on the jewel.

Then my eyes roamed toward the dresser behind Ms Mook, and found a stack of paper in the bottom drawer, still wide open. Next to it I saw a little mound of colorful bric-a-brac, which I couldn't make out clearly from a distance. "What are those in the drawer?" I asked her.

For the first time Ms Mook seemed a little nervous. She walked quickly back to the drawer and closed it. "Nothing that's forbidden," she answered calmly, but a gleam of worry lingered in her eyes.

When I was about to repeat my question, the walkie-talkie on my lap brayed.

"Security has found Grandma Song," the head caretaker yapped, through electric crackles, "She's fallen asleep in the cleaning-supplies room, would you believe?"

From far away I heard hurried footsteps approaching, probably carrying Ms Song back to her room.

I looked at Ms Mook. "Can I see you again?" I asked her.

*

I liked being in the cosmos garden even when all the flowers were gone. I loved being outdoors under the sun, away from the smell of Clorox and dried urine, which permeated every corner of the residents' rooms and the corridors in the nursing home. Besides, the sun has a magical power: sometimes the despair gaping at my feet by night appeared too puny to bother me in the light of day.

Ms Mook, too, seemed different under the sun. It was a dry, windless afternoon. The sun was an ebullient eye in the middle of the acid-blue sky. Ms Mook appeared in a wheelchair, pushed by Ms Docgo, the oldest nursing assistant in Section A. "You have one hour and a half before Grandma Mook's bath time," said Ms Docgo, bluntly, eyeing me and Ms Mook with muted hostility. She walked back to her building.

The sun was so piercing it made my eyes water. Ms Mook narrowed her eyes, made an arching sunshade of her hand and put it on her forehead. Squinting, her eyes covered with a rheumy film, she seemed as helpless and worn-out as most of the patients in Section A. Her hair and her bleached gown looked even whiter under the sun than under fluorescent light. Motionless, she was a plaster cast shaped like a human.

As soon as she opened her mouth and talked, however, she was a full presence.

"You can't wait to write about me, can you?" she said, and lifted one corner of her mouth a little. Strangely, I saw a little boy in her old woman's face.

"I couldn't wait to hear what you have to say. I haven't even thought about writing yet." This was the plain truth.

Ms Mook seemed to be relishing the silence before she unspooled her story. These seconds seemed to suck all the air around her into her meager body. And as I listened to her talk, I wondered what exactly it was that lured me toward her words. It wasn't obvious. Her talk was mostly slow and her voice always low. Still, she was the kind of person people naturally paid attention to, whose talk they rarely interrupted. The very antithesis of me. I wasn't born with such charisma. I was *a person who's easily won over by others*, according to my husband. Too easily impressed, and fooled.

And fooled was how I felt as our conversation progressed. Though fascinating, the introduction of her story was filled with elements far larger than life. When asked about her age, she said she would be "one hundred the day after tomorrow." And yet she couldn't have been that old. She looked at most eighty-seven. I'd seen my fair share of ancient people nearly a century old in Golden Sunset but none had ever sounded as acerbic or cheeky as she did.

I wasn't sure what role I was supposed to play. Should I be angry at being taken for a fool who would believe such nonsense? Should I be level-headed, like an investigative journalist, trying to uncover logic in an illogical situation? Or should I be an eager spectator at this theater of the absurd? Reluctantly I opted for the latter and kept listening, fighting my urge to interrogate her for facts.

She said she had had three nationalities in her life.

"I was born Japanese, lived as North Korean, and now am dying as South Korean."

Her generation was born under Japanese colonial rule so technically she was born Japanese. But I couldn't grasp *lived as North Korean*. I asked her if she had escaped to the South during the Korean War, and she told me she'd earned South Korean citizenship only after her hair had turned gray. "I spent my youth in Pyongyang," she added casually, as though Pyongyang was a normal part of the world anyone could visit whenever they liked.

Half of me cocked an eyebrow in doubt, but the other half

nodded. The latter felt that this back story solved at least one mystery about Ms Mook: her accent. Though very faint, she had unique intonation that rose and fell in unexpected places, an accent that sounded blunt and sing-song at once. I wondered if it was a faded version of the Gangwon-do accent but I couldn't quite place it.

"Japanese. North Korean. South Korean," I repeated. "You already have your three key concepts for your obituary. Don't you think they represent your dramatic life pretty succinctly?" I forged a smile on my face.

"Why are you so obsessed with *three concepts*?" she asked, head tilted like a crow's. "Is there some sacred meaning behind it?"

I shrugged my shoulders awkwardly and said no. "I find it practical, that's all. One and two are too limiting, while, let's say, nine is too bulky and therefore a turn-off. Three is just the perfect number for everyone to fill."

Ms Mook turned abruptly to the side, like a pigeon bobbing its head away. *Ha.* It was a hybrid sound between laughter and a snort. She was now directly facing the honey-gold sunlight that was hitting the cosmos garden sideways. It made her squint again. "Eight, then," she said.

"What?"

"Eight. I will give you eight words. Our middle ground. You said nine is too many and I say three is too few. So eight. Take it as a sign that I respect your method, Ms Writer."

She looked at me and winked. A wink that looked more like a twitch of an eyelid muscle.

"So what are your eight words, Ms Mook?" I asked her, noticing the cheeky one-sided smile return to her face.

"Slave. Escape-artist. Murderer. Terrorist. Spy. Lover. And Mother."

I sat in silence. I saw her eyes light up like a Christmas

tree – she was elated that she'd floored me and was dying to hear my words.

"Those are seven words. Not eight," I told her.

"So you really listened," she said. Her cheeky smile grew wider.

She asked me which story I wanted to hear most and I said: "Murderer."

That made her laugh. It surprised her, she said. I didn't strike her as someone who would go straight to Murderer. She'd thought I would run first to either Lover or Mother.

I told her she'd gotten me wrong. "Who did you kill?" I asked her.

She clicked her tongue. "Not so fast," she said.

The 5th Life

Virgin Ghost on the
North Korean Border

1961

She wasn't a real ghost, of course. We weren't sure she was a virgin either. Yet we called her so because of her clothes: the light taupe *hanbok* made of thick, coarse hemp cloth, a dress worn only by funeral-mourners, or by virgin ghosts in folktales, the bewitching, ethereal beauties who met an untimely demise, and were thus forever tortured by the angst of having never possessed a husband. I enjoyed the chilling frou-frou her starchy hemp clothes made when she was cavorting like a mad puppy in the tall wild silver grass field by the Imjin River. She had an unruly thatch of hair, which was always adorned by a fresh flower of her choice. Since she made her appearance only in the fall, it was usually either a cosmos or a dandelion. On a rare occasion, she went for an overripe dandelion that had already turned into a prickly fluff of seeds. Thanks to the wind, her hair looked like somebody had vomited watery rice porridge all over it. But I loved that quirky side of her.

No one wanted to acknowledge it openly, but we all knew she was pretty. Boys were both scared of and charmed by her; they said she could see ghosts, even talk to them. I guess it was due to her slightly lazy eyes; the irises were unusually large, as if she had chewed a poppy for an hour. Her eerie gaze, often accompanied by a high-pitched, staccato laugh that made you wonder if she was choking, seemed to go right through you, as though she was gawking at some spooky creature lurking behind. So, every time we ran into her in the tall wild silver grass field by the Imjin River, our hearts started to race. There was, of course, so much mystery around her. Nobody knew her age; her overall uncanny look could put her anywhere between fifteen and thirty-five. Nobody knew her folks, where she'd come from.

But strange people drifting in and out of the region weren't uncommon at that time. The war had produced countless orphans, whose parents were either dead or stuck in the north when the country was split into two. My best friend Yong was an unlucky example. His older brother Wan was the only family he had, and was, to Yong, a larger-than-life figure of mother, father and God combined. Yong wasn't the type you would choose as a friend. He was the shortest, loudest boy in class, and his left ear often bled for no reason. My father referred to him as *that circus-runaway punk*. Yong always daubed his greasy, unkempt hair with his brother's brillian-tine made of lard, perhaps to mask the dirt, which resulted in a funky odor of sewer-met-slaughterhouse. I threw in my lot with him from the second grade, when he stood up for me against the five fifth-graders who had bullied me, calling me *a Commie's boy*, because I was born in the north. We were beaten up together till one tooth of his and one of mine loosened. I learned that Yong had been a northerner at birth as well, and although neither of us had any recollection of the other side of the border, this common inglorious past had united us, turning us into blood brothers.

Our small town, called Geumpari, was located in the upper region of the Imjin River. It was so close to the 38th parallel that on a clear, windless day you could even hear the North Korean radio propaganda –Yong and I had often tried to imitate its odd, simpering, histrionic accent. Yong told me that, near Panmunjoem, Imjin River had a secret *yeoulmok*, the neck of the rapids, that was shallow enough even for a kid to cross. After that, there was only a couple of soldiers, and then the DMZ, the demilitarized zone, explained Yong in excitement. He was always asking me to join the secret trip he would take to North Korea one day. I always said yes, knowing full well it was one of those things we planned yet would never carry out. At any rate, Imjin River was our mother lode: we'd swum away our summers there, appeasing our hunger with its muddy fish and frogs. In the fall, we snooped around the tall silver grass that covered the riverbank and sometimes came up to our chins, in the fingertip-tingling hope that we might catch a glimpse of Virgin Ghost there. My mother told me many times to stay away from the riverbank, warning me that the Yankees' old mines had occasionally turned up there after heavy rains, but that had never deterred me from frequenting the place. I was at the stage of life when a firm *no* invites a curious *yes*.

Yong liked pretending to know more about Virgin Ghost than anyone else. One day, flipping through his brother's dog-eared *Playboy* magazine, Yong abruptly said he knew where Virgin Ghost had come from.

'I heard the other day she's actually from the Red House in Moonsan, the one near the Yankee military base. She was sold there when she was very young, and she escaped a few years back. Ever since, she's been roaming around the country, pretending to be crazy and retarded, you know, so that she wouldn't get dragged back there.'

Yong made this claim with impassioned sincerity, and I nearly bought his version of the myth.

'*Fuck*, no! That bitch ain't from the Red House!' his own brother disagreed.

Wan said he'd already asked the old madam of the Red House, as its second most important customer after the Yankees. She told him that under her watch no girl had walked out of the Red House yet, unless she'd got lucky enough to marry an American soldier and move to the US with him. 'Which means *that* pussy's still fresh to eat!' said Wan, smacking his lips. He and Yong laughed the crooked laugh of a small-time villain in an American comic book, which made me, for the first time, despise my best friend.

No offense to Yong, but I'd always hated his older brother. I hated his weaselly face with its pointy chin and narrow, bashed-in nose, always reeking of *soju* and trouble. He was every parent's nightmare: a foul-mouthed, spine-bashing hoodlum, who idled away his days quaffing cheap rum, smoking pot, and befriending the ignoble Yankee princesses. Since I'd never seen him work during the day, I often wondered where he'd acquired all the money he squandered on alcohol and the Red House. But whenever I sounded Yong out on the subject, he closed his mouth.

Not long after, I learned the truth from my father.

It was a day of heavy rain. My father returned home late at night, exuding the sour scent of over-fermented *makgeolli* and vomit. Without a word, he dragged me out to the front yard, turned on the pale night-lamp under the eaves, and began to feed blunt blows to my ears, my collarbones, my sternum, my knees. My little sister, shaken from her sleep, was now hunkering down under the dim-lit eaves, anxiously clutching her cold bare feet, watching in silence. Both she and I knew what to do: we didn't scream, we didn't cry. *I told you, you little piece of shit, I'll break your fucking neck if I catch you one more time with that circus-runaway punk!* Father yelled. Our experiences had taught us to take it, our mouths and minds muted, till his anger fizzled out. It usually stopped when I looked like a washed-up boxer, at least two different parts of my body bleeding profusely.

My father worked at the US military base. They called him a disposal manager, as his mission was to take care of their garbage. It was everyone's dream job: you had full access to the American-made paradoxical paradise, which they called trash but was treasure to us. Anything could find its new use and purpose in our hungry hands. From their melting pot of food waste, which they called pig's porridge, came our best protein and calcium supply: shreds of sausages; mauve, bloated lumps of Spam— Look bad but taste good, as my mom put it; and beef bones still carrying some juicy meat on their curves, with which she made thick *gomtang* stock to help our bones grow as steely as those of the big Yankees. Their worn-out military uniforms, dyed black, became our school uniforms, the thick wool lining blocking the blustery winter wind from the north. Their dog-eared *Superman* and *Batman* comic books became our bedtime Bibles, the indecipherable text translated into made-up stories that I imparted to my little sister, inspiring a deep sigh of contentment before she gave in to sleep. To cut a long story short, we grew up on American trash.

And Yong's brother's job was to steal it. He supposedly started out by breaking into the disposal yard where my father worked, pilfering some food and rags. Over time, it had spiraled into a riskier form of robbery: after gathering together a few other jobless goons, he began to plunder weapons. When a military truck stocked with supplies decelerated along steep, serpentine roads through the Geumpari mountains, Wan would slip into the back, like a ghost monkey; while his decoy lackey broke into the front to distract the driver's attention, Wan would rapidly toss as many guns as possible to other guys waiting outside the truck. By the time the driver scented the trap and hurried to the back, all the mousy bushwhackers had already hidden in the thicket of Geumpari Valley, which they knew like the back of their hands.

Wan's gain meant my father's loss.

My father also got his hands on pieces of US machinery. Once every four months or so, he woke me at dead of night and ordered me to dig a hole with him behind our outhouse, where we buried bulky sacks of cold metallic clatters. A surprise visit of uniform-clad men always ensued, and they rummaged through every nook and corner of our bedraggled home. So, when my father threatened to report Wan, Wan threatened him back, with a toothy grin that hinted at the secret dirty job we'd engaged in behind our toilet shed.

I guess, by calling me a piece of shit as well as beating it out of me, my father wanted to teach me: our life, near the North Korean border, was a zero sum game – an ongoing battle in which you could either beat or be beaten, steal or be stolen.

At a certain point boys stopped referring to Virgin Ghost and switched to Yadada, as they came to realize Virgin Ghost was too common a name for someone so surreal. We desired a proper one, something of our own making, something that couldn't be mistaken for anything else.

Yadadadada was the sound she made when the boys chased after her – or she chased after them. She'd bellow the first syllable, *Ya*, in a resonant baritone, then speed up, hit the treble clef with castrato precision, and finally segue into the last few *das* in a metallic shrill that clawed at your nerves like a lynx's forepaw. The boys found this sound alarming yet amusing, saying she had male *and* female in her voice. They endeavored to find new ways to upset her, just to get more of the sound.

They said *Yadada* was her sole verbal expression that conveyed certain meaning because it was the only thing *they* had heard from her.

I laughed secretly at their simplicity.

I was often there to protect her when the others tried their usual tricks to drive her mad, one of which was stealing the flower in her hair. It was the day she was adorned with the most extraordinary bloom: a colossal cosmos, petals longer than my father's mid-finger, their color an odd gradation from blood-purple at the center to cotton-candy pink toward the edges. The flower was of such an uncanny size and shade that it made her bouffant hair look unusually smaller, her eerie face eerier. They snatched the cosmos while she was taking a nap in the silver grass field, hoping to squeeze a *Yadada* out of her. They failed.

That afternoon, she had an unprecedented emptiness in her eyes: a hazy, foreign kind drenched with fatigue. I couldn't know what had caused it, yet I hoped returning the flower would help her feel better. I waited patiently till the boys lost interest in bugging her and finally parted ways. I picked up the flower they'd tossed away on the muddy riverbank and carefully picked at the tiny earthy blotches on the petals. When it looked clean enough, I ran back to the silver grass field, to find Virgin Ghost on the same spot where she had been dozing, now staring at the gurgling Imjin River with the same void in her eyes. As soon as she saw me, her brow furrowed; when I gently handed her the cosmos, her face instantly lit up, like my three-year-old sister's at the sight of a chocolate bar smuggled home by my father.

While I was basking in her happiness, my face catching her dazzling smile, she lurched forward, and yanked my hand toward her. My heart skipped a beat as she looked into my eyes. Hers had a ghostly glow.

In the tenderest falsetto ever conceivable in this world, she said: *Yalu, Yalu.*

After flashing another eerie smile only a centimeter from the tip of my nose, she gamboled farther into the tall silver grass field.

I stayed put – immobile as a dead frog, my feet glued to the earth where a patch of silver grass had been trampled down by her sleep.

My head was still gonging with the frou-frou of her *hanbok*, with her *Yalu Yalu.*

So I refused to call her *Yadada*. To me, she was always Yalu – my own private Yalu.

As my feelings for Yalu grew stronger, the friendship between me and Yong weakened. Maybe it was what people call part of growing up, losing, whether gradually or abruptly, your childhood friend. It wasn't solely on my side: Yong himself began to drift away as he looked up to his brother more and more, straining to join Wan's squad.

Yong skipped school more often. Before, it was only for Moonsan market day, the huge once-a-month congregation of merchants from all over the country, selling and buying anything they could get their hands on, from a raging bull to a toothpick. Instead of feeling lonely, however, I began to cherish my privacy, as it meant I could spend more time around Yalu.

She turned more elusive, though. I covered all of her usual spots: the silver grass field, golden rice paddies near Panmunjeom, the abandoned pig farm by Imjingak. The haunted farm purported to be Yalu's nightly shelter. It had belonged to a family who settled down in Geumpari a few years after the truce between North and South. The father committed suicide after losing all of his pigs to foot-and-mouth disease, and the bereaved family left Geumpari for good shortly afterwards. People stayed away from the place in fear of the plague and lingering ghosts. Only a handful of windbags had supposedly visited it after nightfall, spreading the rumor that they had seen Yalu there, jabbering in an incomprehensible tongue, presumably possessed by the specter of the pig-farmer.

Despite my affection for Yalu, I never went to the farm after sundown. I'd already had harrowing nightmares about the place: bloody pigs, their limbs chopped off, darting about in the rank pen, filling its air with their thunderous grunting and needle-sharp squeals. So I went there only during the day, when the place was steeped in the crisp autumn sun. I never went inside, just left my little presents for Yalu at the entrance: gorgeous dandelions and cosmos I'd gathered from Geumpari knolls; gutted, salted catfish, and leopard frogs I'd caught in the Imjin River.

It took weeks for her to reappear.

It was a day after the belated rainy spell had finally ended. Feeling lucky, I ran toward the entrance of the abandoned pig farm, my pail full of plump catfish I'd just caught from the river, which was now turgid with flash-floodwater. It was a day of opal-blue sky, not a single patch of cloud visible. Yet the air surrounding the entrance remained chilly, nearby weeping-willows blocking the sunlight with their cascade of rifle-green branches drooping and dancing to the rhythm of gentle autumn wind.

Then I felt the sun shattering in my skull, filling my vision with neon paisleys, undulating, throbbing in time with my slowed heartbeat. At a snail's gallop, I felt the whole world waltz clockwise, my right ear sink into the earth, its rusty tang on my tongue. A brassy, muffled shriek buzzed into my left ear, like a hungry hornet.

And the pain came – sharp like an icepick. The pain – so famished it swallowed all my senses – came back to me only in fits and starts. Through my blinking mind, I saw two small feet gliding toward me. She lifted me in her wiry arms, held me tight into her bosom, then began to run.

My side-glance perceived Geumpari pass by at the speed of light, its river, knolls, rice paddies saturated in daguerreotype foreignness. Yet my gaze stayed on Yalu: Yalu's nostrils bulging and tightening with her breathing; her sharp collarbone brushing against my cheek; her sinewy neck tempered dark by the sun. *What a speed! What a grip!* I murmured in my head, marveling at the strength coming from that small frame. And her eerie gaze occasionally dropped to meet my eyes, smiling through her tears, asserting that everything would be okay, with her odd counter-tenor voice whispering: *Yalu, sweetheart – Yalu, Yalu.* I swear, by the sweet love of God, I heard *sweetheart* between *Yalu*, clear and sonorous like the temple bell ringing at night. Sweetheart, she murmured to me. Yes, she did; no, it wasn't my fevered brain conjuring what I wanted to hear. It was from her own tongue, her own ethereal voice. Then I saw the two figures clad in blinding white running toward me. And – that was it.

They called me a wonder boy.

They told me I could have lost my left calf for good; they told me I could have gone entirely deaf in my left ear; they told me, in the worst-case scenario, I could have died – I could have been lolling by the pig farm, unconscious, bleeding to death.

I woke up to my mother's tear-stained face. *I told you not to go there after heavy rains, you fool*, it murmured. Despite the streak of reproach in her tone, I knew she was ecstatic to have me back, fully conscious and put together. The doctor said my recovery was a near miracle. He'd expected an infection, which would have left my left foot mangled, my left ear eternally soundproof. But I kept them. Of course, my left leg still limps, my left ear has lost 70 per cent of its hearing, and they are covered with scars of varying sizes and textures. But who cares? They survived – thus *I* survived – the blow of an antipersonnel mine. The doctor proudly declared I was the only mine victim he'd ever known who had walked out of the hospital with not a single limb missing.

But I knew I wasn't their wonder. It should have been Yalu. They said she'd arrived at the hospital heaving like a wild animal, her *jeogori* scorching red, soaked in my blood.

She'd run non-stop, clutching me to her chest, from Geumpari to Moonsan, roughly twelve kilometers along the rugged, winding mountain path, unsparing and inhospitable even to the mighty kraken of an American military truck. The villagers said it was the male ghost inside her demonstrating his grit. To me, though, she seemed like a small god, disguised in a feeble frame.

The days of my convalescence were sweet. I didn't have to go to school; I became, for the first time in a long while, the center of my mother's attention; and the townspeople treated me like some kind of war hero, visiting us with freshly steamed rice cake and bittersweet ginseng juice for my recovery. The only downside was that I couldn't see Yalu as I wasn't allowed to go out. My mother feared I would go near the river again, so she did everything in her power to make sure I didn't. I heard my father did, though: he went back to the site of the explosion to collect fragments of copper and gunpowder he could sell for a decent sum.

Strangely enough, I wasn't in a hurry to see Yalu. I felt that she and I were now linked to each other irrevocably, our future paths somehow destined to cross. I took my time in hope, carefully honing the speech I would deliver to Yalu, once I got back on my feet, to express my gratitude, my feelings for her – without the slightest clue that I was never to see her again.

Yong came to see me on a night of full moon – an autumn night before the beginning of the long Chuseok holidays. He knew my father had a night shift. Now me and my brother know *everything* when it comes to the military in this region, said Yong, dripping pride.

We sat on the wooden bench in our backyard. And we gazed at the corpulent moon, basking in its golden glow, for a minute, in full silence, like a pair of turtles. I tried not to show it, but I was glad to see Yong. I'd missed him, sad that he hadn't come to see me.

As I confessed this, I saw Yong's face stiffen, a glisten of sweat budding on his upper lip.

So you have no fucking idea what happened.

What do you mean?

I mean about the Seoul people roaming around our village and all?

I shook my head vigorously, catching an ominous glint – a yellow flicker of anxiety, of excitement – in his eyes.

Promise you won't tell *no one* about this, no fucking single living soul, not even your mother or your little sister, Yong whispered, voice faintly tremulous.

I bit my chapped lip. I felt blood wetting my tongue. I pressed Yong to continue.

I know rumors have been circling, but it's only me and my brother who know the whole thing. You know my brother had an eye on Yadada for some time.

He paused for a couple of seconds, studying my face with a sidelong glance. Contrite, curious, cruel, all at once. As a true confessionalist should be.

One night, my brother went to the pig farm, you know, to keep her company – he often does something like that after drinking too much.

Yong stopped to giggle, his head full of some disgusting memories he shared with his brother – about which I couldn't have cared less. All I wanted to know was what had happened to Yalu. *Continue*, I told him drily.

Luckily, she was there that night, so my brother tried to strike up a conversation, then, you know, feel her up a little . . . That poor girl must have been awful lonely, living out there, all by herself.

Yong's voice echoed Wan's. My face hardened into a slab of granite. I couldn't move my tongue. In my mind's eye, I saw my fingers tightening around a neck – Wan's or Yong's, I couldn't tell.

They tussled a bit and gosh, my brother said that skinny bitch was tough as a bull's tendon. When he finally got his hand in her knickers, you know, it all went fucking sick! Fucking crazy, man! 'Cause down there, he found—

That she was a boy? I cut him short, wet with dire hope.

No! yelled Yong, his sooty brows knitting. *What the fuck?* No, you little pervert. Yong glared at me, long and deliberate. My brother felt a cold, heavy piece of metal, which was – a *gun*.

A *gun?*

Yong gestured to me to hush, ducking his head, scanning the air around us with wary eyes, as though someone might be lurking behind the bush, recording our conversation. Then, in a lowered voice, he broke the short silence. They wrestled quite a bit again and, of course, my brother was winning, but that cunning bitch secretly picked up a rock and hit my brother's head with it. Then she ran. But my brother had already taken the gun, so he fired at her. He heard her shriek.

Shriek – the word kicked a boulder into my throat.

The pistol she had, it wasn't the usual kind. You know, my brother can tell M1900 from M1911 by grabbing them once in the dark. But this one wasn't even American. On its hand grip, it had this weird little circle that had a tiny star in it.

Yong took a deep breath. Then he stared at me with soliciting eyes, waiting for a certain reaction I was too puzzled to provide.

Don't you get it? He sighed. It was fucking *Commie*-made. *That fucking bitch is from the North.*

Silence – sharp as a needle.

I saw an elephant: an outré elephant of a truth, just thrown out there naked, its colossal rear end now blocking my entire vision. My mouth opened, but nothing came out.

Yong took out a cigarette and lit it.

They said it was a Makarov pistol. It's fucking Soviet-Commie-made, man. Even my brother's never seen anything like it before. Yong took a deep, anxious drag at his cigarette. My brother and I, you know, we're patriots. So we told them everything. Within a day, the whole village was overrun by all these men from Seoul. Most of them weren't even wearing uniforms. They're a fucking serious group of people, man. They made us pledge not to say a word about this. So you'd better watch your mouth too, Yong intoned, in cathedral-solemnity, squeezing my shoulders with both hands.

But I don't get it. What kind of things could she do here exactly?

How the hell would *I* know? *Fuck.*

Yong's fingers nervously tapped on the wooden bench, his breath hissing. It at least explains how that little bitch was so tough, so fast, and all that shit. They couldn't even find her, you know.

At this, my eyelids fluttered rapidly, like moth wings.

My brother heard her shriek when he fired at her. But she ran away again. And they couldn't find her. No trace of blood. The bullet could have just grazed her. We should have gotten the bitch, though. *Damn* Commie-mole – she almost killed my brother, you know?

Looking at Yong, I felt a pang of guilt. At that very moment, I couldn't have cared less if Wan had been shot to death. I couldn't have cared less if Yong died the slowest death by a thousand burning needles – if only Yalu lived.

Right then and there, I made a deal with God, whom I hadn't even known I believed in: if he let her live, our future paths need never cross: I could happily get on with my life without hearing a word about her ever again – if only she lived.

I couldn't have cared less about politics, about the ideologies that had drawn the border. Even if she were an enemy, I wanted her to survive.

Yong babbled for quite a while – about the trading business he was in with his brother, about the many different girls he'd been dating – leaving me feeling more at odds with him in every passing second.

It was only when Yong said goodbye that I saw a glimpse of his younger, softer self. He said he was happy to see me doing well, said I probably wouldn't see him a lot at school from now on. I felt sad and glad to let him go.

After Yong had left, I stayed alone in the backyard for a while. I gazed at the moon ringed with its ashen haze, so full and calm, indifferent to the drama of us mortals down here at the border. I sucked in its pale luminosity till my lungs tingled, knowing it would always remain the same, beautiful and callous, the next year, and the year after that, while we down here would fade away, drift apart from one another, or simply change.

I got back inside. And I began to sob.

I felt the little monster that trembled at the bottom of my guts now throbbing at the soft pit of my sternum. It was the tiny bird of the childhood I'd deserved but had been robbed of. From that moment on I knew I would no longer be a child.

My little sister, who would turn four in a week, was shaken from her sleep. She gaped at me in her dream daze, her mouth half open. Crouched in my lap, she gave the house a quick once-over, checking automatically for the presence of our father. Looking more puzzled now, she put her little hand on my shoulder, still shaking up and down in silence, while the other nervously clutched her cold bare feet. I saw her eyes fill with familiar terror. I knew now it was my turn to console her, tell her everything would be okay. I held her in my arms, stroked her hair with my fingertips, as I always did before putting her to sleep, and I told her, Yalu, sweetheart – Yalu, Yalu.

The 1st Life

When I Stopped Eating Earth

1938

I ate earth when I was young.

It was neither poverty nor curiosity: it was just a pure urge that made me eat earth, the same one that makes you crave water when you're thirsty.

Every once in a while, my body was thirsty for earth, and I had no choice but to grant its request.

But that doesn't mean I ate earth simply to fill my stomach: I savored its taste, its tang and texture that are like no other in this world. And my ability to appreciate fine subtleties allowed me to master the art of eating earth at an early age. I know this is quite hard to grasp for the non-geophagists: they commonly assume that when we eat earth, we eat it like hyenas gorging a mouthful of meat, blinded by hunger.

But I never took a mouthful: it was always a dollop, rarely bigger than my little fingernail in size, hardly heavier than a ten-won copper coin in weight. Only in this way could you relish its rusty tang to the full – you could spread all of its fine granules on your tongue, making it easier for your palate to grasp its texture, at once tender and bristly.

I always waited till I found the perfect earth. Its viscosity should be that of steamed jasmine rice, pasty enough to form a dollop, yet also crumbly to the point of drifting away under a harsh puff of breath. Too much moisture ruins it, turning it into a sludge that your mouth might associate with shit. The shade should be milk-chocolate brown at first glance. When you look closely, however, you will discover its tiny particles in manifold colors. The fine nut-brown kind forms the majority, giving the bead of earth its signature warm, nutty flavor. The sooty ones are the dark horses, whose rough hooves prod your tongue with their black-coffee bitterness. The white granules, shiny as gem yet hard as flint, are the rarest: they give a sleek, metallic kick – like blood on your lip. The right combination of all of these could turn a pinch of earth into a pinch of heaven in your mouth. I loved the way it slithered, crackled under my palate, like a caress from a cat's tongue. Although I knew it was chipping away at my teeth, I couldn't stop.

Father thought it was the work of a spiteful ghost. Old people in the village agreed: they said it was usually the spirit of a starved child preying on a living one, trying to appease its hunger through gobbling soil. Father said we needed to drive it away. So, each time he caught me eating earth, he beat the living daylights out of me. Sticks and stones couldn't deter me, though. They only made me worse, adding a thrill to eating earth, the secretive pleasure of the forbidden.

Father didn't know me. We had nothing in common except the blood pulsating in our veins – he said so himself. He was an illiterate fisherman who never believed in the importance of education. He lived in the world of simplicity, capable of seeing things only in black and white; the different hues of gray were lost on him. He drank only to get drunk, ate to fill his stomach. He couldn't appreciate the myriad different tastes of food and drink, as words like *nuance* and *subtlety* had never existed for him. He could never become a connoisseur of anything. He wasn't like me; he wasn't like Mama.

Mama, on the other hand, was a woman of sophistication. She had fine skills in differentiating flavors and scents. She taught me how to tell medicinal herbs from their poisonous cousins: *sahwa* smells bitter, while *sanak* gives out a pungent nutty aroma, like fermented soybeans, said Mama, frowning. She also showed me how to tell good persimmons from bad without touching them: the stalk of a ripe one is withered and brown, you see, while the fruit itself turns nearly vermilion. As her pupil, I observed and dwelled on the world of full color, my eyes wide open for the various shades. In our world, red was never just red: it was vermilion, like a ripe persimmon, scarlet, like early-autumn maple leaves, claret, as sticky stale blood, and fuchsia, as a fresh bruise.

No wonder Mama and I were rich in vocabulary. We had to be, to describe all the nuances we perceived in our world, all the different colors and flavors and smells and feelings. So by the time I reached twelve, I already had a vocabulary at least three times larger than that of Father: when he could only say he was *hungry*, I was able to say I was *starved*, or even *famished*. He didn't like a girl using words he didn't understand. Each time he heard me uttering a term esoteric to his ear, he slapped Mama hard, turning her face *fuchsia* with his handprint.

Mama was a woman of perfection: intelligent, beautiful, refined and loving. Yet she had to pay harshly for the only speck of imperfection she carried: excess of sympathy. I figured that was the reason she'd stayed married to an obtuse stewbum like Father: all because of *jeong* – that twisted feeling of attachment, that needless pity. She was originally from an affluent family. Her father was a renowned doctor of Oriental medicine in Seoul, from whom she'd learned how to read and write, how to appreciate literature and gastronomy, how to select the right herbs to brew for thousands of different illnesses. But the Japanese occupation had turned everything upside down: her father was accused of being a member of the Korean Resistance, and the Japanese stripped him of everything he'd ever owned. Afraid of losing his daughter too, her father married her off to a country farmer's son in the north, far away from Seoul. She never saw her parents again; they both died in prison. And not long after, she had me.

We lived in Heoguri, a small farming village near the northern outskirts of Pyongyang. Heoguri was nothing like the center of Seoul, where she'd had access to libraries and theaters, but Mama always knew how to make the best of everything. During the season of tuna- or whale-hunting, Father was out on the sea for months at a time, and those fatherless months were the happiest of my childhood. Every day Mama and I walked to the Sacred Heart, an orphanage-cum-match-factory located on the border between Pyongyang and Pyongannamdo. The Sacred Heart was one of the first *modern* buildings in the North. And in our flat town of thatched-roof cottages, this three-story concrete fortress loomed over everything, its imposing body angular and ash-grey. It was founded by Canadian missionaries, and Mama made pocket money helping them with odd jobs and house-hold chores. But money wasn't the main purpose: Mama and I were taking English lessons there with the orphans and factory workers. Our English teacher was Pastor Arnaud Peltier, a Canadian missionary from Québec, who also spoke French and Korean fluently. I couldn't breathe for a few seconds when I first saw him: he was the first Westerner I'd laid eyes on, the first human whose eyes weren't dark brown, whose hair was neither straight nor raven. On his head sat sizzling flames, all curled up in their *vermilion* heat. A *ginger-curly*, the pastor called himself. Despite his eerie appearance, I liked him almost immediately. He was an avid traveler and a human encyclopedia, who could tell us endless stories about the other side of the globe. I loved the tales from the Old Testament, especially those of Noah's Ark and Samson, and nearly everything by Shakespeare, whom I considered a heck of a storyteller, always pepping up his dramas with death and love and betrayal, like *Romeo and Juliet* and *Othello*. So, with this foreigner carrying fire on his head, in his bleak tower of ashen cement, Mama and I traveled the world.

Some people in the village badmouthed us, claiming that by learning their language we were selling our souls to the foreign devils. Mama told me to ignore them. She said those townspeople didn't understand the significance of language.

"Words are not just words, honey. They are much more than a simple tool for getting your intention across. Words themselves can affect the way you think, and with them, you can influence the way others think. It's never one-way traffic."

Although my understanding of her speech wasn't perfect, I nodded passionately, my heart swollen with pride. I couldn't have asked for a smarter mama.

"You can think of it as a soft weapon, dear. Why do you think Daddy feels hurt when you use vocabulary he doesn't know? You see?"

I kept nodding, despite being irked by that word *hurt*. What an irony – Father felt hurt while all he ever did was punish Mama? But I didn't want to contradict her so I kept quiet. And I went on attending English classes; not because I saw it as an important weapon, but simply because I enjoyed it.

Mama was also the only person in the world who told me eating earth was okay. She said we all had different tastes, and sometimes some of us developed an unusual one. "But *unusual* doesn't mean *wrong*, honey," Mama added, her eyes smiling like two crescent moons. I asked her what kind of weird things other people ate.

"Pastor Peltier told me that in France people eat *snails* as a delicacy!" Mama answered, her brow creasing like that of a child looking at boiled cabbage on her plate.

"Disgusting!" I whispered, covering my mouth with both hands, envisioning the glossy little living phlegm slithering its way into my stomach. Then I giggled a bit, feeling relieved and much less like a freak. Mama giggled with me, then told me that eating earth was fine as long as it didn't cause health issues, that I would eventually grow out of it, the way I'd grown out of all my childhood clothes and tantrums.

But Father disagreed. He found and imposed his own way of settling the matter. And, as always, he needed nobody's approval for that.

It was a godforsaken stevedore who gave Father the idea – a menial worker as uncouth, thick-headed as Father himself. A complete stranger who didn't know a thing about me.

Father befriended this idiot when they anchored off Busan – together visiting seedy harborside bars and whorehouses, no doubt. It turned out this old stevedore had a younger sister who also ate earth. He said she'd begun nibbling it as a little girl, then over time she'd turned into a complete addict, who would gorge fistfuls every day. It got worse. She started to eat other oddities, like spiders' webs, cicada larvae, and even her own feces, driving herself further and further into madness, at which point she lost interest in human clothes and even human language.

He confided in Father the cure the stevedore hadn't been able to afford for his sister.

Goot – an exorcism performed by a shaman.

Father told me and Mama nothing. We knew what was going on only when the shaman arrived in his shiny silk vestment, striped in blinding red, yellow and blue. Yet Father had tied me down before the shaman showed up, knowing I might run away into the woods if I knew what he would make me endure.

I was thrown into the middle of our backyard, trussed like a chicken to be dropped into boiling soup, surrounded by dozens of townspeople, their eyes gleaming with excitement for the upcoming spectacle. I saw Father among them, his face impassive, inanimate as a wooden leg. He was holding Mama. Her arms folded behind her back, she writhed in his grip. She was crying silently.

The ruthless noon sun hammered down on my head, leaving me sodden with sweat. Three men the shaman had brought with him began chanting, their voices soaring, sharp and heavy, like funeral wailing, the jarring cacophony of their gong, drum and willow pipe shredding my eardrums.

When the music died away, the shaman came in, brandishing a long, shimmering sword in each hand, his own chanting higher in pitch, like a tomcat yowling, hovering above the howl of his chorus. He hissed at me. He spat at me. And he cursed me in the most menacing tongue, his feigned baby voice full of venom. He made my bones shudder, my eyes run with scorching tears.

Then Father came to me. His arms were wide open, yet his face was still cold. I saw a knife beaming in his hand and he cut the ropes tying my hands and legs. As soon as my limbs were free, I felt a bone-shattering weight on my back. I looked up and saw Father on top of me, his knees crushing my torso, my thighs. He fastened my right hand onto my right thigh. Then he clutched my left hand, pulled it over my head, and held it down on the ground, the palm facing the sky.

The shaman sashayed toward me. He put down one sword on the ground. He waved the other over my head in circular motions, as though writing a letter in the air. Then with the tip of his sword, he cut open my palm.

Through the haze of heat, my pungent sweat and tears, I saw a beige lumpy fluid gushing out of my open palm. Its sour smell was like puke. I watched, helplessly, the muddy clots spilling over, soiling the ground – till everything went black.

I came back to myself at dead of night, my body wrapped in cold dampness.

I looked down at my left hand. Covered with layers of sack-cloth, it resembled a makeshift boxing glove, its color dirty claret with sticky blood.

Father and Mama were fast asleep. Father was snoring slowly, his breath exuding the stench of alcohol. His arm encircled Mama's neck. Her face was swollen, marked with the dried paths of tears.

I sneaked out into the darkness of the night, breathless, gasping like a minnow out of water. I ran till I reached the grove of birch trees on the southern border of Heoguri, the safe place of my private musings, where the gnarled branches and their lush moss-green leaves keep the soil moist and warm all year, inviting the somber lives of ferns and mushrooms and poisonous herbs. It was where, I knew for sure, I would find fine milk-chocolate-brown soil, the earth of perfection.

In the gloom of the grove, I did something I'd never done before.

I knelt down, plunged my fingers into the silky soil, and clasped it in my hand. I shoved a fistful – not a dollop – of earth into my mouth, and I swallowed without tasting it. I pushed down one handful after another, and another – till my heart rose and pushed out the heavy knot.

After the big tremor had passed, I lifted my head, struggling to focus. I saw a mound of regurgitated earth in front of me, its surface glistening jade with my bile, my acid hatred and contempt for the monster with whom I shared nothing but the blood pulsating in our veins. His heart, when cut open, would show nothing but black.

A month later, the monster left home: it was the season of whale-hunting, which would keep him out on the sea for months, away from us. Forced to see him off, Mama and I stood for a while by the entrance to our village, occasionally waving at him when he turned back – as though to measure our obedience by how long we stayed there.

Watching his back dwindling into a speck of dirt, I prayed for the first time in my life. I prayed to the Canadian God, the sole creator and overseer of the world, whom Pastor Peltier had been eulogizing with fervor in his endless stories.

Please make him never come back. Then I'll be your disciple forever.

It was the language of the White God that brought on the beginning of the end.

The irony – it was only a word: a single word of a single syllable, of merely three letters.

The clincher was that they were *English* letters.

SEX

The townspeople found the word written on the concrete buttress under the Heogu Bridge. It was the only modern bridge in town – the Canadians had built it along with the match factory; though small in size, it was used by every villager, including farmers commuting to their rice paddies with their oxen, and children taking naps under its arch, hiding from the searing noon sun.

A little boy saw it first: the mysterious word written in sooty black, probably with a piece of charcoal, each of its letters as big as his small body. Then he showed it to his friends, and his mother and father, itching to know its meaning.

I went there a few days later. I could recognize the shapes – the capital S and E and X – and I told the other kids that they were English, the tongue of the white. Whoever it was, I guessed, the writer was making sure the word stayed: its letters were neat in shape, yet when you looked closely, you could see their curves were drawn multiple times, making them look *colored* rather than written. I didn't think a kid had done it. No kid in the village, except me, was smart enough to pull off such elaborate work, which required knowledge of a foreign language.

I told them I had never seen that word before and didn't know what it meant. I didn't think I was telling a lie, as I couldn't recall learning it in class. In the back of my mind, however, I'd already figured it out. I felt the significance was self-evident in the way the letters displayed themselves: the sensual curve of S; the stern forbidding X; and the E in the middle, like a trident about to pierce its neighbor on the right. I sought Mama's words for the final confirmation of my hunch. To my surprise, she refused to talk to me about it. So, in the end, I had to consult the English dictionary, a gift from Pastor Peltier that Mama had hidden in her sewing box.

To me, Mama's refusal to talk about it was more shocking than the word itself: she rarely kept a secret from me. Only in hindsight did I understand her intention: it was her way of protecting me. She knew all too well the reality of the world we were living in. Heoguri was a place in which understanding a sinful language could turn into a sin, in which acquiring a foreign tongue meant selling your soul to the foreign devil.

On the surface, no one in the village seemed to be talking about it. Yet the rumors spread, like silent wildfire, igniting people's curiosity and suspicion, their desire to point fingers. By the end of the week, like magic, the entire village knew what the scribble meant.

Mama was right. Words have power. Magic, even.

And the black magic of that single word took hold of the entire village.

It made people disappear: the bridge, the thriving Mecca of Heoguri ever since its construction, turned desolate overnight. The townswomen, carrying baskets of lunch for their husbands working in the rice paddies, took a detour that made their journey an hour longer. All the mothers in the village forbade their children to play there, some even whipping their little ones when they caught them staring at the scribble. They treated the bridge as if it was doomed. As if it was raped, desecrated by the filth of the foreign devil's word. As if any kind of association with it could turn you into a moral leper.

The monster arrived back in the town in the midst of this frenzy, while accusations flew through the air, like invisible daggers. Mama kept quiet as she had no desire to be embroiled in the madness. The silence didn't help, but in retrospect, nothing would have helped. That's the funny thing about suspicion. Suspicion isn't really suspicion: it's *conviction* wearing a soft mask. All it needs is time, and it will eventually grow into full-fledged certitude.

And it wasn't long before Father's took its full shape.

The fact that there were thirty more people in the English class – twenty-two orphans and eight full-time factory workers – somehow wasn't important to him. While those thirty people were free to roam around the village in their free time, unrestrained by the rules of nosy parents, they were never under the radar of Father's suspicion. His burning eyes, from the very beginning, were on Mama and me.

I saw the green-eyed monster growing, evolving into its

concrete form each time he questioned Mama about it. The beginning was the usual *whodunit* censure: *What kind of nutjob would do such shit?*; *Whoever it is, we gotta burn that dirty sod alive*; *If you let our kid go near that bridge, I'll whip you till you weep*; *You better tell me who done it, woman, 'cause I know that you know.* By the end of the week, the certitude was there, baring its sharp teeth: *You tell me the whole truth right now, then. I'll be kind and I'll forgive you, darling, you won't be punished*; *How can I make you open your mouth, without hurting you?*; *You want me to kill you and that white devil of yours? Is that what you want?*

Then he found the dictionary.

The truth was that the hardback English dictionary itself didn't prove anything. He already knew we were taking English lessons, and Mama was earning money helping the pastors at the Sacred Heart; that was how we paid for our rent and food, as the amount he made as a fisherman was hardly sufficient for him to stay drunk. He was simply craving a visual trigger, no matter how meager, just as Othello needed his wife's handkerchief. When Mama fiercely denied the accusation, he blustered at her, demanding why she had to hide the dictionary at the bottom of her sewing box, under the skeins of yarn and pincushions.

Mama didn't bend. Father snapped.

He seized Mama by the hair and dragged her to the bridge, the other hand waving the dictionary in the air, like a street preacher wielding the Bible – his legs occasionally kicking me to the curb, whenever I tried in vain to bite his hand, kick his ankle, to free Mama.

"Can't you see? Can't you recognize your own handwriting, you dirty little cunt?" asked the monster, bumping Mama's forehead on the concrete buttress.

"No, I don't, please, it isn't mine," Mama begged.

"You don't see it? Then I'll make you see," answered the monster. He was pounding Mama's face with the dictionary. When the cover grew slippery with Mama's blood, he flung it into the stream, then continued to pummel her with his bare fist.

He only stopped when Mama and I could no longer make any noise.

And I heard him whisper in Mama's ears, panting: *You fool me again, I'll hand you over to the Japs. Then your daughter will grow up without a mama. Think of that.*

Mama lost an eye that day, under the bridge.

And I lost my last shred of hope for help from God.

I knew, from then on, I had only myself to trust for our future.

It took Mama three days to become fully conscious again. And on that third night, I had to witness the sickening sight again: the monster sleeping with Mama, clinging to her like a starved leech, his arm wrapped tight around her neck.

I looked down at the pair lost in sleep. Then I felt the gut-wrenching contempt.

The serene face of the monster was wearing a faint smirk. *I have your mama*, it seemed to whisper, in a feigned baby voice, full of venom, like the greedy little brother I'd never had. *She is mine, I own her. You'll never get her out of my grip.*

And for the first time in my life, I felt disdain toward Mama, too. I hated her for being unable to throw the devil's arm away from her; I hated her for being so powerless.

I realized, then and there, what I had to do. The duty I had to carry out before the monster squeezed the shining light out of Mama, before the monster choked my love for her out of me.

I ran out again into the damp darkness. I darted toward the grove of birch trees, where I would feel more at home than I did at our house. The green place where all the small, somber lives of mosses and mushrooms thrived, the spot where I knew for sure I could find the perfect earth.

But it wasn't earth I was after this time. I was looking for a smell.

A smell of sun-warmed garbage, slightly sweet and repulsive. A smell of stale sesame oil, and of fermented soybeans. I was searching for the snake's peanut – *sanak*. The herb that took its nickname from its peculiar scent: the poisonous cousin of the medicinal herb *sawha*, the snake's flower.

Only people with a heightened sense of smell and taste, like Mama and me, could recognize its toxicity.

Only *I* could do the job, though: Mama's excess of sympathy wouldn't allow it. So in the end, I had at least one little thing I could thank Father for: I was indeed his daughter after all, and shared with him the blood pulsating in our veins. And his blood in me would offset the excess of sympathy I'd inherited from Mama, preventing me from showing mercy to the devil, who didn't deserve it, the alcohol-breathing demon that I was about to exorcize.

Later in life I heard that all murderers, in their own eyes, have legitimate reasons for their crimes. I was no exception: I believed my decision could be justified, if not forgiven. And, in truth, I didn't even feel much guilt.

But I guess the difference between me and a psychopathic killer was that I at least felt guilt for not feeling guilt. Besides, I didn't enjoy the *process*. For the psychopath, I heard, it's all about the process, about watching the victim suffer and die.

I didn't want to watch him die, regardless of how much I loathed him. So I fixed him the meal early in the morning and then I took Mama out for the long mushroom-gathering. We returned home late in the afternoon.

The sight we walked into wasn't a beauty.

His lips, webbed with blood and foam, glared pink. So did his eyes, the black rolled back in his head. The two bloodshot bulges doggedly resisted my fingers' efforts to shut them. In the end I removed his quilted vest and put it over his head.

Mama wasn't stupid. She knew instantly what had happened. She was in a daze for two days, refusing to talk to me. But I knew it would be all right in the end – we just needed a bit of time to let the new reality settle into our lives.

We couldn't have a funeral, so we'd have to tell the villagers he'd gone for another round of whale-hunting. On the third night, when the entire town fell under the midnight gloom, we wrapped the body in a potato sack, dragged it to the birch grove and buried it there as deeply as we could.

On our way home, trudging side by side in silence, I wondered how long it would take for the body to fade away. Thanks to the warmth and humidity of the soil under the dense birch grove, I figured it wouldn't take long for his body to be one with earth. With only the sackcloth between him and the soil, it might not take as much as half a year.

I imagined his face in the earth, his eyes gently closed. His cheeks and lips would probably be the first to go, inviting the soil into his jaws as though he was eating earth. The decayed fragments of his flesh, fallen out of his frame, would mingle with the soil, dirtying, tainting my perfect earth.

Then, in my mind's eye, I saw my greatest fear come alive.

I dipped my hands into the smooth earth under the birch trees, grabbing a fistful to shove into my mouth. When I pulled my hands out of the ground, I saw my fingers run black with Father's blood.

And that moment, the moment when I faced the color of my sin, was when I stopped eating earth.

The 3rd Life

Bring Down the House

1950

We seldom slept with a roof over our heads; often the only choice of nightly shelter was abandoned houses brought down by fire. Starlight lingered above our frowned faces, rapt in sleep. Despite the nocturnal chill gushing through the mangled ceiling, we slept well. We ate what we could. We survived.

We, during the Korean War, was a slippery concept. It could mean both a Northerner and a Southerner, either a Commie or a capitalist, it didn't really matter. Every night I tried to form *we* with a stranger, another human body next to me in pale darkness, to keep myself warm and shielded from loneliness. First I would curl my body, gently put my forearms and shins to a person's back, and if they didn't wince, I would bring my belly to the warm wall, slowly shrouding their shoulders with both hands. Most people didn't resist, to my astonishment. The next morning we might fight each other tooth and nail for a sliver of balloon-flower root; at roofless night, though, we were just warm bodies in need of more human heat. Sometimes, once the others fell into a dead slumber, I slipped my fingers into their inner pockets and pilfered anything of value: candies, silver coins, a tiny vial of snake-oil for typhoid fever.

I remembered talking about this war even before it began. I was younger and naïve. I was in the English class taught by Pastor Peltier, a Canadian missionary who ran an orphanage-cum-match-factory in my North Korean hometown. While giving us a crash-course on American history, he talked about a peculiar kind of war in which brothers are turned against each other. War is not always a fight among different countrymen, emphasized Monsieur Peltier, his milky complexion growing light pink, like a piglet's buttocks. Westerners call this type of war *civil war*, he said, and my juvenile mind secretly laughed at white men's stupidity, the inane irony of calling fratricide *civil*, of this *civil* war being in fact much more brutal than a regular war.

At first the war was just a nuisance. When I returned to my hometown after years of absence, the comrades with red armbands had already infiltrated the daily lives of the villagers, pestering them with mandatory gatherings and weekly rallies, often summoning even married women to train as sentries. It made townspeople disappear. Rumors about the warm South, free of forced partisan duties, began to lure certain Northern dreamers, like my mother and sister, who, according to the neighbors, had gone South long ago.

More started to evaporate. A family in the neighboring town perished overnight, people whispered, hit by a misguided missile. After a few months of ongoing overhead fireworks, townspeople finally saw the arrival of the Yankees, and what they called *sawing* began. The town became divided into two, like a penurious concubine serving two partners, not yet sure whom to worship for survival. During the day, the Yankees with Southern soldiers roamed the village in their military truck, doling out food and asking questions; after dark, gaunt guerrillas who had been hiding in the mountains descended and skulked around the village, like hungry ghosts, gathering food and information by stealth. A family feud, or a petty quarrel between neighbors, blossomed into a bloody disaster under the strange circumstances. Under the sun, a villager accused his neighbor of being a Communist sympathizer; under the moon the victim's son split on the former for being a Yankee's stooge. The alleged Commies, taken away by the Yankee military truck, never came back, while many of the rumored Yankee-lovers were executed on the spot. Red-baiting and traitor-hunting took turns day in day out, the jagged scythe of war swaying from side to side each day, pulverizing villagers at random.

I refused to be a helpless victim. I headed South, the childish dream of being reunited with my mother and sister still half alive in the back of my mind.

During the day I walked and scavenged, every day expanding the definition of food, from barley porridge to crabapple, boiled nettle to tree bark. At night I stole warmth from the body of a stranger, under the ashen moonlight leaking through a burned house.

The night when I decided to be a boy, however, it wasn't a house. It was what used to be a school. The biggest nightly lodging thus far. Once a modern school building constructed by the Japanese Army during the Second World War, the place had been remodeled as a billet by the Yankees, and was now, in the midst of the Korean War, used as a temporary refugee camp. I was lying down in one of the classrooms, looking up at the patchwork of roof, a shell-shocked chasm covered with sheets of corrugated tin. Under the tin roof, though, I could still smell the pallid moon. The glassless windows were inviting its icy breath, making my body ache once again for human warmth.

I found a perfect back. It belonged to a woman, neither young nor old. She had round shoulders wrapped in plush flesh. Her rich hips roiled each time she tossed and turned. I waited till her squirming faded. I let out a soft, high-pitched sigh behind her ears, to disarm her, even in her sleep, with my tender female breath. I was about to latch onto her, as gently as possible, my arms folded like those of a praying mantis. But the night predators poured in through the window. They were murmuring, their breath rushed. I understood the nature of their whisper; I understood their language. They were the Yankees. Two. One white, one Black. They shoved a ball of cloth into the woman's mouth. She writhed furiously as they took her away, her hips jiggling at each protest, till a smack across her face stilled her. Through the glassless school window came the straining sound of quiet rape.

Next morning I roamed the streets, searching for a body of a dead boy. I found one easily, about the size of my own frame. I stripped him of his male clothes – a pair of long johns, a thick vest and pants made of burlap. Color of rust; smell of stale stingray. Before I put them on, I bound my breasts flat with my cotton scarf. Thankfully, my hair had already been cut short.

I was tall for a woman, short for a man. Perfect for a boy.

I'm only a half-woman anyway, I thought, grinning, my belly empty of womb.

Father used to say, before slapping me or Mama, women were like boys in a way: forever stuck in immaturity, never to learn and grow up, thus in need of permanent spanking. I wanted to whisper to Father, if he were alive, that boys were never to be drafted, only men; besides, their loins were more likely to be left alone than those of girls.

I've survived way worse before, I told myself. I can survive this.

On my journey through the North to the South, I didn't once see a house unburned, uncrippled.

The sky was pregnant with noise, fighter-bombers its permanent occupants: when grazing the air in relative leisure, they grumbled softly; farther away they purred like a cat, or growled like a hound just above the bushy hills; then, when least expected, they farted thunder on my eardrums, setting fire to every thatched roof in sight.

Days later, I could take a dump in the bushes without stirring an eyelid, through the ensemble of howling planes and their fiery droppings. The bombing was so omnipresent that after a certain point I felt surviving was just a matter of luck.

So, my heart leaped with wonder when I first saw the train crossing the border. It shocked me that so many people had survived such hellfire: the train was teeming with refugees, its surface alive with fidgeting bodies, like barnacles cloaking a sunken ship.

I was among hundreds of people riding on top of the boxcars. The wind on my face grew sharper as the train accelerated through the night chill. But stealing warmth from another body was unthinkable. Every sliver of strength had to be squeezed out for holding onto the ridge of the steel roof. Failing to do so meant loss. I saw several little bodies disappearing, falling behind the relentless thudding of the night train. The thin strips of space their small bodies had once occupied were now filled with their mothers' keening.

For me, the South was the place of sootless houses.

Busan was the final destination of countless war orphans. One of the southernmost cities of Korea, Busan hadn't been seized by the Communist force, so it was the only region in the country that had escaped the bombing. Houses in Busan, like the newly arrived phalanx of Korean refugees who had fled Communist rule, were survivors, their walls and roofs never claimed by flames.

Nevertheless, the number of existing houses was hardly sufficient for the ever-growing flow of human survivors. The rocky hills of Ami quarter quickly turned into a shantytown. Every week, new rows of clapboard houses sprang up there, like mushrooms after heavy rain. The latecomers who failed to take shelter in the hills swarmed to the cemetery. The public cemetery for the Japanese, a burial ground constructed under the Japanese occupation, gave way to the *pondok*s of Korean refugees, their roofs made of rusty tin panels, walls of abandoned packing-crates and mud. The once occupied were now occupying the resting place of their dead occupiers, turning the last resort of the dead into that of the living, tombstones into cornerstones, and giving the place its new nickname: Biseok Maeul, the Town of Tombstone.

Markets mushroomed as the refugees, driven by hunger, bunched up on the streets to sell and buy, to barter and haggle anything they could get their hands on. The most popular was Can Market. There, the refugees traded Yankee-made canned food: the American military C-rations were one of the few stable sources of food. The *crème de la crème* was meat and spaghetti in tomato sauce, while frankfurters and lima beans always remained among the most popular. Demands for candy-coated chewing gum and Lucky Strike were ceaseless, while the stolen dog-tags of dead soldiers were sought out as rarities by some wartime oddballs, to serve as souvenirs and can-openers.

The concubine had no confusion now as to whom to turn to for survival: from the waist down at least, below the 38th parallel, all walks of life revolved around the Yankees. I couldn't care less whom I was to serve, either capitalist or Communist, as long as they gave me a warm meal and no beating – I was, among other things, a survivor.

One day, I walked up to them. The boy's attire was protecting me, I believed. With my nearly accent-free English, I asked them, nice and simple: "Do you have a job for me?" I caught them off guard, a bunch of GIs on their cigarette break at the entrance of Can Market. Speechless, they stared at me for a couple of seconds, two of them with their mouths agape, smoke swirling out. "Go away, kid," a Korean man among them answered in Korean, waving his hand in the air as if shooing away a gnat.

"I speak good English," I said again slowly. "I need a job, sir." I wasn't even afraid of beatings anymore: my stomach had been empty for four days.

"Where did you learn English, kid?" they finally asked, after exchanging laughter and a few curious glances. One white soldier, a burning cigarette still hanging from the corner of his mouth, gestured to the Korean man to come closer, and mumbled something inaudible in his ear.

I followed the Korean man – thin-lipped and owl-eyed. He said, with a lopsided grin, that they had a job for me, even though I was too young, too skinny to be a soldier. With my good English, he told me, I could be an interpreter. He promised they would feed me, put a roof over my head. My growling stomach uttered yes even before my mouth did. "You're a war orphan, right? What's your name, boy?" he asked.

"Yongmal," I answered. It wasn't my name, though it wasn't a boy's name either.

They took me into their military truck.

"Where do we go?" I asked.

Without looking at me, he told the driver: "To the House."

"Where do we go?" I asked the driver, looking into his eyes reflected in the rear-view mirror.

Instead of an answer, the driver gave a dim smile; and made a strange noise – choppy caws, like a little animal panting. His right hand pretended briefly to scratch his cheek.

The House wasn't a house. It was what used to be a school.

The building was unscathed. No scar of an old chasm on its roof. No window missing.

The window glass was as thick as a thumb, protected by iron bars as chunky as a man's wrist. Tears of rust, running down from the metal bars, streaked the concrete walls, like stripes on a prisoner's uniform.

Another modern school building – constructed by the Japanese, repurposed by the Korean War.

They called it the House in short, the Monkey House in full. People from the nearby village sometimes called it the Truck, for the building, pigeon-colored and perpendicular, looked like a giant military truck.

I saw the faces of women through the windows on the second floor. They were hanging onto the welded wire mesh behind the window, eyes filled with silent moaning, fingers tightly clenched.

Like monkeys, clinging to a caged wall.

Their heads constantly bobbed, shoulders twitched. "I know it's not a pretty sight," the man whispered to me, "but you'll get used to it." He said those were sick women, and they cured them there, on the second floor of the House. I was to help them, as their interpreter of maladies, he explained. My task was simple: to translate Korean into English, or English into Korean, among the girls, two doctors and visiting Yankee soldiers.

In truth, the House needed no introduction. I knew

everything from the moment my eyes met theirs. I knew the kind of pain they had, all the bobbing and twitching and screaming and sweating – I knew it was from too much penicillin forced into your body. I already knew, from top to bottom, the list of their *maladies*. I already knew what the House was, what it was really *for*.

A little shiver ran down my nape and spine, and stopped around the pelvis, lingering there for a while. I put my hands on top of my belly, where my womb had once been.

I felt immolated from within.

Like my own existence, the structure of the House was an irony.

Contrary to its modern cement-gray exterior, nearly every element of its interior was in warm-hued wood, including the floors, rafters, crossbeams, and columns. The parquet floor, made of cedar, always gave off the pleasant spicy aroma, even after it had acquired copper-colored bloodstains in four corners. The women told me the building hadn't been intended as a school. It was supposed to be a summerhouse, they whispered, for a concubine of a Japanese prefect. The official wanted to construct a sumptuous wooden villa for his mixed-blood lover, but he died in the early stage of the Pacific War (a name I found as paradoxical as 'civil war'), thus leaving the vacation home incomplete. Much later in the war, it was hastily repurposed and finished as a modern school, where they dreamed of molding snotty Korean children into loyal defenders of the Japanese Empire.

Now, the House. A home for twelve homeless women – though the number tended to fluctuate. According to the owl-faced Korean warden, their real homes had either been destroyed by the war, or rendered inhospitable to them by their own double-dealing. "While calling themselves freedom-loving Southerners," he explained, "they were receiving free bags of rice from the Commies through their back doors. Now they've been given a second chance, here at the House, to serve their true country through serving the soldiers of their country's biggest ally, the American forces, the heroes who came to rescue us from the evil hands of the Communists." The warden emphasized that their *health* was a matter of importance, for it could directly affect that of the in-and-out Yankee soldiers. "That's why we have the second floor, where we try to eliminate any budding signs of trans-mittable diseases."

The second floor was the place that had given the building its nickname, and also the place where I first saw Jenny. Her real name was Jae-soon, yet all the soldiers called her Jenny. In time it also stuck with us. I saw her naked body from the beginning: pigeon-breasted and pigeon-toed, she seemed like a tall bird. Unlike other women, she never dropped her gaze to the floor. Her eyes, without shame, constantly followed mine and the Yankee doctor's during the whole medical check-up, as if she was striving to read some secret code behind our actions. It made me uncomfortable. I felt as though she saw through me, somehow poking at the trickster me beneath my male disguise. In my mind, I marked her down as *Jenny the hawk-eyed*. On the medical chart in my hand, I marked her down as *pass*.

Jenny was the only woman who tried to escape the House, albeit unsuccessfully. One night the warden woke me up, ordered me to ring the alarm. He ran up to the second floor and I followed him. Through the barred window I saw Jenny. She'd somehow made it out to the backyard, and was now run-ning, barefoot, toward the woods. I saw a soldier, the truck driver, following her in big, leisured strides. "*Run baby, run!*" he shouted, with laughter, one hand pulling up his pants, his fly half open. Soon they disappeared, almost at the same time, into the darkness of the woods. When they returned, Jenny was sent directly up to the second floor. She spent the following three days there, in the dusky corner of the Monkey Room, veins in her thighs bulging black with the cocktail of injections forced into her body, her screams filling the entire House like a never-ending banshee wail.

Jenny reminded me of an old friend of mine. And I admired and pitied her for that. I fancied her courage, her foolhardiness. Yet I wondered if there could ever really be an escape from the House.

I thought I had escaped, too.

Before the House, there had been the Station, the place that had sucked my adolescence dry.

The junkyard, or the butcher's floor, where the memory existed only in shivers and fragments.

The Station in short; the Comfort Station in full.

We learned the hard way their meaning of *comfort*. A group of hungry Korean teenage girls, leaving our home country for Japan. A factory, they'd promised. No factory of things, it turned out, a factory of men, Japanese soldiers, in the jungle of Semarang, of mosquitoes, blood and rusty perspiration.

Soldiers, day after day. Sober and drunk. Sometimes missing an eye, a tip of a finger. Grease of their hands. Of sweat. Semen, salty as fish, dripping. Screams came first. Silence of give-up the second. They let opium, penicillin, mercury swim in our veins. They beat us up, then sang us a lullaby. Girls died. One after another. Of malaria. Or from flogging, choking. And of all the maladies that dye the thing between your legs black, purple. Of wombs stolen, without full anesthesia, half-open eyes watching the warm tight knot pulled away from your body, a small clenched fist wrapped in blood.

Suicide was a dream forbidden to us.

At the Comfort Station, I met Yongmal. The owner of my pseudonym: an odd name actually, with characters of dragon and horse put together – two letters rarely used in a girl's name. Yongmal was the fool, the clown. The story-teller who kept us up at night. They could never shut her up, even after they took away two of her front teeth. When the lights were out, she whispered, breathing tales down on our necks. Words spilled out: the name of her mother, sighs of her dad, the year her first pony was born, the day of her first period, first wine tasted, the tall tales of her horse-riding and puppy love, all the sweetness and stupidity of her childhood, tales of home. We were in love with her gap-toothed smile, her giggles. Every night, with her stories, she brought the house down.

The idea of home was fading inside us in that place, but Yongmal kept it alive. Though she died in the Station, she'd wanted me to survive. She'd wanted me to escape the damn place and go home. In a way she was lucky, I thought, for she would never know that what she called home would no longer be there, eaten up by another war; she would never know I was to be thrown back inside those walls, by the same hands that had saved me: those of the Allied forces, of American soldiers, which had put a grand end to the Pacific War.

As time went by, it became clear why they put me on the job, as the unofficial manager and interpreter of the House. In their eyes I was a little boy, never a man, thus an unlikely tomcat to put his dirty little paws on their meat, the wartime victuals reserved for the Yankees. They were intent on keeping it as unspoiled as possible, their military bodies healthy, work-ing. They must have thought that their House, along with its secret, was safe and sound. They didn't know they'd let in a bug – a wrong one with sharp little teeth, slowly gnawing at its four corners.

When Jenny was locked up in the Monkey Room for three days, I was to watch her, make sure she wouldn't run away again, or die. Most of the time she wasn't fully herself, only able to moan or scream. In rare peeps of moments, however, when she did flash her real self, we talked. As much as I was drawn to her, I was appalled by her: I knew where her audacity would take her. I'd seen it, and I couldn't afford another loss. Yet still we talked. And I smuggled in more food and water for her. I was a listener mostly, she the talker. Though I had some stories to spill, I tried to keep quiet – I knew it was better for both of us. Like Yongmal, Jenny talked a lot of home. She also told me how she'd come to the House: all it had taken to get her there, she said, was two bags of barley. "My little sisters had been starving for days, so I happily took their food and wrote down my name on their list. How the hell could I know what *Namrodang* was?" she howled. "A young girl who couldn't even go near the school gate?"

With time, I got used to the routine of the House – Jenny also helped me learn its ins and outs. Two doctors visited: one Korean, the other American. The Korean one came more frequently, each time with a nurse and a box full of needles and phials. The white man appeared only once every few weeks. He never engaged in the treatment directly: he was, rather, an observer, reading charts, taking note of progress or deterioration. And once a month, just like they did in the Station, they took all the women out, put them into the back of their truck, and drove to the big military hospital in the city, where the women underwent a more thorough check-up.

I knew where they kept the medical supplies. They were stacked in the makeshift storage room on the second floor, near the entrance to the Monkey Room, to which I had no access. The night-prowling Korean warden carried the key with him always. I figured he never fully trusted me with the girls or the valuables. It wasn't an issue for me: I was a natural pickpocket, who'd survived the war, with no shame, through stealing. Not only did I steal warmth from other bodies, I also took their valuables. Their meals, money, medicine – you name it. Whatever they'd buried in their bosoms got me through one day after another.

And poison wasn't a stranger to me – not at all. It was a face in a crowd, familiar, shooting me a furtive smile. Or a little sentinel, keeping guard on my pocket full of dark secrets. *With you, I've already toppled two men*, she whispered, into my ear. Yes, it was *she*, not *he*, for it was, they say, a *feminine* way of doing it: underhand and insidious, therefore never a manly enough means. For me, it was the only conceivable method, as helpless as I had been, stripped of choices and dignity. When the hands that ought to protect you come to strangle your life out of you, you feel no shame in turning to the only set of teeth you're left with. Poison, for the love of God, was true democracy: it didn't discriminate – it would get you, rich or poor, Communist or capitalist, woman or man.

Though I was tempted, I never revealed my true self to Jenny, or to any other woman of the House. As much as I longed to save them, I avoided attachment. I had no small talk with them. I evaded, or ignored, their pleading eyes. I knew those faces would visit my dreams even long after the smell of shell-fire had died out. I strove not to remember their names, all those familiar disyllables that would roll off my tongue if I let them. All except Jenny's, of course.

I felt that Jenny, like Yongmal, had come into my life through a certain force over which I had no control. I wished her hawk eyes, those disturbing yet exciting little glares, would always remain as treacherous, as full of fight. I wished I would always remember her that way. So when the day dawned – the morning of the monthly medical check-up in the city, the morning when I tied those deceitful slip-knots under all the women's wrists, which would easily come undone with one long, gentle tug, after putting the warden's revolver in Jenny's knickers, the gun with only one bullet missing, the one now wedged somewhere between the sleeping guard's ears, the gun, I told her, to be pulled out only when the truck decelerated along the steep, serpentine path through the mountain, to be fired into the back of the driver's head as soon as she and the other women quietly freed their hands from the slip-knots, the morning when I fed the truck driver the half-true lie that the warden had passed out *under the influence* again, the big morning, if their luck held, of their only attempt at escape – I did something to Jenny I hadn't really planned on: I hugged her. I pulled her toward me and held her tight from behind, stealing a shard of her warmth, giving her a little of mine, too, so now I had a piece of her, she of me. I felt her jutting rib cage purr gently in my arms. Neither of us moved. Albeit briefly, no woes of the world could touch us.

The biggest problem lay within the House. Even with the warden, the driver and the guard down, the House would always be there, making it impossible for us to escape from it, even long after we were taken out of those walls. So, I'd started to pilfer fuel. Anything that was a fan of flame in fact: gasoline for the truck; kerosene for the stove; rubbing alcohol out of the doctor's white box; even the stinking liquor the warden had stashed behind the kitchen shelf. I'd poured a wee bit of cloudy toxic fluid into his liquor bottle instead and filled my syringe with morphine. I'd felt an ironic gratitude toward the doctors, toward the warden; like many other slaves, I'd learned how to wear the look of a halfwit while keeping an eye and ear wide open, constantly picking up crumbs of knowledge from the master. How odd it had been in the end – to watch the warden's face in peace, in surrender to the big sleep, at odds with his usual air of anxiety, the big nervous eyes incessantly on the rove, his readiness to swoop on a scampering mouse. I gave him the respite he'd needed yet could never give to himself.

I knew the raw, tender guts of the House beneath the sturdy skin. The iron-gray outside was a veneer, sheltering the fragrant frame of wood.

If we really couldn't get out of the House, I thought, why not turn it inside out?

Carefully, I injected the stolen liquid into its skeleton, dousing every column, crossbeam, every corner of the parquet floors with the piercing perfume of the inflammables, its sweet and sinister aroma lifting my head to float around the House, as though I had no body, an odd grin curving my lips.

I could have left the area immediately. Instead, I walked slowly up the mountain at the back of the House, and stole into the thickness of its woods. I spent the entire morning there, hidden, watching.

I saw the flapping wings of firebirds through the barred windows, warming their little bodies to take flight. *Burn, baby, burn* – my lips moved without a sound.

What a beauty. What a pleasure it was. To burn, to see things smolder, disappear into the dance of the amber tongues, driving each other wilder, at each caprice they conjured. It happened much faster than I thought, a hundred strands of those scorching tongues poking out through the bars, licking, caressing the wall, painting blazing black over the dull gray. Soon, along with a change in the course of the wind, the House blew one of its last breaths, sending the flickering fireflies in my direction, the beautiful remnants of flame that tickled my face, leaving little smudges of darkness on my skin, which I would probably never be able to wash away. Rather, I would wear them proudly. Now the crossbeams began to rumble down, giving up a roaring round of applause. For one last time, I put my index finger right under my nose, breathing in the lingering scent of kerosene. I drank its headiness to the lees. Then I took one last good look at the collapsing maws that had once been the steel-guarded windows. They'd probably thought those iron bars could keep their dirty secret in forever. They didn't know they'd let the wrong bug in – a *firebug*, a coat-turning trickster that set their roof on fire, set to bring down the whole damn House.

The 2nd Life

Storyteller

1942

They were good storytellers, after all. They used so many different stories to woo us.

For Soori, it was the promise of her father's release: they said all she needed to do was to work at a Senninbari factory in Japan for two years to free her father, whom they'd taken in for tax evasion he'd never committed. For Nami, it was education: at the top of her class, yet poor as a mole, she saw it as a once-in-a-lifetime opportunity when they offered her a scholarship to a high school and college, in exchange for two years of her labor at a shoe factory. For Jayoung, the bait was caramel: born as the unlucky fourth daughter in an impecunious sonless family, she didn't think twice before saying yes to the job at a candy factory in Osaka: they promised her daily toil would be met not with censure for being a girl, but with ample pay and a fat sack of caramel that would indulge her incorrigible sweet tooth.

For me, it was an eye.

They cajoled me into believing they could undo the damage that had taken away my mother's right eye. Tokyo's best modern hospital can perform such a miracle, Officer Kinoshita said, So the benevolent Empire will redeem what your Joseon father destroyed. I couldn't say there was no room for suspicion but I was too desperate to care. After my abusive father died from sudden food poisoning, his beastly hands leaving Mama half blind, her health deteriorated rapidly. With her poor vision and vertigo, she could no longer work at the match factory. To make matters worse, three months after his death Mama discovered the parting gift he'd left for us: a seed growing inside her belly. So, by the time kids of my age from rich families entered middle school, I became the child breadwinner of a newborn sister and a purblind mother. My endless labor, however, was barely enough to provide us with three meals on our table each day. Thus, when Officer Kinoshita came to us with the proposal – a decent salary and eye surgery for my mother in exchange for two years of my work at a textile factory in Nagoya – I took it, thinking there was no way my situation could become worse.

Sometimes when they were too tired to make up stories, they didn't bother. They took random fresh-faced teenage girls off the street, loaded them into the back of their military trucks, and drove away. Mija and Yongmal came to the Station in that way. They were at the market in broad daylight, in front of the confection vendor, watching him cut gooey pumpkin taffy into perfect golden rectangles. Mija was counting coins when she felt the arm encircling her waist and a hand grabbing her braided hair. She was too stunned to scream. But she heard Yongmal, who fought hard, kicking the soldier's shins, biting his forearm. Yet she ended up, just like Mija, in the back of the truck, spitting out a bloody tooth lost to a military boot. Mija and Yongmal told me they were jealous of the rest of us as we had had a chance to say goodbye to our families. They said it broke their hearts: their parents might have assumed they'd run away from home. But I thought there was no difference in the end. I even figured their parents were better off assuming their daughters had run away than knowing the truth – knowing what we were made to go through at the Station.

With their own storytelling, they redefined everything.

First they changed our names. Jayoung became Sawako, meaning *sweet*. Jobasan declared the name a perfect fit for her love of caramel and chocolate. Mija, for being the youngest and smallest of the Station, turned into Akiko, which means *child*. Yongmal's was handpicked by Officer Kaneda, who had her before all the lower-ranking soldiers: "Call her Anzu," he ordered Jobasan, grinning, "for her rear end tastes like a young tangy *anzu*" – an apricot. Yongmal, of course, refused to let us call her that when they were not around, swearing she would never touch another apricot. Soori was now Saori and Nami Namiko, probably for the sake of phonetic similarity. I didn't refuse to use mine: by adopting their *nom de guerre*, I wanted to separate the woman at the Station from the old me, the shrewd, bubbly little girl of Heoguri, Korea. So from then on, I was Kaiyo. "Never forget that you girls are the loyal subjects of the Japanese empire," proclaimed Jobasan, "so abandon all your old Korean ways, especially the language."

Not only did their plot redefine our names, it also altered the meanings of certain words we'd been familiar with. What they called *factory* wasn't a factory at all, and the place they called Japan wasn't the Japan we'd known of. Our final destination turned out to be Semarang, Indonesia, one of myriad locations in Asia for the Imperial Japanese military bases. And we were to serve at what they referred to as the Comfort

Station inside the base. On our first night at Semarang we learned, viscerally, what their *comfort* meant. The Station was a small makeshift lodge mainly made of bamboo, its interior comprising twenty-five tiny rooms separated by thin walls of interlinked tree bark. Each of us, twenty-four in total, was locked into one of these rooms. Then, a few hours later, the officers came in. And they did to us what thousands of other soldiers would repeatedly do on every single day we spent at the Station, until the end of the Second World War. On that first night I heard the whole spectrum of sound that a human in terror could make. It began with shrills and shrieks, then quickly ripened to a guttural roar, like that of a cornered beast. At times the noise came to an abrupt halt, following a dim metallic clunk, or a wall-shuddering thud, accompanied by cursing in Japanese. In the end, after the exit of the last gloating officer, there was muffled wailing in unison. Before long, the deep, damp trench of the night swallowed it all up, then belched out a smidgen of panting sobs and, finally, silence: a resigned stillness as heavy and gray as my mother's dead eye.

During the day, numerous soldiers robbed me of *comfort* – around fifty on each weekday, two hundred at weekends. When I slipped into unconsciousness, they poured a bucket of icy water over me so I would wake up and continue my duty till sundown. When our groins swelled with burgundy blisters, our backsides bled, and the pain stopped us walking, they injected opium into our veins, eight or nine shots at weekends, to meet the soaring demand.

At night, we whispered to each other in secret, in our mother tongue, our bittersweet memories from home, which would make us smile, sometimes choke in laughter, then cry. Yongmal seemed never to run out of words. She was quite a talker, the one you couldn't shut up. She'd even persisted in speaking Korean for the first few days in front of Jobasan and the soldiers, until they took away another front tooth and gave her a permanent limp on the left. Missing two front teeth resulted in Yongmal pronouncing every *s* as *sh*, which would often make us giggle. She knew this and turned it to her advantage in her night-time chat – "That shtupid shucker-shonova-bitch!" she once called Jobasan, setting a stifled snigger that spread among the girls like brush fire. We never tired of Yongmal's stories. I envied so much the childhood she'd had, and the flair with which she described it.

She had been born into a wealthy farming family in northern Pyongan-do. Yongmal's father, who'd inherited a big pear farm from his childless uncle, was a sweet-natured, soft-spoken man, with a velvety voice and meek eyes as round as those of a calf. Her mother, who ruled the household and farm with an iron fist, was endowed with the quick eye of a businessman and sturdy forearms, taut for travail. Despite the difference in their nature, Yongmal's parents hatched a hearty home full of love, laughter and food. She even had a horse. She named him Baram, which could mean *wind* and *wish* in Korean. Baram had a sweet tooth – even worse than Jayoung's, Yongmal added, with a cheeky grin. She had a hard time keeping up with his demands, often giving up her own sweets, stashing them inside her pillowcase for their future training sessions. Sometimes she had to pilfer her mother's expensive white sugar from the kitchen, or purchase pumpkin taffy from the market with her pocket money. Unlike most men, who found a woman straddling a horse vulgar, her father was happy to see her and Baram together, how vivacious she became with him.

The story we loved most was that of Yongmal skipping

town on the dawn of her wedding day, the legend told and retold on countless occasions. One day, to her shock, she found out her parents had been arranging her marriage. A sneak peek at her future husband's photo filled her with horror: a pale, lanky man, seemingly at least ten years her senior, with two big pockmarks perched just above the arch of his right eyebrow, like a semicolon. It turned out he was a well-to-do tailor from Pyongyang whose father was a childhood friend of her father, a widower thirteen years her senior. Yongmal felt stabbed by a sense of betrayal – how could her father, the liberal dove-eyed gentleman, conceive such an archaic plan behind her back? He explained it was for her own good. 'The word on the street is that the Japanese are taking away unmarried girls,' he said, unfamiliar gloom drawing his brows together. Now she had grasped his meaning all too well, but her younger self had been too innocent to understand. All she recognized, clad in the shiny gown of blood-red taffeta on the early morning of her wedding, was the prospect of rebellion. Left alone in her darkened room behind a white muslin curtain, while all the women in the house were busy preparing food for the banquet, she shed her crimson dress. Like a snake slithering out of its dead skin, she sneaked out of her room through the window facing the back-yard, scurried to the stable, and mounted Baram. They made it out of the back gate with no one noticing. And when they reached the safe path through the woods, she urged Baram into a gallop, making her horse, for the first time in his life, run worthy of his name.

They were racing toward the bridge, just a dozen meters shy of exiting the boundary of her hometown, when they spotted the tiny figure. It was a man, a short, pudgy one, shoulders bowed under two huge brown bundles he was carrying. His eyes were fixed on her and Baram. "What a sight it must have made," Yongmal whispered. "A young girl on a high horse, dressed in thin silky undergarments, dashing toward him like thunder!" She saw his knees wobble, then a bundle on his shoulder fall to the ground, spilling its powdery contents across the bridge. She didn't slow. But Baram gave a sudden hiss. He neighed loudly, and came to an abrupt halt, catapulting Yongmal into the air. The icy river hitting her nape was the last thing she remembered before she passed out. She woke up later in her room, surrounded by her parents, servants, a doctor, and the tubby man from the bridge. He turned out to be a sugar pedlar, carrying the sacks of white sugar her mother had ordered for the wedding banquet dessert. While Baram was consuming the snowy dust that covered the bridge, the pedlar rescued her from the river. Fortunately, Yongmal suffered only a minor injury. And thus, unfortunately, the wedding proceeded as planned – despite Yongmal sneezing every two minutes, her upper lip swollen to the size of a walnut. And, she said, for the following few days, the sugar-dusted bridge remained a hot spot for the town's puppies and passing mules.

We waited, with curiosity and horror, for her account of her first night with her unwanted husband. She said she knew vaguely what was supposed to happen, and was ready to fight him off with tooth and nail – and even with the burning candles in the room, if necessary. "Life is full of surprises," Yongmal murmured. "He didn't lay a finger on me." He said she needed to rest after such a long, hard day, his voice smooth and silvery. What she'd expected to happen took place on neither the next day nor the day after. And she came to realize he wasn't as bad-looking as she'd assumed from the photo: his awkward, lanky figure seemed sleek in real life – stately even, at times – in the maroon Western suit he had made for himself. She liked the way his eyes smiled before his mouth did. She was also surprised that he spoke to her in the honorific Korean despite the age difference. She liked talking with him, his gentle voice flowing in measured cadences, as if reciting a poem. She even began to find the two pockmarks above his eyebrow endearing – they seemed to give him an extra edge, as though the brow was permanently arched with curiosity or wonder for the world he described with such passion. He loved Pyongyang, and thought she would, too, yet he made sure there was no rush. "It's you who will decide when to start things," he told her, his eyes gleaming.

Some of the story's minor details shifted a little at each encore: Baram was once called a *pony*, not a horse – slip of the tongue – and the bridge over the river sometimes sounded more like aligned steppingstones over a stream. Those changes never undermined our love for the story, though. It always made us sigh with satisfaction, then with longing for the world that had been lost to us. We never asked her to repeat what had happened afterwards: Yongmal and Mija, Yongmal's house servant who had grown up more like her little sister, vanished on their way to the market to buy sweets for Baram. "I should have held my husband in my arms" – Yongmal spoke under her breath, her voice raspy with regret – "and told him how much I'd grown to care about him even over such a short time." Mija started to sob, her breath choppy. In silence, we endeavored to absorb a shard of their sorrow, and keep it buried in the pit of our bellies. Jayoung, lying next to Mija, held Mija tight to her big bosom. Then she fumbled for a piece of caramel she'd stashed in her pocket, and slipped it gently into Mija's little hand.

Yongmal and I were similar in many ways. We were both smart and stubborn, they said. We resisted showing tears in front of the comfort robbers. We even looked alike:

about the same height and weight, with high cheekbones and slightly square chins that men found eye-catching and off-putting. "You girls could easily pass as sisters," Jobasan once blurted out, after he had called me Anzu by mistake from only a couple of steps away. We also shared a passion for stories.

Unlike Yongmal, however, who relied on her stories from home, I avoided dwelling on mine. My last memories of Mama especially. How she had shed a layer every passing day since Father's death. How her swelling belly had seemed to sap her sanity, her rapier wit. This wasn't the story of Mama I wanted to hold onto. It was a chasm too vast for me to bridge – between my beloved mama, a bright, modern woman who would take her little daughter to an English class run by foreign missionaries, and the gray-eyed woman, whose will to live had shriveled away with her abuser's demise.

My hard-scrabble life was riddled with violence. With his fists and mouth, Father consumed my childhood. The Station took my adolescence. Yet it didn't leave me feeling like a woman. Instead, I saw an old man in my eyes – crumpled, surprised by nothing any longer, expecting nothing, too, from life, save its inevitable ending.

Every now and again, though, when I was caught up in the desperation to hold onto my sanity, I thought of the earth of my hometown, Heoguri. I thought about its birch grove, where the lush moss-green leaves kept the soil moist and warm all year round. As a child, I used to eat its earth. I loved savoring its texture that was at once tender and bristly, its warm, nutty taste that harbored a surprise bitter, metallic kick. After Father's death, after we had buried him in the birch grove, I'd given up eating earth. I started again only at the Station, after the first death of a comfort girl. It was Soori:

homesickness had overtaken her. On the eve of her passing, I was gripped by the urge to eat the earth at the Station, hoping it would return my senses to the once-familiar world outside, to the birch grove of my hometown. But the soil of Semarang was nothing like that of Heoguri. It was too fine, too silky, its texture akin to that of dust or chalk, devoid of the sharp metallic bitterness I craved.

When eating earth failed me, I stole into someone else's asylum, lost myself in the stories of Yongmal, pretending I was living her childhood, no matter how transient that would be. During the imaginary escapade, I was her, the darling daughter whose life had known no evil before the Station, and I gave her story an alternative ending instead of death in this place: a return to her dove-eyed father, her sturdy mother, and the delicate arms of her willowy lover, who had never stopped waiting for her.

The reality wasn't as beautiful as the stories we told each other in secret at night.

Some of us fell pregnant, our babies and wombs ripped away from us. Miraculously we survived the procedure, but we lost the chance to bear another child.

It was Soori's fall that made us all wonder who would be next. Soori was the first to lose her grip on reality. She began to call every soldier *Appa*, Daddy in Korean, prattling endlessly and incoherently about her family in a chilling baby voice, often letting out panting, throaty giggles. It seemed she'd forgotten Japanese, unable to respond to the language at all, including her Japanese name Saori. She never stopped babbling in Korean while she was awake, and one day Officer Kaneda decided to shut her up. First by jamming the muzzle of his pistol into her throat. Then by smashing her lower jaw to ruin with its hand grip.

We knew she wouldn't make it. They didn't take her body away, though. They left it there, by the entrance to the Station, for all of us to watch. It took almost two days – her breath gurgling like that of a newborn, half of her face, a flattened web of blood, twitching intermittently – until her body slowly bled itself to silence.

Then, one day, Mija fell down, grabbing her belly. The littlest and the sweetest at the Station, Mija was the last we ever wished to lose. But a coil of pain in her loins pulled her down. She spent the early morning moaning, curled up on the floor like a shrimp. Strands of blood trickled down to her knees. When Jobasan and a medic took her away, many of us wept, Yongmal the most, of course. Half an hour later, Mija came back – her arms still coiled around her belly, shoulders slumped, yet smiling. It turned out, to our utmost relief, Mija had no serious illness: it was her first period, her first cramps. Yongmal held Mija in her arms for a long ten minutes, word-less. Mija was twelve.

The angel of death descended on another girl, though. It was Nami, a month later. Nami the brightest, the girl who spoke the best Japanese, the little genius who wanted to become the first female doctor in her hometown once the war was over. Nami's belly had been bloating, bleeding for weeks. When her escalating fever caused her to faint, the medic took her away, only to return her an hour later, half conscious, high on pain. Whatever the medic did failed to improve her condition, and perhaps worsened it. Nami died a week later, the color between her legs purple-black, like the sky during a thunderstorm.

As the war dragged on, dulling our already threadbare hopes, the soldiers' cruelty increased. Beatings and railings accompanied the rapes. And our flimsy night-time peace was invaded by much more frequent visits from drunken, howling officers. I smelt fear – a hint of frailty disguised in harshness. Only in this did they seem remotely human.

One night Officer Kaneda came to me, completely inebriated. "Take off my clothes, Kaiyo," he said to me, his voice surprisingly tender. I knew what he wanted: he wanted me to play his sweet concubine, taking off his war-sodden clothes, washing his weary feet, all the while telling him a sugary lie that everything would be all right. I said *no*. "I won't do it," I told him. If they rape me they rape me, I thought, I have no power to stop it. Catering for their emotions, however, was another story. His eyes squeezed into slits, the pupils gleaming dark as sealskin. The following was no surprise: slaps and punches, the warm, tinny flavor of blood seeping through my gums. I heard the mocking falsetto of my *no* echoing from his contorted lips. He wrapped his fingers around the hilt of his sword, and pulled it out of its scabbard in one long smooth swish.

This was my turn, I thought. I closed my eyes.

They were opened again by a voice: "Go ahead, cut me," she said. An uncanny one, yet with the familiar wheezing, raspy tinkle.

"Aren't you supposed to cut off an enemy soldier's head with that?" she continued. "You're not going to smear helpless little Josenpi's blood on the precious sword bestowed by the Emperor?"

Kaneda was motionless, his jaw slack. The tip of his sword had been already lowered to the floor, despite himself. Yongmal's wooden voice continued: "What sort of man are you? You call yourself an officer of the Imperial Army? Shame on you."

Yongmal's gaunt body was standing in front of mine, her pelvis jutting out to the left – toward the lowered sword.

Kaneda's face was turning livid. The shock was draining away, I could tell.

"*You filthy Josenpi*," Kaneda barked, his voice shivering up the walls. "How dare you mention the Emperor with your filthy mouth?"

His hands tightened around the hilt of the sword, fingertips growing pale. Then slowly he lifted it, drew its curved edge near Yongmal's chin.

She cocked an eyebrow, slowly, with a faint grin. A thought raced through my mind: *She wants to die.*

"Go on. Let me see what it feels like. My heart is right here."

She pulled down the loose neckline of her blouse, baring the left side of her chest, the skin parchment yellow, mottled with cigarette burns.

The following day I went over the whys in my mind. Was it her uncanny voice, so full of eerie serenity? Was she really willing to die? Why did he dither? Most of all, why did he put the sword away? Yongmal and I, how had we survived the night unscathed?

Not long afterwards, I saw Yongmal coughing up a thick clot of blood. "Don't come any closer!" she yelped at us. It was tuberculosis. It had developed after she had suffered a bout of malaria. "I don't have much time left. I know my body," she murmured. Then she let out a whoosh of air – sigh or snort, I couldn't be sure.

"That was why you weren't afraid," I told her – and myself.

"Oh dear, I *was*," she said, with a smile. "I thought my heart would pop right out of my chest, to tell you the truth."

"Then how?" I asked.

"Well, I thought, I know I'm going to die anyway, so what's the difference? Plus, that coward knew I have tuberculosis. He didn't want my blood to splash all over him." She winked at me, her gap-toothed smile widening. That disarming smile of hers, emanating the cheek and innocence of a child, was the picture I would carry along with her name. Yongmal died a month later.

Yongmal's stories couldn't save her, even though they saved the lives of many others at the Station, including mine.

But life after her death wasn't the same. Our night-time chats were often punctuated by silences. No girl was half as willing or as gifted a storyteller as she'd been. The stillness of our nights constantly reminded us of her absence. It also stole Mija's tongue. She stopped talking. She seemed to have thrown herself into complete resignation, probably the only passive aggression she could afford.

Officer Kaneda had begun to visit me at night after he found out about Yongmal's illness. After her death, his visits became part of my regular routine. I knew I was second best, a substitute for his absent favorite, who shared the same streak of doggedness that was maddening yet tantalizing, the same rugged facial features that invited his elaborate punches, the high cheekbones standing out white under the gas lamp. The kind he loved to torture, tame, and fuck. On one of his many drunken nights, he blurted out that he had created Yongmal and me: "*I named her Anzu, and you Kaiyo*," he mumbled, asking me if I knew what my name meant. I said I didn't want to know but he told me anyway. "*Forgiveness*, Kaiyo – forgiveness." Eyes full of clammy nostalgia, he stared at me, as though waiting for my nod. I told him "forgiveness" might be my least favorite word. A fake, make-believe vocabulary to be precise. My breasts had to bear a dozen cigarette burns that night, just like Yongmal's.

A daily life wallowing in misery sometimes made you find beauty in the least expected crevice. After Yongmal's death, and the unbearable silence of our nights, what got me through the looming madness was an image of what might have seemed stark banality to most others. I saw it, once every week, outside the walls of the Station, of the military base, when we were sent out to the military hospital in the village for the regular medical check. Crouching in the back of the rattling military truck, the fuzz on my forearms soaking up the shimmering Pacific sun, I devoured the sight of the locals. Their glowing nut-brown faces filled me with joy. They were the few human faces I saw, other than those of moaning Japanese soldiers. I felt as though they were my closest allies, intimate friends to whom I could confide my darkest secrets and sorrows. The picture of them going casually about their daily business – a small toothless grandfather slowly driving a cyclo in the lazy haze of the day; a group of farmers chatting their commute away, punctuated by throaty laughs; a stocky mother with a gurgling baby wrapped to her bosom and another dangling from her forearm – was the essence of delightful mundanity. Sometimes when the truck was slowing for a throng of heavily equipped water buffalos, I could even hear them talk in their native tongue, so sweet and comforting that my eyes brimmed with tears. Its tone, chirpy and playful, reached my ears like a nursery rhyme my mother had hummed, full of intimacy and ineffable solace. Time ceased to matter during that eight-minute bumpy truck ride; that transient moment was a weekly dose of strength, hope, and beauty, which allowed me to survive another week in hell, my core still recognizable as mine. The moment was truly mine – something they couldn't taint, couldn't take away from me. I held onto it for dear life.

The weekly medical check-up, of course, provided me with practical aid as well.

Although there was an infirmary inside the base, the

increasing occurrence of venereal diseases among the soldiers forced us to undergo a regular check by a real doctor from the military hospital in town. Dr Mitsuyama, on my fourth visit, revealed his real name to me: Kim Young-soo. Born and raised in Seoul, he had been finishing his medical degree in Tokyo when he was conscripted into the Japanese Army. "We're all striving to survive the battlefield that isn't ours," he whispered to me in Korean, his deep-set eyes glistening with sorrow.

It was through him that I could start collecting the pills: *keumgyerab*, for malaria, made of quinine. On each visit I asked quietly for one or two. My goal was to collect forty. This had begun only after Yongmal's death: I thought it was the only measure of dignity I could turn to, ending my own life, one day when they would squeeze me dry of every last drop of hope.

Then I started to feel it, the beginning of the end. The air around us was growing thicker with it each day: the sour and sinister breath of fear. We sensed it in their drunken cries. We saw it in their downcast eyes that occasionally surfaced through their hard exterior. Even the foot soldiers were showing up sloshed at the Station in broad daylight. Certain officers were rumored to spend more time getting high on opium than mapping out military tactics. For the first time I saw Officer Kaneda, under the double influence of whiskey and opium, pass out in front of me. Jayoung told me one private soldier with an unstable temperament had committed *seppuku* in the barracks – suicide by disembowelment, the old practice of Japanese samurais who had lost a battle. "The *Yankees* are coming," Jayoung whispered, her breath quickening with excitement.

Dr Kim, with his rutted brow and dark philosophical eyes, once said the end of things always comes at first gradually, then suddenly. The day he handed me the fortieth *keumgyerab*, he told me the end was just around the corner now. "Soon the American forces will attack the base, could be tomorrow, or in a month," he whispered. My heart fluttered like a trapped bird as I thanked him, and said goodbye. He put on a thin smile. Then he called me by my Korean name one last time, and beckoned me to come closer. He asked me sotto voce to promise him one thing.

"Once the attack starts, the Japanese may herd you girls into the air-raid shelter. Do not follow them into the shelter. They're trained not to acknowledge the word *surrender*. They'll spare no one, not even themselves. Do you understand?"

That night, Officer Kaneda visited me – half drunk as expected. As always, he brought his own glass and opaque teal bottles of cheap liquor. Looking down at his measure of desperation, breathing in his tart insecurity, I suddenly realized there were so many things in this world Kaneda wasn't aware of. First of all, he would be surprised to see me do something I'd never done before without him forcing me: I would pour him his drink with both hands, my eyes lowered in decorum. He had no idea that I would let him wallow in my sudden surrender as well as his smirking sense of conquest, quietly nodding to his intoxicated reminiscences of Yongmal and his days of glory. "Like I've created you," he would mutter, "you are to die as my little forgiveness, Kaiyo, just as Anzu did as my sweet little apricot." Then he would carve, in his off-kilter laughter and tears, a jagged shape of an apricot on my flank with his small army knife, which was already familiar with the taste of little girls' blood. He hadn't the slightest idea that quietly I would bear it all.

How little did he know me – after all these years of him cutting into every hole on my body. This realization squeezed silent laughter out of me, the kind tinged with pity. What he didn't know was that I was a storyteller. Just like him and Yongmal. Of course, it was I who'd woven the finale of my own father: after his violence toward Mama became unbearable, resulting in the loss of her eye, I hatched the plan of putting an end to it all. I poisoned him, and I created the make-believe context of his death for the townspeople. I buried his body deep in the birch grove in secret and told the neighbors my fisherman father had left for another round of whale-hunting, only to send myself a fake telegram a month later that a storm had got the better of him out on the sea. Although I abhorred the physicality of the death I'd had to cause, making up its back story came naturally to me. Later in life, I came to ponder if my impudence had driven Mama addle-brained after Father's death – the shock that her sweet little daughter was capable of such chicanery without batting an eyelid.

What he also didn't know about me was that Kaiyo wasn't the first alternative name I'd been given. Before him, there was already an older man, a white man, who had christened me with a foreign name. I was called Deborah by Pastor Peltier, the Canadian missionary who taught an English class near our hometown, to which my mother took me every week when she was still the bright young modern woman I'd admired. So here's another thing Kaneda would never know about me: Japanese wasn't the only foreign tongue I knew. Trained as Deborah in my late childhood, I was a good speaker and writer of English. Yes, writer was indeed what I was; when Dr Kim learned about my secret skill on my thirty-eighth visit, he asked me to help him write the crucial note in English – the tiny slip of yellow wallpaper that harbored an SOS for the American forces, describing the location and the overall situation of the Japanese military base in Semarang – which he would furtively hand over to a local laundryman to be delivered to one of the Yankee scouts.

There was yet another story I was to weave, entirely of my own accord this time. Kaneda had invented my new name; I would write him his new secret ending. I had no choice, as death was marching toward me from both sides anyway. With my plan at least I had a shot, however meager it would be, at revenge and survival. I would play the ultimate concubine, the submissive geisha he wanted me to play for him so badly, pouring him wine, lighting his corncob pipe full of the sinful flower, all the while feeding his whiskey bottles with powdered quinine pills by stealth whenever he tottered out to take a leak, till his body gave in, slowly sinking into the cloying slumber. Dr Kim said the death by *keumgyerab* was a messy one: You would bleed profusely, through every little open hole of your body. So, to mask its bloodiness, I would have to perform the final act of submission on his behalf: *seppuku*, suicide by disembowelment. I would meet a sure death if they found out I'd poisoned him. If they believed he'd turned to their own warrior-worthy way of suicide, though, I might outlive the murder.

Dr Kim was right. As he'd philosophized, the end of things comes at first gradually, then suddenly. With Kaneda's samurai sword in my hands, I was looking down at his body, its limbs mutely twitching, fighting the last fight he would never win, against the ample trinity of spirits and opium and quinine. I held the sword high, its tip pointing at the left end of Kaneda's lower abdomen, astounded by my own calm, the icy steadiness of my grip. I was just wondering what kind of thoughts would cross his mind if his little tadpole-shaped eyes were open when I heard the first thunder.

It reverberated from the far-east corner of the base in dull ripples – dreamy and intangible, as if it was somebody else's thunder. The second came like a sharp slap in the face that would leave your ear in dense silence for a while. This one was close, I knew, feeling the floor shiver under my bare feet. Then the siren wailed. I dropped the sword and stormed out of the room.

Amid the sirens, I heard a man shouting: "*All of you girls, if you wanna live, run to the air-raid shelter!*"

Another bomb dropped. Clods of dried mud fell from the roof, filling the corridors with sallow mist. Fits of coughing echoed. Muffled grunting, whimpering. "To the air-raid shelter! *Now!*" squealed the male voice again, followed by the smacking click of a rifle being loaded. Knocked to the floor, I gasped to regain my voice.

Soon a whorl of little sloppy footfalls clattered the Station. *Girls running for their lives.* My head ticked like a clock as I realized they were in fact dashing toward death. I wanted to bark the truth out loud. Through my narrowed vision, however, I saw a Japanese soldier holding his gun a stone's throw away; at the entrance of the Station another was eyeing each girl darting out of the smashed door. I ducked down, hid behind the closest corner of the main corridor. I waited. Then I tripped the next set of little feet that showed up. With a thump, the girl stumbled down next to me. It was Jayoung. I quickly pressed my hand to her mouth. Then without removing it, I stared at her, slowly shaking my head. Wide-eyed, Jayoung nodded. I pointed at the latrine near the back door, and we started crawling toward it together. "I think we're the last ones in here," whispered Jayoung, wheezing. "I was running around looking for Mija."

When we had dipped our bodies into the tobacco-colored pool, the shooting roared. It came from the air-raid shelter. The first round of bullets was quick and tight, the second rather lazy, intermittent. Jayoung and I remained dead silent, still as a peg, hoping the thatched roof of the outhouse wouldn't cave in on us. More thunders, thumps, so heavy you could feel them in your throat. Then the earthquake that ate at one corner of the latrine, inviting a silver lining of the peppery morning sun. The hiss of bullets, the dense crooning of shells piercing the air, the guttural screams of dying men. Our ears survived the hour of the deadly hulla-balloo that felt like an eternity, until they could discern the real silence again.

The fog-like silence – the ghostly bleep, dull and sharp at once.

The soundless noise one can feel only in the wake of an air-raid.

When Jayoung and I crawled out, through the gaping chasm at the corner of the outhouse, the hems of our dresses dripping snuff-colored crud, the entire base seemed to be blanketed under such silence.

The air was rife with the piquant smoldering of gunpow-der. With the fetid smell of burning flesh. The ironic scent, cupreous and musky, of all the blood spattered, spilled, and spoiling.

All that was still standing was our lopsided outhouse and the northern tip of the Station. The southern end, where Kaneda's body had been, was now a jagged mound of rocks, slivers of blackened tree barks and branches. Even through the smoke I could recognize the dark stubby forearm poking out of it. An oil-scummed puddle was collecting next to it, the color of ox-blood, its surface iridescent in the rise of the sun.

Both Jayoung and I were in tears. That my frail body had outlived this impossibility was sharply gratifying on a deep animal level. Yet hulking sorrow began to unwind in my gut at the same time. *Gradually, then suddenly*, Dr Kim had said. I mulled over the word *suddenly*. I wondered how what had seemed impossible to us, putting an end to this slavery, had been achieved so easily by the American forces, almost in the blink of an eye. The Comfort Station, the impregnable fort of evil, had come to ruin so abruptly, so readily.

I stumbled along, my hands in the air in surrender, toward the air-raid shelter. Jayoung followed in silence. The Japanese soldiers must've been in a hurry, I could sense: a couple of dusty feet were already visible at the entrance. They hadn't waited till the girls covered themselves in the darkness of the shelter. They'd started shooting when the last girl had just passed the threshold. After the rushed first round, however, they'd taken their time, checking on each little body, and shooting if there was any sign of life. They'd remained true to their motto till death: *What happens in the Station dies in the Station*. But I bet they hadn't expected the worst mouse to scurry out: the plotting trickster, the storyteller.

We found Mija effortlessly. I recognized her little feet before I recognized her face – in Yongmal's mildewed leather shoes a size too big. The feet looked pale and languid now in their slumber. I took the shoes off. I had none, and I wanted to own something to remember both Yongmal and Mija by. Mija's eyes looked into the void. Jayoung sat down next to Mija's body, smoothed her tousled hair. Then she plunged her hand into Mija's pocket, and one last piece of caramel covered in crinkly foil appeared. She unwrapped it, then gently slipped the caramel into Mija's little hand.

We trudged out of the shelter. The rivulet of blood streaming down from the entrance had now grown thicker, both in color and scope, dyeing the soil a rich burgundy. I hunkered down and stared at the new earth. Soaking up the pained blood of comforters, the silky soil of Semarang, always too meek and bland, had taken on a new grit – the rough metallic bitterness still full of fight, its kick warm red and biting. I sank my fingers deep into the dark earth. Then I grabbed a fistful, and swallowed it whole.

The 4th Life

Me, Myself, and Mole

1955

This is a story about a mole.

About the size of a pea, light aubergine in color. He still remembers how it felt under his fingers: how it stood, pert and taut, when pressed down, yet how pliantly it leaned over when caressed sideways. A little oddity he would always remember her by.

How he relished all the tidbit idiosyncrasies of her body – how endearing they were to his eyes. Her high cheekbones and slightly square jaw, two uncommon features that most men rarely found pretty on a female face. As for her bony shoulders, two ripples that surged voraciously upward every time she let out her guttural laugh ... The sound plays on a perpetual loop in his head.

He has imagined seeing her again, certain he would recognize her instantly. Countless times he has dreamed about the moment he spots her among the crowd. Once it was a roaring red throng on the streets of Pyongyang, celebrating the Supreme Leader's birthday; another time, a collection of shapeless faces in the valley of Daedo, a former home of an illicit leper colony. Whatever the circumstances, he has never failed to spot her right away.

In reality, however, it is she who recognizes him first.

When she arrives at his tailor's shop, she sees three men behind the sleek glass window. As she steps through the door, all three pairs of eyes converge on her face. The men are in suits, all in dark gray, all tall and lean. Yet she approaches her husband directly. She knows what to look for: two pockmarks perched on top of his right brow, like a tilted semicolon.

She cups his face with both hands, as though she is about to stroke a delicate animal. "My husband. *My husband.*"

Twice she repeats. The first rings on a high note, like a question; the second sinks, like a warm, heavy relief. Her eyes well up. Yet she smiles loudly.

A ghost. An apparition. For a few seconds he doubts his eyes. Yet soon he realizes he can't doubt the touch of her fingers on his cheeks. He searches her face for the signs. Those prominent cheekbones and the angular jaw – they are all there.

It is her. Yongmal. His wife.

His beloved, short-lived companion, who had, one day, vanished from his life. Like a scattered daydream – without a proper goodbye, without a trace. It was more than a decade ago. She left home with her handmaiden, saying she was going to the market, to buy some sweets for her pony.

Some people said she ran away, to escape from the arranged marriage. Everyone in the village knew she had already tried. In the early morning of their wedding day, she executed her first breakout: she sneaked out through the window, then the back door, to get away from her hometown before the unwanted companionship could begin. This attempt failed, though – she fell into the river while crossing a bridge – and their wedding took place as planned.

But her second disappearance was different, he thinks. Although their relationship started off as an obligation, as all traditional marriages do, they managed to fall in love. Quiet and introverted, he took to her boldness, while Yongmal, full of spirit, became drawn to his patience and gentleness. They pulled each other, like the opposite poles of a magnet. Each passing day they shared more and more of their minds. More of her laughs, of his sidelong glances, which shielded his thrashing heart. And some collective secrets. The murmurs of their conversations ripened into knowing smiles. Over the course of the first three months of their marriage, they had become lovers.

Was the feeling one-sided? Was I that blind? Despite his initial conviction of their mutual affection, ever since he has found himself asking those questions.

Up until now.

The first day of reunion passes in a daze.

Their heads are in a cloud, both dumbfounded by the stroke of luck that has come their way, the bliss so sharp it leaves them numb.

Yet she needs to think clearly. She knows she's the one to tell stories. She is obliged to fill the gaping hole that includes two wars, the Second World War and the Korean War, a dozen years of her disappearance. She will tell him only the truth. The question lies in what to tell and what to leave out.

When to tell is another matter of importance. Fortunately, she knows him well. One of his characteristics dearest to her is that he can wait. She is already familiar with his patience: although he had had every right by law and by custom, he had never laid a finger on his young wife without her consent. "It's your choice to make, Yongmal," he told her, "not mine." She knows that to love him is like being soaked by light drizzle:

it happens over time, little by little. The moment she sees him at his tailor's shop, though, she knows she's drenched already.

In truth, he takes her by surprise. He is much handsomer than she has imagined. She was expecting him to be a gangly old man with a sallow complexion. But he is neither lanky nor pallid. He is a slender man with a straight back, his posture as elegant as that of a flamingo she'd once seen in her English textbook. And she is rather fond of his *old look*: his salt-and-pepper hair goes well with the graphite gray suit he is wearing. She likes watching the little silvery parts of his hair glisten, whenever he tilts his head in thought, under the incandescent lamps of his shop. What isn't surprising is his smile: it's as lovely as it should be, spreading from his eyes to his mouth, not the other way around, like that of most people. She realizes, as a survivor of two wars, she has long forgotten what a genuine kind smile looks like.

This is my husband, she whispers again, in her head. Though appearance matters little to her when it comes to love she revels in the unexpected physical beauty of her spouse. She can't believe her luck: she has never imagined that someone she fancied for his words and warmth could be also physically gratifying.

For the first time in her life, she feels a surge of desire for a man.

She wonders how long she can put off their *first night* – their marriage has never been consummated. She is not sure how to reveal her new body to him. She is not too worried about the scars: the darkness of night will hide them. Her real concern lies elsewhere: Yongmal's body before her disappearance had known no man. Now, however, it has known thousands. The first war forced the repeated introduction. How can her body fake ignorance? How can she unlearn what she's been force-fed for years? One thought reassures her: her body has never known lovemaking. It is a plain truth. In that light, she doesn't need to fake anything: she has nothing to unlearn. In that light, it will be the first night, *her* first night, true to its meaning.

She stares at his face again. She has already grown fond of his scars above the brow. She likes their texture. It's one of the slight signatures that makes him *him*, she thinks. She wonders whether he would feel the same about hers, if he knew. She thinks he would. But she doesn't want to gamble – not yet. She would rather make sure his feelings for her grow strong and sound again, before she reveals anything too jarring.

She is touched that he noticed her shoes. It took him only a glance. They were the ones that got him to say her name. Yongmal! He mouthed it, the sound barely audible, his voice husky, eyes moist. She guesses the shoes were the clincher for him. He'd had them made for her. He picked the calfskin, the dark maroon color. He designed their fronts to be round, not pointy like most ladies' shoes of the time, so that she could even ride a horse in them. Now they look nothing like their beginnings. Weathered by time and wars, their shimmering maroon has turned moldy mustard. Their heels are a hair away from holes. Still, he can see them for what they were, or what they have always been. As expected, his attentiveness moves her. It moves her deeply.

Ironically, however, the same attentiveness can also alarm her. So she chooses to talk to him at night. They lie face to face, her back against the window, letting the moonlight hit his face, hers immersed in shadow. This way, she can study his face, every reaction it may display, while hers remains illegible. One of the first things to test is her plausibility. She decides to go for it directly. Bold and clean.

'Have I changed a lot? Do I look different?' she asks him. Voice amiable and steady, although her heart is thundering in her ribcage.

"Yes," he answers slowly. He remembers, earlier during the day, seeing those little things on her face that hadn't been there before. Tiny round dots that resemble pockmarks. Or, one would argue, small burn scars from sputtered cinders. He finds the latter convincing, keeping the endless bombardment of the war in mind, still painfully fresh in his memory.

She also sounds different. Her voice has softened, it seems. It has lost a little of its former vigor. And yet he knows she was a teenager when she disappeared. She's a fully-grown woman now. Certain changes are natural and inevitable, he tells himself. What matters is how he feels about her. He still feels the same energy, the same delight. The affection may have grown even deeper in her absence and in his constant waiting.

'You're even more beautiful,' he tells her.

She feels her heart sink again, as joy and sadness come together to stroke it. A strange giggle escapes her, making her sound like a child, a happy one. She does feel happy; she feels very anxious as well. She asks herself if she deserves this happiness. She likes to believe she does.

She is a fast learner. Postwar Pyongyang is a good place to be for someone like her. Only a couple years ago Pyongyang was in complete ruins: saturation bombings by American forces during the Korean War had left nothing but jumbles of burned structures here and there. There was no satisfying closure to the war, no gloating winner: a bloody stalemate had led to an armistice signed between the US and North Korea, leaving the country cut in two. The people of North Korea have been in high spirits, however, fresh-drunk on the Communist Party's ideology and propaganda, still young and handsome in the making. The Party have said they are keen on making it on their own, unlike their disloyal Southern brother who's already turned to foreign aid, especially to the Yankees. People and machines have been working as one mind, to make their country the greatest in the world – "The Workers' Paradise on Earth" is their exact term, branded in blazing red above every entrance to factories and laboratories, along with many other slogans eulogizing the nation's Godly Founding Father, Kim Il-sung. The Party has consistently provided its people with words and images against their brother-turned-enemy; people know, as a fact, that the streets of Seoul are still filled with starving orphans and panhandlers, while in their city of wonder, Pyongyang, a brand-new modern building goes up each day. Like many others she is fond of the city, even though she doesn't really buy the propaganda that dominates every cityscape: she knows too much of foreign tongues, has seen too much of the world already, to believe it wholeheartedly. Yet she has no trouble playing along while the city remains a shelter for the loving, stable family she has never had before.

They live in one of Pyongyang's many *harmonica apartments*. It resembles a harmonica's reed, a load of straight lines bound by right angles: all for efficacy, none for privacy. Like the kernels of a corncob, dwellings are divided by flimsy walls so eavesdropping becomes a natural part of life, as does breathing in the moldy air of the long, narrow corridors, the boxcars rarely touched by sunlight. Sometimes when the night wind rushes through from one end of the hallway to the other, it howls in high falsetto, like a harmonica.

To her, nevertheless, it is a happy home. It is their own place, where the tender husband comes back every evening to be greeted by his wide-eyed wife. In public he is a man of few words. In fact many Party officials, primary customers of his tailor's shop, respect him for his industry and, most of all, for his quietness, as the coterie of promotion-seeking sycophants at work has cloyed them. At home in bed, however, with the lights out, he is one of the most delightful conversationalists.

He shares with her his honest (sometimes a little dangerous) view of life, of the world. One night he whispers to her how much he misses real cinema. "In the old days," he lowers his voice to a silky murmur, "movies could be about anything." He speaks of European and even American films he saw when he was young, the captivating story of Scarlett O'Hara, of honey-voiced Dorothy and her Wizard, and of the imaginary underground city named Metropolis, which, ironically she reckons, sounds not unlike their own dear capital. "Good cinema can effortlessly transport you to a different place and time," says her husband, with a nostalgic sigh. How sad that nowadays the Party cookie-cuts every film to their political purpose. She nods to his blasphemous reflection, fighting the urge to spill out her own cinema stories, the ones she'd heard from her mother who grew up in Seoul. Normally she has little difficulty listening to him all night. She's in love with the way he talks: he speaks as though he's writing, livening his sentences with words and metaphors that others hardly use in workaday conversation. This side of him reminds her of her mother: a rare woman of her time, well-spoken and well-read, a collector of words. It is fascinating to her, this newly found meaning of family – how a good union of a man and a woman becomes more than just the sum of two individuals.

A family. There's no other word to describe it, she muses.

Routines. Daily and weekly. She abhorred them in her former life. Now they are little particles of pleasure she will never grow tired of breathing in. On most weekdays her husband dons a cerulean three-button suit or a silky gray double-breasted, both slim in the waist yet wide around the shoulders, accentuating his figure, sleek and elegant as a greyhound. On holidays, he often puts on his old tweed jacket, loose-fitting and worn at the elbows. She likes its cinnamon shade and enjoys sniffing the faint aroma of gasoline it acquires from dry-cleaning. On weekdays she calls him *yeobo*, a common term of endearment for a spouse, like every other Korean wife; on weekends, she calls him by his first name, Young-min. She likes how their first names share the same initials, Y and M.

Her favorite part of the day is around sunset. Sometimes she waits for Young-min at home. Other times, more often than not, she goes to his shop and walks with him home. She has already become friends with Mr Shin, a bespoke tailor in training, working for her husband. Mr Shin is a quiet man, tall and thin like her husband, whose face can seem quite austere when not smiling. When he does, though, he seems like a nice country boy who's just arrived in the big city, naïve-looking, easy to fool. She loves the moment when she's gazing into the shop, before the two hardworking men notice. When they finally do, they pause and grin. And she walks through the glass door, feeling the sunset behind her, caramel and lazy, tickling her nape. As she and her husband walk out arm in arm, saying goodbye to Mr Shin, she watches his face beam, like honey, drenched in the golden sunset. She recognizes a pinch of harmless envy in Mr Shin's smile, which leaves her a little more elated. Though they are in the north, sunlight feels warmer in this part of the world. Every day, through repetition, she sees new meaning in life.

She has found a job through her husband's connections. She works at the Foreign Currency Store of Pyongyang. It's not a dream job for most highborn Pyongyang ladies but she is satisfied, as every day she can discreetly get her hands on foreign money and high-end goods. Her knowledge of foreign languages helps her. Her good English and decent French, both of which she learned from the French-Canadian missionary as a child, allow her to read and understand manuals written in Spanish and Italian – making her a competent manager, who can explain how to store and appreciate Cuban cigars properly, how to wash Italian cashmere knitwear without compromising its initial softness. Even the forced acquisition of Japanese comes in handy when she sells Japanese television sets to the fashionable wives of Party cadres. Yet it turns her head toward the big irony: while on the surface everything Japanese is evil in their self-sufficient country, most Japanese goods are high in demand among the powers-that-be, considered far superior in quality to Chinese and Soviet ones.

Once a month she and her husband go to Hyesan, the northernmost city near the Chinese border. It is both a business and family trip: they travel together to see Young-min's sister, Young-shim, who manages a Party-controlled trading set-up in Hyesan, through which Young-min has quick access to imported fabrics. They could get travel permits easily, thanks to Young-min's connection to the Party cadre customers, the only class of people who have the luxury of pursuing the latest fashion without persecution. She finds Hyesan fascinating. Although she has no desire to cross it, being near the border excites her still. She knows where this exhilaration comes from: the impression of mobility, whether it's illusory or not. As a former expert at border-crossing, both literal and metaphorical, she's familiar with the sense of escape, the proximity to new possibility. Her favorite spot is the narrow neck of Yalu River, the natural border that separates Korea from China, less than a hundred meters from Young-shim's house. It is a site where countless trades take place, mostly between Chinese and North Korean merchants. It's a shrine of lawful thieves, Young-min once said, with a roguish grin. It is shocking to witness, even for a down-to-earth woman like herself, how easily one can get hold of foreign products that are supposedly non-existent in this country, with bribes and a little bit of luck.

Sometimes she sneaks out at night to stare at the Yalu River. Under the full moon, the river seems to take on a life of its own. As moonlight hits its surface, the water splits into thousands of little black gleaming bodies – raven carp, one could see, or simply an army of snakes, might as well be a swarm of small seals, persistently on the move, all in one direction. The river hums sharply as it runs its course, breathing with thousands of its dark supple gills. She finds the sight and sound magical. When morning comes, however, the sun turns the water back into its usual rifle-green drab.

She decides Young-min's sister doesn't like her. Young-shim is a no-nonsense woman, thick-bodied and sharp-eyed, nothing like her little brother. Young-shim finds her sister-in-law suspicious and she has already told her brother so. Young-shim might have caught sight of her sneaking out at night, she guesses. She tries not to make a fuss about it, though. She acknowledges their country is a place of paranoia. It's their national sport: to be suspicious of others, to spy and tell on them. They're trained to do so from early childhood. It begins in elementary school as *life purification time*, or self-criticism session, during which children should confess any of their impure deeds or thoughts against the Party, followed by reporting on the wrongdoings of their friends and neighbors whom they are to observe closely. Yet she thinks she can't really blame others, for she sometimes eavesdrops on Young-shim's conversation with Young-min. "She's changed so much," whispered Young-shim once. "How do we know what kind of things she's done for all those years?"

"Don't worry, sister," her husband answered softly. "I know my wife well. She has nothing but good intentions."

He is right. She has nothing but good intentions. What she has done is for the good of herself and her husband. (The only person of importance who might mind is already dead.)

They love each other. They are happy together. This companionship gives her something she's never possessed before: sustainable happiness. Although her childhood memories of her mother are full of love and joy, they are punctuated by her father's many dark blows, frozen in time with the smell of *soju* and stale blood. She has learned, through her relationship with Young-min, that everyday life can be a series of steady pleasures, blissful tedium one could complain about with a contented grin. Her whole life she was denied such happiness. Now she has finally earned it, and she's enjoying every bit of it. When it's still warm they stroll by the Daedong River at sunset; in winter they ice-skate on it, dormant children inside them awoken by the pounding snow; on windy nights, the northern gusts rattling their harmonica apartment, they watch smuggled films, American or South Korean, under the blankets, the sound nearly muted, their hands clammy and sweet with sweat; under the same blanket, on countless nights, they make love.

The first night. How she dreaded and desired it. She made sure the first three months went by before it began – the same amount of time Yongmal had had with him prior to her departure. Yet fear kept her away from it for a couple more months. Then another month, deferred by her lingering cowardice, until it struck her one night, an unwelcome awareness, that she couldn't put it off any longer. If she wanted to pursue this life, she should face it. Revealing her new body meant revealing her past, of which she would speak with only truth – accompanied by necessary holes and blanks of her choice.

After that night, she came to love him even more. He let the blanks be blank. He didn't delve into the holes of her memory. After the act, he cried. No sound, just streaks of tears running down his cheeks. He grabbed her battered feet and studied them with a sad gaze. Then he kissed them. "Do you remember when I said I would make you a new pair if you grew out of them?"

She nodded. He grew quiet and remained so for the next few days. He held her in his arms, however, even more than before. By the time his words and smiles returned, he began to call her *yeobo*, my dear wife, instead of by her name.

It took time for her to appreciate sex. She tried to separate it from her past by calling it lovemaking, but that didn't always work. The act, each time it happened, seemed to bring the place back to her skin: the lewd taste of the jungle; the dampness that cleaves to your every pore, choking you out. Memory of that sensation never seemed to grow dull.

Yet Yongmal's metaphor hit home as well: certain appreciation could grow on you only little by little – *It's like getting your clothes soaked by light drizzle.* And the steady drizzle – not the bombardment of showers – was exactly what her body needed. It began with small, subtle changes. Like getting used to the movements of the hips. The rhythmic up-and-down thrust of male buttocks, which she'd associated with nothing but revulsion before. Over time, with Young-min, it shed its layers of dread. It began to appear awkward, then silly ... and a little funny. Paired with his gentle whisper in her ear, it brought a sense of intimacy. Soon she began to see some oddly calming effect in the consistency of those movements, hypnotizing and reassuring. By the end of the year, she was able to lose herself in it.

She remembers the first night of acute pleasure. It was one of many nights they spent in Hyesan, near the border. A vision woke her – the enchanted sight of the Yalu River, throbbing black with the spell of the night. She longed to see it again. She knew what to do: she had to pull her feet, silently, one by one, out of the blanket. Instead, however, she burrowed deeper into it. Her fingers searched for the patch of fleecy hair above his navel. She stroked it slowly. He woke up. She pressed her hand against his mouth – they couldn't afford to wake his sister and her little daughter sleeping in the next room. In strained silence, two skins clung to one another, like bound pages of a dusty book that no one opens, lost in time.

Now I know him, and he knows me, like an open book – almost, she thinks, with an inward smile. Now she's happier to be called *yeobo*, instead of Yongmal. So far names have mattered little to her; she'd had three different ones and each time she simply accepted it as it was thrown at her, without protest. But Yongmal was different. Yongmal was the first name that hadn't been given to her – she'd taken it. She longed to possess it; she longed to become it. Now she has done so, however, she has begun to resent it a little. She's begun to feel ensnared by her own trap. She feels as though the love she deserves is divided between herself and the shadow of her own making.

She wonders how much he knows. They have made love only in the dark so he hasn't seen the scars clearly, yet he should have felt them. She told him the stark truth about the beginning: that they were abducted by the Japanese on the market street. Then she gave him a slightly altered, simplified version of the story, which isn't entirely a lie: that they were taken to a labor camp in Japan, where each day they were forced to perform continuous physical labor, which eventually claimed countless lives of the captured, including that of Mija, her maid, and that a small number of survivors were freed, sent back to their homelands by American soldiers. The location isn't spurious, she argues, within herself. Our Station was in Semarang, Indonesia, but most of South East Asia was under the rule of Imperial Japan, so why can't one call it Japan? The same goes for the nature of the labor, she thinks. What she left out were the details. *Too big a wound to be touched yet* – that was what she gave him, a rain-check of words. He seemed to have accepted it with no doubt, like the patient, tenderhearted man he was. I'm in a safe place now, she feels. No one can call her bluff: those who would be the hardest to convince, the parents, passed away between the wars. She's already won – or *won back*, in Yongmal's perspective – the most crucial hand in the game: her husband's faith.

She wonders when it all really began, this *game* of hers.

It wasn't when she walked into Young-min's tailor's shop.

It began when her name was Kaiyo.

Kaiyo was her name when she met Yongmal. Yongmal was also given her new name, Anzu, but she refused to use it. The seed was sown, maybe, from the very beginning, when the fellow Korean *comfort women* at the Station began to call them, her and Yongmal, the *bone sisters*. She and Yongmal were about the same height, slightly tall for teenage girls, slim but broad-shouldered. Other girls said they both laughed with their shoulders – they tended to go up and down vigorously to the staccato rhythm of their guffaws. Most importantly, they shared the same dogged jaw and cheekbones, which later became a symbol of their irritating stubbornness – a destination of numerous punches. No wonder Jobasan once shouted, "*Anzu!*" at her, not even a meter away. No wonder Kaneda, the Japanese officer who'd visited and tortured Yongmal nearly every day, began to come to her cell every night after Yongmal's passing.

She loved Yongmal. Yongmal saved her life. In many different ways she could never have imagined. Yongmal's stories of home taught her there was still some beauty left in this world: something worth living for, not merely to survive by. She also learned from Yongmal that certain voices can't be shut off. They would rather die than be silenced, and she guessed that

113

was what Yongmal had chosen eventually. In a way she felt she was the closest person on earth to Yongmal, for they'd spent her last years together whispering stories. Inside the walls of the Station, Yongmal was their sage and she her enthusiastic scribe. Devoted to her role, she strove to carve every whim of Yongmal's story into her memory. That was how Kaiyo survived the Station: immersed in Yongmal's past, daydreaming of herself in Yongmal's shoes.

Even when she took Yongmal's leather shoes, however, the idea hadn't taken hold of her yet. Before she died Yongmal had given her famous shoes, the custom-made wedding gift from her loving husband, to her little friend Mija. And when Mija passed away in the air raid, she had removed them from Mija's small feet and put them on her own. She simply wanted a token she could carry, something to remember Yongmal and Mija by. The idea budded somewhere along the second war thrown at her path, when everything around her turned into fire and brimstone all over again. She needed to give herself another scrap of hope, yet it had to be something stronger this time. She promised herself she would pursue the greatest happiness ever known to her, even if it meant for her to live vicariously for good. *I took her shoes – why not her life as well?* In this game, she thought, if well played, no one would be hurt and everyone would win. She wanted to think of it as an ultimate gift from Yongmal.

Yet now she asks: Am I to share this happiness with the hull of Yongmal – *for life?*

Before, she was happy to feel that a part of Yongmal, even long after her death, was still living inside her, like a beloved changeling. Now that she has earned the love she'd yearned for, what she had seen as blessing begins to weigh like another skeleton, piling in her closet.

*

This is a story about a mole.

About the size of a pea, light aubergine in color. He still remembers how it felt under his fingers: how pert and taut it stood when pressed down, yet how pliantly it leaned over when caressed sideways. A little oddity he would always remember her by.

So when the light goes out and the clothes slide down, his fingers try to crawl their old way back to her signature, her little *grain of beauty*. His hands remember clearly what his head finds hazy. They slip and scurry past the ravine between her collarbones, her small, pouty breasts – they don't even stop or flinch at the speed bumps of scar lines, a whorl of sandpaper blooming around her belly-button – then finally saunter around her right pubic bone. To be exact, it's where the lower tip of the bone meets the fold, which, if followed further, will lead you down to her fluffy bush. There is the home of her lovely little mole.

But the mole isn't there.

In disbelief, his hand skids toward her left pubic bone, ferreting about its perimeter for a sign of a tiny, petulant bump. Yet he fails again.

He asks himself if he's been truly blind the whole time.

And he knows the answer already.

She seemed the same and different. The same shape of face, of shoulders, the same laughs, the familiar shrewdness. Yet she was strangely shy: he caught her stealing glances at him, even blushing on occasion in doing so. She also gaped at him in his Western suit at his tailor's shop, a chipped front tooth peeping out through her parted lips, as though she'd never seen him dressed up before. Nevertheless, in his head, time has been the sole culprit. They say a decade could change even a mountain and a river, he reasoned. In fact he found this new facet of hers was rather charming. He also found her more beautiful. He liked her skin darker and shinier, seasoned by the sun. He enjoyed her smile, childish and self-forfeiting – her face awash with honest delight when she glided through the door of his shop. Her energy seemed contagious: even the reticent Mr Shin, caught unawares, would pick up her smile and put it on his own face. A tiny tweak of jealousy he felt was surprising to him, yet also exciting.

She listened more. Before, despite her youth, Yongmal had talked much more than she had listened, often eager to lead the conversation in the direction of her whims. He would happily hand over the key and let his thoughts drift in Yongmal's currents, as she was a nifty storyteller gifted with disarming honesty and harmless hyperbole. After her return, however, she hadn't talked much about herself. She seemed content, rather, to listen to him, countless accounts of his humdrum life, the sundry lists of his desires in the present or the past – an old man's fit of nostalgia maybe, or a small verbal act of revolt through which one strives to find meaning in their world of absurdity.

Sometimes, during a whispered conversation, he caught the glare of yearning in her eyes: they grew wider, then blinked twice, quick and firm. He could sense she had things she longed to say. But she always held them back. He wanted to beg her to get it off her chest, let him share the burden with her, but he didn't dare. The last thing he wanted was to frighten her away, to add pressure to her already bruised mind. He couldn't afford to lose her again. He would never forgive himself if he did. What he should do, he concluded, was to wait. Until she made the decision on her own. And whatever truth she chose to tell, whenever she chose to tell it, he was willing to embrace it just as it was. No question, no condition. It was what he'd always thought in her absence: that nothing else would matter, as long as she could return, alive.

He wondered what she would do if she knew that he knew. He wondered if maybe, on some deep level, she did know, yet was simply too frightened to acknowledge it. He was familiar with the sweet solace of denial, the deferral of facing reality. He knew, albeit vaguely, what those maidens were taken for – that was why Yongmal's father had married her off hurriedly in the first place – for somehow the rumors survived while those girls never did. None had been lucky enough to escape and return, to spread the visceral truth of what their bodies had undergone. Even if they did, he understood, they would never dare to bring it out into the open. Even their own society, their Korean fatherland, would silence them, branding them whores. Calling those girls prostitutes would be a lot easier, with much less of its petty pride to be wounded, than look truth in the eye: that the fatherland had failed to protect its own. And without a victim, no crime exists. He knew all of it.

What he didn't see coming, however, was that she might no longer be who she had been before, in a literal sense.

He realized there had been another sure sign, before the absence of the mole.

Yet how willing he was to overlook it.

He was able to recognize them, no matter how beaten-up they were – the leather shoes he had prepared for Yongmal. He had designed them to please her, to serve her teenage needs, both practical and aesthetic. He'd chosen that pricy calfskin because he'd wanted to spoil her with the very best. He'd chosen the single dye of maroon for he'd known she would spurn any medley of flashy chromatic colors, calling them *too girlish* for her, as though she wasn't a girl. He chose them to be heelless and round-capped so she could ride her horse in them, walk with her pony through the woods in them.

And he chose them to fit perfectly. Since she was still young, he knew her feet might grow a little, turning the expensive present into useless strips of leather sewn together. But that was the whole point of offering this wedding gift to Yongmal: he wanted her to know he would always be there, growing and changing with her, to help her at each milestone through her adulthood.

"I will be glad to make you a new pair if you grow out of them," he had told her, looking into her eyes beaming with joy.

So when he laid his eyes on the worn-out shoes, he felt happy rather than sad. He began to picture a new design of boots: something simple, sleek, yet sturdy, supple black leather that she could wear every day to work and also to the Daedong River for their stroll. Through the gift he meant to tell her that now they had a new start, whatever had happened before didn't matter.

He wanted it to be a surprise. So he waited till she seemed fast asleep, body curled up like a fetus. He crouched down, lifted a corner of blanket with painstaking slowness, and then he brought the measuring stick close to her right foot. He noticed a change – which wasn't unexpected. The number he remembered, from the first time he had measured it, had now shifted by a size and a half. What he couldn't foresee was that the number had grown smaller, not bigger.

He checked three times, his heart thumping like a night train, cold and heavy.

One of the trivial things he'd learned in his career, working closely with other bespoke tailors and shoemakers, was that the foot size of someone so young may increase, but never shrink.

Now, the mole.

His mind can't seem to work up another back story.

He looks at her feet again. They look as fatigued as Yongmal's war-surviving boots, three toenails gone. At first glance he'd thought those were the result of her grown feet, her sweet insistence on surviving wars in their token of love. And the love, for him, was never to be compromised. Yet his memory, if necessary, could be. He convinced himself his graying head might have dredged up the wrong number. If a shoe size can't grow smaller, an old man's memory may grow foggier. Such self-indulgence seems to work no longer, for, once again, his fingers remember clearly what his head finds hazy.

Who is this woman? asks his head. Yet the rest of his body already knows her so intimately. In the end, he has known her longer than he ever did Yongmal.

She's certainly someone who was very close to Yongmal, he thinks, to know all the stories of her life, about their marriage.

But not close enough to know the mole. A little secret between Young-min and Yongmal.

After their first night, before Yongmal sneaked out of Young-min's room, she had whispered that this should remain a secret between just the two of them. She made him swear.

It was a month after their wedding. The day they had had their long stroll through the grove of birch trees. They talked about the future. She told him about her horse-riding. He told her about a life in Pyongyang. She listened with fierce eagerness for the first time. He felt their eyes stumble upon each other, again and again. He wanted to grab her hand.

That night Yongmal came to him. Except for the kerosene lamp flickering at his bedside, everything was drowned in darkness. Even the crickets had stopped chirping. The nocturnal silence was only punctuated by the rustling of autumn leaves and languorous hoot-hoots.

She gestured to him to stay silent, first by putting her index finger gently to her lips, then again by wrapping her hand around his mouth. Salty pressure of her palm on his lips – so pleasing that he forgot to breathe.

He was, of course, no stranger to a woman's body. He knew how to work his way into it, how to share the pleasure. She was nearly half his age. Yet her boldness made him bashful and nervous as though he were a teenager. He saw his hands tremble. He saw hers drawing near the kerosene lamp. Instead of blowing the light out, however, Yongmal pulled it closer to them. Her eyes brimmed with the innocent audacity of a child, curious and unflinching, head slightly tilted to the right, like an innocent animal, watching. She fumbled, rummaged his face and his naked torso, with her round eyes. Then she ran her fingers, painfully slowly, through his hair, glistening with sweat. As if it was his first time, he didn't last long.

She didn't mind, though. She wasn't too keen on the in-and-out act. They spent much more time studying and caressing each other's bodies, like adolescents in love.

"We should do this again," whispered Yongmal, just before she exited into the darkness of the night. And they did. Nearly every night.

Although they were married and in love, both emotionally and physically, they kept to their own rooms. Yongmal wanted it that way. Every night she sneaked into and out of his room, like a second-story man. He never asked her why. Maybe, he thought, it was her teenage coyness. Or it might be an act of defiance, faking indifference to her father's arrangement. Perhaps she just liked the excitement of harboring a little secret, their double-dealing assignation.

Unpredictable and wily, that was who Yongmal was.

Who is she?

He raises his head and looks back at the woman before him.

An intimate stranger he knows and doesn't know.

A girl with battered feet and scarred loins. With a chipped front tooth. Bridge of her nose dusted with tiny burn scars.

A self-forfeiting child's smile.

Can you risk losing her? he asks himself.

He cries silently. Then he kisses her feet.

"Do you remember when I said I would make you a new pair if you grew out of them?" he asks her.

She nods.

He realizes deception, like making love, is a two-party act. No foolery complete without the person to be fooled. And how he yearned to believe – how willing, desperate.

He knows what he will do.

The thing he's best at – what he's always been doing, and always will.

He will wait.

The 6th Life

The Spy Who Writes Yellow

2005

"So how does one become a spy?" asks Mr Park, in his signature monotone.

I smile, thinking he sounds like a philosopher or a poet. Once again I marvel at his calm, which I've come to appreciate greatly over time. Even though he has already asked the same question dozens of times, he still manages to deliver it as if it's the first. I guess the secret lies in wording: he is a man of few spoken words but a large vocabulary. He doesn't like using the same words over and over even when talking about the same concept. This makes me grin, as it reminds me of someone both you and I love so much.

"Same way one becomes a mother, Mr Park," I answer, without suppressing my grin.

Silence, slippery as ice, cuts the air between us in two.

I drop my grin as I read his face. It's been trained to be illegible, but three months of observation wasn't a waste of time on my part. I see the jaw muscles near his ears tighten briefly, veins in his temples stir to life. His index finger taps the desk slowly – once, twice.

He thinks I'm pulling his leg again. I'm not. I'm using the best metaphor I can think of. I feel sad he doesn't get it. Yet I'm smart enough to catch his drift and know my limit.

"Just a figure of speech, Mr Park. No intention of annoying you. And if you want the conventional version of the answer, you've already heard it countless times."

A shallow sigh escapes from him – not a bad sign.

"You know how it works, Ms Choi. Tell me again."

Tell me again?

It was your favorite sentence for a while, after the year-long period of *Why is that?*

You asked me to tell you the same stories over and over, although you already knew every detail, every nut and bolt of their narrative structures, every comma and every sigh, simply because they were your favorites and you loved hearing them again and again. It was a great form of entertainment for you, and a tough game of patience for me. And it got harder at each retelling as you never failed to come up with a new question to annoy me with: How come Nolbu's wife hit Heungbu with a rice paddle? Why not a winnowing basket, or a cane?; Can't a magpie or a pigeon help? Why does it have to be a swallow?; How come the Supreme Leader didn't feed Heungbu when he was so hungry? He always feeds us, right?

At first those words were fascinating, then, after a few months, maddening. Sometimes I felt outright scared, for I knew that in our society the road to the firing squad or labor camp is paved with questioning.

Questions. Oh, you loved them. As soon as you could put two words together to form a sentence you started asking questions. And you never stopped till you became a teenager. From then on, I guess you began to turn to your peers more, finding them a cooler, smarter source of information.

They say every mother finds her toddler a genius but eventually he or she turns out to be just a normal kid. I was different: I never thought you were a genius. Yet I knew you were a lot smarter than most others.

What kind of three-year-old asks questions about death?

One day you asked us why you had no grandparents. "Geumjoo has two grandpas, how come I have zero?" you grumbled. I answered that they had passed away. This sucked us into an endless loop of new questions. "What is *passed away*?" It means they died. "What does that mean, *they died*?" It means that they are no longer here with us, that they left for the sky and they can't come back. "What do they do there *in the sky*?" Nobody knows that for sure, Mihee. "Why is that?"

I knew I shouldn't use that old Korean expression, the euphemism for death: leaving for the sky. They'd banned it for they'd thought it had a religious undertone and, of course, religion had no place in our society. I still used that metaphor, though. I thought for your little mind it would make the concept easier to comprehend.

A few months later, you saw your first airplane up close. We were passing by the gate of Hyesan airfield. It was long before the beginning of the end and there were still quite a few airplanes that regularly flew in and out. You noticed the noise first. It began like the rumble of distant thunder, putting you instantly on alert – you ducked your head, squeezed my hand. The next second we were standing right under a colossal airplane, looking up at its sleek gray underbelly, and watching it glide further up in the sky, till the reflection of the sun on its tail vanished into a bed of clouds. Transfixed, you stood still for a while, even long after the plane's vapor trail was gone.

For the rest of the day you stayed quiet – quite unlike you.

Then at night, when I tucked you in, you blurted out a question, your fingers clutching the edge of the blanket.

"Mom, you said my grandpa left for the sky, right?"

"Yes. All of your grandparents, in fact. Before you were born."

"An airplane can fly high in the sky."

"Yes, as you saw today."

"So one day, if I ever take an airplane, I can catch my grandpa up there?"

"You know, I've never jumped out of a flying airplane or a burning building. Contrary to most people's imagination, physical fitness isn't really the priority. It's not where most of us begin," I told Mr Park.

"Then where do you start? What's the first thing?"

"Languages."

Mr Park tilts his head, just a little, to the right. It means I should go on.

"The classic place to start is the Pyongyang University of Foreign Studies. They select the smartest students there, the ones who excel in foreign languages. And they conduct a thorough background check. The kids should be from good upper-class families, with most of their family members still alive, to prevent a situation in which they feel tempted to defect to their enemy countries while they're working out there."

"But that wasn't your case. You never went to college."

"Of course not. I've been a maverick. Always."

Maverick. I notice I uttered the word with a twang of fake pride.

I realize his gaze has left me. His eyes are now drifting in midair, near the right corner of the room, where there's a small gray bloom of mold. His face remains blank. This time

I can't seem to read his intention. I don't know if he's thinking intently, or getting bored. I continue anyway.

"When I returned to the North, I was very happy to be reunited with my husband, whom I hadn't seen for a decade. It was the best time of my life. Living with him in Pyongyang. The economy was good, then. Kids on the street were still rosy-cheeked and plump."

Despite myself my eyes well. This failure of self-restraint angers me. I clench my fists under the table. I feel my fingernails dig into my palms, leaving imprints of tiny crescent moons. A little pain to anchor myself back to now, here.

This seems to wake Mr Park as well. Though he remains silent, his eyes give him away: the irises grow darker and rounder, like a cat's at night.

"I guess we were *too* happy, and so a bit stupid. Too much happiness can do that to you. It makes you loosen up, let your guard down. In retrospect, it would have been odd if they hadn't found me suspicious right from the beginning. How was I so blind? A woman who turns up just like that after ten years of absence?"

"What did they find most suspicious about you?"

Mr Park asks the question drily. He already knows the answer. He wants to drive the conversation faster toward his destination.

"Languages, of course."

"What about them?"

"I knew English. I could speak it fluently."

"Before, you couldn't."

"No, not at all. And also my Japanese. Though I'd already known it a bit before, when I returned I could read and speak it perfectly."

"How did they discover your new linguistic skills?"

"I guess it was my vanity. I worked at the Foreign Currency

Store of Pyongyang where only the high-born can legally buy foreign goods. I often translated the manuals written in foreign languages into Korean for the customers. I thought I was helping them while harmlessly flaunting my intelligence. Some of them must have reported it to Bowibu. I admit that I was naïve. Or plain stupid."

The airport. The place where you saw your first airplane. It was also the place that killed your naïveté. You weren't a child anymore after that.

At Hyesan airfield you saw your first public execution. You were just shy of eleven.

They made sure every kid watched it early on. It was their preferred educational method, designed to instill fear and obedience.

It was odd to see death under the sun. Daylight crisp and loud as the propaganda speaker.

There were two young men, each bound to a wooden pole at the head, the chest, and the ankles. Their eyes were covered. One man was arrested for watching pornography, American-made, the other a romance film, smuggled from South Korea. Both were to be punished equally with death by firing squad.

They fired three times, each shot aimed to shatter the ropes tying the bodies to the poles. At the first shot the heads exploded. The second brought the bodies to fall forward on their knees, as though begging pardon. The third brought the corpses to the ground. It was quick. Pink mists were still floating around the wooden poles streaked with warm blood.

In a sane man's world I would have covered your eyes.

A couple of months later you turned eleven. You declared to us the gift you wanted.

A bicycle. *Period*, you said.

We bought you a pair of shiny red loafers instead. You were furious. "Do you know how rare these are?" said Dad.

"Other girls your age would die for a pair of red shoes like these," said I.

We didn't bother to tell you the plain truth that girls were not allowed to ride bicycles. We felt you already knew, and that was exactly why you'd insisted on this particular gift. The world around us said a girl's body atop a bicycle was impudence – her thighs open, straddling the saddle like a farm boy on a horse, while her little bottom slow-dances side to side to pedal. A sight of horror and impurity, people thought.

You rode it anyway. You sneaked out with your dad's old Japanese bicycle, which was still too tall for you. You fell down badly by the Yalu River and nearly broke your collar bone. Dad and I knew we couldn't stop you. So we ended up getting you the small bicycle you'd wanted. We made you promise you wouldn't ride it when there were people around.

But you did. People saw you on that bicycle and started to say things. Some boys called you names. Several old men and older women shouted at you as you slalomed by them on the main street. Your schoolteacher summoned me to lecture under her sour breath: *It will tear her bottom! You don't let your daughter lose her virginity to a bicycle saddle!*

The scene of public execution did something strange to your mind. A little side effect they hadn't desired. It set your curiosity alight. You began to crave a piece of what those young men had thought worth risking their lives for. Luckily, however, you were also smart. You knew the danger in your weakness and when to step back. You played with fire without getting burned. Because I taught you so.

Dad and I knew you were bound to tamper with the forbidden. Things that were much riskier than a bicycle ride – which was socially taboo but not a target of criminal punishment.

We realized simply telling you not to do something would only make you scoff. I had to tell you not to get caught. I taught you how to pretend and hoodwink, the specialty that I'd acquired through surviving two wars.

One of the first things you learned from me was storytelling. At school, intelligent as you were, you excelled in every subject, except one: *life purification.* This was the weekly session of self-criticism, during which everyone had to take turns to confess sins they'd committed against the Party – any verbal, behavioral, or mental deviance at odds with the ideals of the Supreme Leader. It began in elementary school, training children to spy not only on others but also on themselves. The Party said *introspection,* while the rest of the world would call it *self-surveillance. A real pain in the ass* was your take. "Mom, the teacher forces me to confess even when there's absolutely nothing to confess! Then she gets mad at me, yells at me that I'm sinning just now by lying, not telling the truth!"

"*The Art of Storytelling,*" I told you. "You pretend that's the name of the class, Mihee." The trick worked for you, as you were a zealous reader of literature, a fan of fiction. It was a delicate job to make up stories for the self-criticism session. One had to invent accounts of small dalliances that were believable and bad enough to confess as sins, yet at the same time innocent enough to dodge any serious punishment or blacklisting. You learned fast. You became a little storytelling machine. *This morning, before leaving home for school, I was still sleep-drunk and forgot to bow down to the holy portraits of Our Great Leader and the Dear Leader. Please forgive my pitiful self-indulgence. When we learned about Our Great Leader's ideology of Juche in history class, I realized I'd committed a major crime the other day by trading my extra pencil with Comrade Young-hye's eraser, and now I'm dying of shame that I engaged unwittingly in a wicked practice of*

Yankee capitalism. When I received candies and new clothes on Our Supreme Leader's Birthday, I was so happy I hugged my dad and said, "Thank you," forgetting that those gifts are in truth provided by Our Respected Father Leader, not my own father!

I also taught you how to cry. As kids got older, they were meant to display more and more enthusiasm in the life-purification session. It sometimes ended in a mass hysteria of weeping and wailing. Students started by shedding little tears of guilt and it expanded into full-fledged crying that often involved the whole body, kneeling down and rocking the torso back and forth, fists thumping on the floor. For you faking a story was one thing, faking a cry another. "How can I cry of guilt, Mom, when I feel none?"

Every other Friday you would come home frustrated and angry, a failed attempt at tears still sore in your voice. But I knew you were a girl capable of crying. You just needed a different fuel. I told you to use your anger. "Think about the people who made you angry – for instance that big bully boy who threw a rock at your bicycle, made you fall, then called you a *spoiled cunt*. You turn that explosive feeling into crying, dear." I also offered you a biological trick in case the psychological one failed. "Lower your head and cover your eyes as if you're crying, but keep your eyes wide open, do not blink. In a minute they'll begin to prickle, then burn, and eventually well up whether you want it or not. Once the first batch of tears is out, the rest will just flow. You'll see."

The crying lesson came in handy, especially later in life when the Supreme Leader, whom people had tacitly considered immortal, died. The entire nation fell under the spell of apocalyptic hysteria. People swarmed in front of colossal bronze statues of Kim Il-sung, as tall as a four-story building, to perform the mass game of crying their eyes out. Asphalt pavement simmered with the July sun and the acrid heat given off by millions of bodies flailing in grief. Countless people fainted. Some died. Meanwhile the *inminban* kept tabs on everything. *Banjang* of each work unit and class recorded how often its members came to mourn in public, and how they cried. Failure to cry meant flirting with death.

Now I'm writing this journal, or letter if you prefer, in yellow. Last week it was purple. The week before, red. When I complained about the red to Mr Park, that I was sick of seeing texts in red, he understood and gave me a purple one instead. I complained again, asking for just a normal black one. Then he told me, in his soothing monotone, that purple is the noble color, a symbol of royalty. "You know, long ago, natural dyes for purple were very rare, so only a small number of people, those with certain social positions and wealth, could use them." He said this image of exclusivity had persisted through time and eventually turned the color purple into an emblem of blue blood. I smiled back and told him I liked his story. To me, purple had been the color of starvation, of dead faces and limbs piled up at the rail station, on the market streets of Hyesan.

Of course I knew Mr Park was bullshitting. I knew he was giving me the purple one simply because it was one of the few left. But his bullshit came with flair, with a nice little story. I liked this side of him, which appreciated good use of language. So, when he handed me back the purple peel-off wax pencil, I grabbed it and started writing with it.

It's a marker rather than a pencil. Unlike a pencil, no part of this object is sharp or hard. The lead is replaced by colored wax, and the wood by thin, narrow layers of paper that you can peel off instead of sharpening. A hybrid between a crayon and a pencil, it's made for little children to color with, yet it's the only writing tool I'm allowed in here. No sharp object of any kind – no pen, pencil, fork, not even wooden chopsticks – can enter my room. They must have some highfalutin idea of me, as if I were James Bond or MacGyver, who could drop a man with a click of a pen. Though I knew how to use certain types of guns and how to poison someone if I had to, that sort of rough job wasn't really my specialty.

My specialty is to weave a narrative, like I'm writing this letter to you now. Mr Park understood this before anyone else did: he was the one who suggested I write it down. He knew I was growing restless at night, my head throbbing with too much thought. "Writing is the best way to make sense of your muddled thoughts, Ms Choi, as well as to pass time," he told me. "You can write it as a journal, or in the form of a letter to someone if that makes you feel more comfortable."

Ever since, I've been writing using these colorful pencils made of wax and paper, which can't hurt me or anyone else. It is a win-win game anyway: I stay sane by keeping my mind occupied and they test my credibility better through reading what I write. They comb my words, both verbal and written, determined to find any glitch or discrepancy among my repeated testimonies – before they decide whether I'm a reliable asset or not.

At first I hated the yellow. I complained to Mr Park that I can't easily see the yellow text against the white paper, especially with my aging eyes. Then he told me yellow is the color of hope. "Something both of us need very badly now," he said, wearing that subdued smile of his, a confusing kind where the brows and the mouth tell different stories.

Yellow as hope. If others had said it, I would have dismissed it as a cliché. But as I told you, Mr Park has a way of saying things so that they carry weight. Even when he's talking about the most banal things.

A laconic listener usually, he knows when to shut up and when to speak. With his velvety voice, his pensive brows. Just like your dad.

You were two. One morning you came to me, held my face with your chubby little hands, and gently kissed me as if I was the most delicate, endearing thing in the world. Then you said to me: *Like Daddy kiss Mommy.*

We had few memories of you before you were two. I never had the moment of holding a bundle of joy in my arms, wrapped in my own blood. Surge of bliss and terror, tears of raw, bodily connection – I had had none of that. I needed time to know you. To like you, appreciate you. I became your mother only little by little, one step at a time. I became a mother through practice. I became a mother through training.

We never knew your biological mother. Your first adoptive mother was actually Young-shim, your father's sister, whom you know now from old family photos as Auntie Young-shim. Her body, like mine, couldn't bear a child. All I knew was that she had adopted the illegitimate baby of an underage girl from the neighborhood, who was considering suicide. Even the fact that Young-shim was a widow couldn't stop her adopting you. She must have liked you a lot.

We had to take you in when Young-shim died in a train accident in Hyesan. Your dad said we should adopt you and raise you as our own. I was afraid of this big change in our lives, having to become accidental parents. I wasn't sure if I was capable of loving someone who was flung into our lives by chance, not by our desire. We also had to move from Pyongyang to Hyesan where Young-shim had worked as an overseer of the Party-backed trading business with China, which we were to take over as well.

It wasn't love at first sight: it was a bond by piecemeal. Like learning how to speak a foreign language. The more you learn, the more you feel invested in it, and the more you enjoy it. Like learning a new language, it takes a lot of practice and patience. The love grows in you little by little, at each cradle song hummed, each tantrum thrown and tamed, and every spoonful of porridge, whether swallowed or spat out. The rewards took me by surprise: the very first call of Mama from your lips; presents of stick-figure drawings of me, titled *My Besty Comerade*; sudden stifling hugs, and sleepy I-love-yous in bed for no particular reason. Never in my life have I seen a creature so vulnerable yet so open, ready to love and trust with no condition.

By acting like a mother in love, I became a mother in love.

And the moment I realized the full presence of this love in me was when you uttered the sentence: *Like Daddy kiss Mommy*. With your gentle kiss, your tiny plump fingers on my face.

As for love, your dad was the complete opposite of me. He was like a baby: a born giver, ready to surrender with no condition – right from the beginning. Like a baby, he was brave enough to be vulnerable and open. That was how he loved me, how he loved you as well. As if a switch was turned on the moment you came into our lives, the love was already there in his eyes when he looked at you. He was a native speaker; he needed no training.

When I first met him, he was double my age. Yet he spoke and listened to me as he would to his most valuable teacher. He was a humble man with a noble tongue. A romantic rebel who wasn't even afraid of holding his wife's hand in public, saying, "I love you," each morning. Sacrifice meant little to him when it came to his family: moving to Hyesan equaled giving up his privileged life as a tailor of Pyongyang, yet he did so without a qualm. "It's perfect timing for an old man like me," said your dad, excitedly, "to have a new purpose in life." Compared to his job as an upper-class suit maker, when his schedule was packed with appointments with Party officials, trade-managing at Hyesan was pretty laidback. Besides, thanks to his Pyongyang connection, importing and distributing foreign fabrics for the high-born went more smoothly than ever, allowing him more free time with his family.

When I was away for training or on a mission, your dad served as both mother and father to you. And he was a better mom than I ever was. To tell you the truth, at first I was a little jealous. I guess I felt like a first child about to lose her grip on a love she'd monopolized thus far. I also felt envious of you as a daughter: I never had the kind of father you have or the kind of childhood you enjoyed. My own father was never a giver: he was a reaper of pain, an existence that subsisted on others' suffering – the origin of my dark side. No wonder I'd been drawn to your dad, even just through stories of him, long before I met him in person. I wanted to love and be loved by him. And in secret, I wanted to protect him. You know I used to tell your dad nearly every day that I was the luckiest woman in Chosun to have a husband like him. Yet at the same time I thought he was as lucky to have *me*. A man like your dad can't fare well alone in this mad man's world. He needs someone like me on his side: a woman both good and evil, capable of bottomless love and willing to commit murder to defend it. A woman who knows the language of mad men.

"Tell me about 130 Liaison Office," says Mr Park.

"It's where I was trained."

"Tell me how it works, Ms Choi. The training process."

"You know I can't speak for everyone on this. Mine was a very unusual case."

"I'm interested in hearing it again. Please."

Today Mr Park's *please* is as insipid as a plastic plant, as though he's being ironic. I'm surprised by how hurt I feel inside by this. I wonder if I'm turning into a pathetic case of Stockholm syndrome: I've been in isolation for too long, with only one man to talk to. Yet I resist being caught up in negative thoughts toward this sole ally of mine. Maybe he's simply feeling exhausted today. Maybe he wants to run home to his wife and kid, sprawl on the sofa and watch TV, forget about work.

"Mine began with torture. They had been watching me for some time. Some people had reported me already as highly suspicious. A decade of absence, a sudden return. Then the knowledge of foreign languages. They thought I was a spy from the South, or Japan. Later I learned that, much to my shock, among the snitches was Mr Shin, a young tailor-in-training who used to work for my husband back in Pyongyang. He had also been working as an informant for the Secret Police, as it turned out. His main job was to eavesdrop on the conversations between the Party cadre customers and my husband. I was surprised to know that even the powers that be aren't completely free from surveillance.

"Though I always felt that Comrade Shin watched us closely, my husband and me together, I thought it was because of envy. I thought he was just jealous of a couple so much in love, and happy."

I sigh. I can't help but snort a little too. At my own foolishness.

"Maybe he felt that as well," says Mr Park, in a low whisper, his gaze down, as if talking to himself. Then he looks up at me. "Continue." His voice turns dry again.

"They tortured me black and blue. I confessed the whole truth about who I was but they didn't believe it at first. I guess it wasn't the kind of story they'd expected to hear. It took some time for them to understand what was going on. To get the absurd truth."

"The truth?"

"That I was an imposter, not a spy."

Mr Park stares at me, wordless.

"I wasn't Yongmal, the girl who had married Young-min, my husband, ten years back, then had suddenly disappeared. I met the real Yongmal at the Comfort Station in Semarang, Indonesia. One of many locations for the Imperial Japanese Army bases during the Second World War. Yongmal and I, and dozens of other Korean girls, had been abducted and brought to Semarang to serve as comfort women. Their euphemism for sex slaves. That's how I happened to perfect my Japanese.

"Everyone at the Station said we looked like sisters, Yongmal and I. We became good friends. Yongmal was a talker. And I loved her for that. She told me all about her life back in Korea. Her family, hometown, her recent marriage. Her husband. I loved her and I envied her. Yongmal died in the Station, of tuberculosis. I survived. I came back to Korea. I'd lost track of my own family, my mother and baby sister. So the idea of finding Yongmal's entered my head. Then I did. And I became Yongmal. I became the wife of Yongmal's husband. *My* husband."

"And you did so successfully."

"Yes."

"Your husband never noticed."

"No," I said, staring back at Mr Park, "I'm good at what I do."

Early August. A rare sweltering summer day again in Hyesan. Humidity bloomed under your armpits, dripped along your temples. I felt dog-tired. You and Dad had already seen two dead bodies on the way to the train station. You and Dad were there to greet me. I was coming back from Pyongyang, from a *business trip*. I hadn't seen you for nearly half a year.

A commotion erupted at the far southern end of the platform. A mother and a child traveling without a permit, caught by a plain-clothes policeman. More and more people had begun to take the risk of travelling illegally, in search of food, which was growing scarce.

The young policeman ordered the woman to pass him the bundle she was carrying. She refused. Befuddled, the policeman took out his pistol, started shouting at her. Then suddenly the woman sprang out at him, on all fours, like a small beast. Behind her, I saw her little boy run, hugging the bundle. Gun fire roared. A sharp scream shot through the station.

An alarm had been set off in my head. It made my blood gallop, heart thump in my throat. But my hands remained steady. Nothing on my body shook. Muscles on my face relaxed. It even put on a mask of a waning smile. Soon my heart followed suit. Wearing an armor of trained calm, I walked past the sight of commotion.

Your dad's face came into focus. Then I heard your scream – *Mommy!* – behind me.

Your dad was shouting my name. I recognized the horror in his eyes.

I turned around. I saw you on the ground. Crying. Half of your face yellow, covered with fine dust. Blood ran down from your open mouth.

I ran to you and tried to pull you up but you pushed me away.

Your dad came and held you in his arms. He wiped your face with his sleeves. Then you both looked up at me. Eyes of a wounded puppy – with a glare of disgust.

At 130 Liaison Office, I'd been trained to pose as a foreigner. A Japanese, Chinese, even an Asian American if a mission required it. Mastering the foreign tongues isn't sufficient: they train you to deny your mother tongue, not to blow your cover by reacting to it. For months I'd been made to live and dream in foreign tongues, speaking of my mind or hiding it with only foreign words. Every time I turned my head or darted my eyes toward an interpellation in North Korean, I was punished. *Comrade! Hey! You there! Hello! Excuse me! Watch out! Help!* One particular call, which had taken me a lot longer to ignore than others, was *Mommy!*

The training paid off in the end. When the gun was fired at the station, you ran toward me, with your little arms open, shouting, "*Mommy!*" You wanted to protect me. You wanted to make sure I was okay. You wanted to save me; you wanted me to save you as well.

But I walked past you as though you were invisible. You stood still, dumbfounded. A herd of soldiers, alarmed by the gunfire, came running. Spectators scattered like scared rabbits. They pushed you and you fell down hard on your face. You lifted your head, bleeding, and cried, "*Mommy!*" till your voice croaked.

"How did they change their mind and decide to hire you?"

"It started when I was telling them how I learned English. I learned it as a child, from a Canadian missionary who ran a match factory in my North Korean hometown. I perfected it later in life, working for American soldiers during the Korean War."

"What was the nature of your job, when you worked for the Americans?"

Mr Park's voice, when he pronounces *nature*, trembles slightly. Quite unlike him.

"I was an interpreter between Korean women and American military men, at what they called the Monkey House. A facility that wasn't far removed from the Comfort Station. You replace Japanese soldiers with American ones, and the Second World War with the Korean War."

My voice trails off. Mr Park's eyes squeeze into slits.

"How did you end up working for the Monkey House? The kind of place that had formerly enslaved you."

"I didn't know where they were taking me. Disguised as a boy, I was struggling alone to survive the war. In Busan I approached the American soldiers for a job, telling them I was fluent in English. I was starving and had nowhere to sleep."

My eyes drift over Mr Park's head and rest on the window-pane near the ceiling. The tiny square opening that isn't really an opening but an illusion of it. The only thing that comes through it is worn-out sunlight. A double window, tempered glass. Latticed with steel bars, it looks more like a big drain than a small window. No noise is permitted in or out.

"Focus, Ms Choi, please. We haven't much time," Mr Park pleads. "Tell us why RGB changed their mind."

"After they knew what I did to the Monkey House." Thinking about Reconnaissance General Bureau, the North Korean intelligence agency, sends my eyes to the grille, to the windowpane. So I close them. *Focus.* "I burned it down. The House. Then I ran away back to the North."

"What made them believe this story of yours?" Mr Park persists.

"They didn't at first, I told you. Then they ran a check and found out there *was* a report of a case that dovetailed with my story. An American military facility near Busan burned down – a few soldiers went with it. And a young orphan boy, who had worked for the House as an interpreter, went miss-ing. As it turned out, the South had assumed I was a spy sent by the North. I was a wanted man to the Allied Forces. A *ter-rorist*. A guerrilla. This, in the North, made me automatically a hero. Their attitude toward me changed overnight.

"They wanted me to be their spy, officially. It was a pretty good deal for them. I was a ready-made agent, who required little training. I knew the foreign tongues, knew how to survive the impossible, to deceive and pose. A successful identity thief already. I was a chance RGB would never let go. So *they made me an offer I couldn't refuse.*"

I say the last sentence in a feigned whiskey tenor. An attempt at comic relief for poor Mr Park going through a bad day. He doesn't pick up on my jest, though. He's turning more and more solemn these days. And I can't help but wonder if this will work for or against my end. Are they close to making the decision? The thought makes my pulse flitter.

"They cut down my training process to the bare minimum. They even let me and my husband continue to handle the import-export business with the Chinese. They had calculated that my status as a businesswoman would work to my advantage as a spy, allowing me to cross borders and contact foreigners more freely. Above all, they promised my *secret* would be safe with them, if I chose to work for them. What they really meant was, if I refused, they would reveal my true identity to my beloved husband. I had no choice but to accept their offer and become their spy."

"Girls," Mr Park murmurs. I watch his Adam's apple go up and down.

"Excuse me?" I ask. I hear the rain begin to patter against the tiny window. What timing.

"The girls, Ms Choi. Those Korean women at the Monkey House. What became of them when you burned the place down?"

Training Day One at 130.

They loaded me and a dozen other trainees into the blackened bus. An armored vehicle – a mongrel of a tank and a shuttle, really. Its narrow strips of window were dark and sleek as sunglasses. Still they blindfolded us. The inside smelled of acid grease. It began to move slowly. A heavy, cold clunk suddenly jolted us into sightless vigilance and I felt a tingle shoot through my fingers, toes. I could locate every single person inside the vehicle just by the ins and outs of their breathing. Then I heard the thick thud again, slightly drawn out, and followed by an echo this time. Doors of the cargo lift were shut. And it began its descent.

It felt like an hour, a dozen kilometers deep. But I reminded myself darkness makes a trickster of time, too waxy and perfidious to grasp. Sightless, other sensations sometimes stretch and bend like a clump of taffy. I had grown familiar with that, surviving wars in the gloom of captivity.

When the metallic whooshing finally relented, silencing all the human fidgeting as well, I found myself besieged by the gray scent. It was the smell of concrete pavement in rain, homespun and musty; of a basement, full of mildewed bookshelves. Reminiscence far from unpleasant. Yet soon the conscious fear grabbed hold of me. It jostled me to figure out what this place could be, this gargantuan underworld buried deep under Pyongyang. Walking in darkness, alert to the cavernous ring of my footsteps, I busied myself with conjecture. An underground bomb shelter came to mind. So did a few other places that I wouldn't want to envision, such as a Re-education Center or Labor Camp – certain variations on slavery.

Removing the blindfolds was blinding. Gentle hue of burgundy, the light seeping through the folded black cloth, snapped into a white explosion, leaving some of the trainees mewing like hurt kittens.

In front of me unfurled the floodlit street of Myeong-dong, the biggest shopping district of Seoul, South Korea.

Luminosity hammered down blithely, left me reeling, my mouth dry and salty. An array of vast glass shop windows on both sides of the street caught and scattered the heavy lighting in an endless loop; it reverberated in all directions, keeping no corner in the dark. Mannequins behind them were wearing modern Western casuals, and so was a medley of pedestrians, pottering about in washed-out blue jeans, colorful T-shirts bearing swanky English logos, Nike sneakers, raven-black sunglasses, a mini-skirt, high heels, and blood-red lipstick. Every single one was banned by the Party; wearing it in public was a sure ticket to the camp. Blood-red lipstick, especially. Last time I saw one was at the Hyesan station. The famine had made prostitutes of mothers. A host of young women with low *songbun* had chosen selling their bodies over losing their kids and siblings to starvation. Since prostitution was a major crime against the Party, those women had no other way of soliciting than casting sheep's eyes at male passersby in the station, their lips daubed in red lipstick – their scarlet letter for survival.

Next to Myeong-dong was Osaka. Neon signs on Dotonbori Street flooded my sight again. Even long after I closed my eyes those bright lights floated around in the back of my head. The gigantic Running Man was already there with his welcoming arms up and open, as surreal and breathtaking as the twenty-meter-tall bronze statue of Kim Il-sung at Mansudae. Across from Osaka was the 5th Arrondissement of Paris, including the mini Jardin du Luxembourg and bits and bobs from the Quartier Latin, where some besotted college kids, the *bourgeois bohème* bored with their privileged Western lives, still jerked off to the idea of Communism.

This underworld deep beneath Pyongyang was their simulacrum of the world. A hyperreal theme park, or the breakneck training field, where the top students from Pyongyang

University of Foreign Studies were molded into the secret agents of the People's Democratic Republic of Korea.

Most days I had my early breakfast in Paris with Amandine, a pudgy, middle-aged French woman abducted in Paris in the early seventies, with whom I practiced my workaday conversation in French; I had lunch in Osaka with Yuki, a reserved young lady kidnapped on the shore of Niigata Prefecture at the age of twelve, picking up Japanese slang and old proverbs; dinner was in Washington DC with Malcolm, a burly American deserter from Huntsville, Alabama, who'd run north during the Korean War after accidentally killing his platoon sergeant in a drunken brawl, and who helped me to brush up my American history and English military vocabulary.

Often at night I was trained to be South Korean. I learned how to talk, eat, smile, walk, and think like one. (And this harrowing process made me realize how big the gap had grown between the North and the South.) A mistake was without exception followed by punishment. I learned fast, fortunately. A couple of months after I'd arrived, when they woke me up in the middle of the night, I could mumble my complaint, half asleep, in a perfect South Korean accent.

My first time at 130, gazing up into the floodlit street of Myeong-dong, Seoul, I thought of your grandma. My mother, whom I had assumed dead long ago. Along with the war, memories of her had been pushed deep beneath my conscious reflections. She was from Seoul, and she'd told me so fondly of her childhood memories of the capital, colored by its theaters and libraries, street markets and ice cream. After marrying my father, she had moved to the Northern countryside, where she had me, severed from the city life she was in love with. I wondered what she would have said if she had laid her eyes upon this uncanny doppelgänger of her hometown, on this secret irony deep underneath the heart of the North. I wondered what she would have felt.

As of now I'm wondering what your reaction was, for *your* first time at 130.

I bet you were deadly excited, rather than intimidated or lost. And I bet you were shrewd enough to hide the thrill.

"On weekends we were to perform various tasks in the Seoul of 130. Daily activities only denizens of capitalism would engage in. Anything that has to do with a bank, such as opening an account, wiring money, updating a passbook. Easier – and slightly more fun – tasks included renting a movie and shopping. Native South Koreans, most of whom had been abducted near the DMZ, took on various roles such as pedestrians, bank clerks, and shopkeepers, coaching our gestures and correcting our diction and intonation."

"Their names?"

"They were given fake names, of course. But you can easily find their records according to the descriptions I've provided, which I'm pretty sure you've done already."

I look up. Mr Park averts his gaze briefly. A flash of guilt. I want to tell him that there's no need to nurse remorse, that we're all just doing our jobs. Instead I hit him with something else: a hiccup of a question. An improvisation. A shortcut.

"How about the other names?" I ask him boldly.

"What names?"

I smile. I caught him off guard. And I know he knows. His lips are pressed into a tiny o.

"Mr Park, I'm asking, nice and simple, if your bosses are ready to trust me." I turn my head to the right and glower at the wide gray mirror that takes up nearly half the wall – a mirror that on the other side works as a window.

Mr Park breathes deeply. Then he looks me straight in the eye. As if urging me to go on.

"If they're ready for the names that I'm here to provide, Mr Park. The list of agents sent from the North, like myself, who have worked undercover here in South Korea."

I thought your resentment towards my frequent absences would last.

But soon, smart and affectionate as you were, you turned it into something else.

When you were two and a half you said you would marry your dad; at eight you declared you wanted to be like me when you grew up.

"I'm gonna be a *businesswoman*, just like you, Mom," you told me in your stern voice – the thespian one you used to get our attention. I asked you if you knew what my work required. You said my job was a cool job. It made me wear lots of cool clothes, which let me travel all over the world that most people weren't allowed to see.

I sighed and smiled at the same time. And I told you only very smart people could be businesswomen. "You need to work hard at school, honey," I said, "especially on foreign languages. In business those are the tools with which you negotiate to gain your end."

You were an eager pupil, I a spitfire teacher. With your hungry passion, the kind only a childlike mind could possess, you absorbed every piece of linguistic knowledge I gave you. And you always chirped aloud for more. You even began to set out new rules, like *English-Only Weekends* and *Chinese Fridays* and *Japanese August*. I'd never taught you the South Korean accent but I figured you had already started flirting with it on your own, like most cool kids of your generation, who watched and shared copies of South Korean TV series under the radar.

I taught you all this because I wanted you to become a businesswoman. Not the double-dealing, moonlighting kind I was, but a real one who could savor her success in broad daylight. I thought you could even make it as a diplomat – why not? I wanted you to be the classic textbook elite I'd never had a chance to be. I wanted you to walk the Silk Road.

So when I learned you had been accepted to the Pyongyang University of Foreign Studies, I was in tears. I was so proud of you. I don't deny that my feeling of elation was vicarious, that I was enjoying through your academic success something I hadn't been allowed to achieve myself.

I enjoyed being a shameless snob for the moment.

Arms akimbo, he stands stock-still. His back is turned against me. I hear him sigh, agonizingly slowly, twice.

I've never seen Mr Park so dramatic. It isn't unexpected, though. I just wait for him to puncture the silence first.

"Why do you want to turn your only sure ally into an enemy?" he asks. His tone is drained. He puts down a piece of paper on the table, right under my nose.

"You don't fancy my list?"

"Quit playing, Ms Choi," he barks. I see his right hand on the table is squeezed into a fist. "First of all, it's not even a *list*, Ms Choi. There's only one name. What happened to the other names you promised us? All the names of RGB's secret agents operating in South Korea that you know of?"

"I've never learned their real names. I only know their aliases for the job."

"Tell me, Ms Choi, am I supposed to swallow your bullshit without rolling my eyes?"

"Have you been listening, Mr Park? Haven't I told you my nation is a nation of spies? Ever since you're old enough to jump rope you're trained at school to distrust and tell on everyone, even your own family members. Haven't I told you that even the powers that be are under constant surveillance? The only free person in the North is Kim Jong-il himself. They trust no one, and they don't want us to trust each other. They always assume there could be double agents among us. So for the love of Heaven, and for one last time, I'm telling you the truth. I do not know their real names."

"Then you're no use to us."

"Untrue. I can provide their code names, descriptions of their missions, their physiques and faces, as far as I know. You can dig up a lot from there. You already have."

I see his fist loosen a little. His eyes dart from side to side. Then another deep exhalation.

"Then the single name on the list. That's a real name," says Mr Park. More a statement than a question.

"Yes."

"It doesn't make much sense, does it, Ms Choi?"

He glares at me once more, head tilting like a raven's. I stay alert. And silent. He makes a sound somewhere between a sigh and a stunted chuckle.

"Choi Mihee. Isn't that too familiar?"

There's a clear moment in every mother's life when she realizes she can't really control her child's life the way she wants. The older her child gets, the more the mother recites this truth to herself like a mantra, to save herself from further fear and disappointment. In the back of her mind, however, her blind faith in her own power over her child still lingers, like droplets of water on a spider's web after a storm, clinging to the thin maternal mirage that she can still save her, that she can put her back on the right track, where she's destined to be.

I thought I wasn't every mother. Different from the others, I've never lectured you not to do anything dangerous. I always knew you were bound to try things. You carried my stubbornness under your tongue, after all. Instead I told you not to get caught. *No Getting Caught, No Cheating* was the furtive motto. And you put it into practice so effortlessly.

Your college life in Pyongyang was sweet, yet the Secret Police was no joke. They could creep up on you when you least expected it. Every once in a while they ran a random inspection of student apartments. And those who happened to get caught in possession of subversive contraband faced the firing squad. You had seen, the previous year, three of your classmates shot in the head. It was the usual public execution on campus, in full daylight. They let the bodies rot in the open pit for days, for everyone to be reminded of the consequence of cheating on the Party. A couple of weeks later, however, the kids resumed their usual affairs.

That night, you had your lethal lover in bed.

You were watching the sappy South Korean drama in which the dashing son of a *chaebol* and a plain, penniless girl fall in love against all odds. (Well, they always do, don't they?) You had borrowed the videotape from a young male comrade in your English class – he was making quite a bit of pocket money from copying and distributing illegal tapes. You and your little friends in the circle called him the Monk.

The Secret Police started, in the dead of night, by cutting off the electricity in the whole building. Then they made a quick surprise visit to each flat. The first thing they did was to locate the VCR and to rest their hands on it. If they felt the lingering warmth on the machine, they would turn the electricity back on, start the player to check its content. If the videotape was of a clean nature, depicting the usual propaganda shenanigans of the Kim family, you were off the hook. Yet the idea of a teenager watching a propaganda film after midnight for fun – finding Buddha in a cathouse would be more likely.

If the videotape was of a dirty nature, you were screwed. You couldn't take the tape out and hide it because cutting the electricity had trapped the tape deep in the machine. If you tried to pull it out forcefully, it would spill its shiny brown guts everywhere, visible evidence of your treachery. Even if somehow you magically got the tape out unscathed, you were screwed all the same. The first thing they did was to feel the machine, remember? They already knew it was warm. They knew you were watching something, that you had hidden. You see? There is no way out.

That was the Monk's fate, the poor boy. He got caught, and was executed within the fortnight. He was nineteen. But the nature of his offense is too atrocious, they said, committing as well as propagating the thought-crime. A handful of other kids also had themselves either bullet-studded or labor-camp-bound under a similar charge.

Yet you, Mihee, you walked out clean. Without a single strand of your hair sullied.

No getting caught, no cheating, you knew. You were always on the lookout for a dawn raid. So you had two VCRs ready all the time. That night was no exception. You turned on the two video players simultaneously, harboring two distinct videotapes: one puffs the brilliant life of our Big Brother while the other croons the star-crossed South Korean love song. Both machines were in full operation, warming up their reeling bodies, but what you were absorbed in was only the latter. The former wasn't connected to the TV, of course.

When the Secret Police cut off the electricity, other kids thrashed in panic. But you were calm. All you had to do was hide the video player hosting the South Korean romance in your wardrobe, and to connect the other video to the TV. It took a minute.

Precisely one minute and thirty seconds after the cut, the

agents barged into your flat. They put their hands on your video player and felt the warmth. They turned the electricity back on, played the tape inside. They saw a screenful of Kim Jong-il's benevolent smile, thousands of people crying, cheering at the mere movement of his fingertips. Everything was perfect. Everything was clean.

When others thought there was no way out, you always found a nook. A tiny opening. A fine crack on the rampart no one else had caught sight of.

When you told me this story, I noticed the glow in your eyes. The same one you'd worn in our first English lesson, your voice croaky with excitement reciting ABCs, only brighter and eerier this time. I realized your teenage sheen was out of my hands now.

Then you began to carry that odd inward grin with you. New secrets you were to share with me no longer.

I gave you the right kindling and now you were burning brightly on your own. And it wasn't up to me to stop it.

Like me, you are a trickster. Yet more for the fun of it, less for survival. It wasn't in your blood: it was on and under your tongue, around the eyes that have looked up to me always. It was my love. It was my vanity.

"And the only way of pursuing it legally in our society was to be a part of the secret service. Mihee was the classic textbook recruit. The Secret Police record remembered her as the gung-ho revolutionary obsessed with the Supreme Leader's propaganda films. She was also a top student from the Pyongyang University of Foreign Studies, already fluent in several foreign languages. No surprise. She learned everything from the very best.

"In the end, taking on different identities is like speaking different languages. When you learn a foreign tongue, you're not merely picking up its words. Along the way you absorb its moods and mannerisms, and the common narrative of people who speak it off the top of their heads. When you really begin to feel that you own the language, it owns you, too, like magic. By simply switching the mode of your tongue, you can turn into a stranger. You put on a new air. You can steal into somebody else's history without even realizing it."

I stop to take a breath. And I realize I'm speaking as if I'm writing. As if I'm giving a speech, instead of talking. It can't be bad for Mr Park; he's a worthy aficionado of good, careful words. I look up to observe his face. Then I know my words own him. At least for the time being.

"You once asked me about the girls. The Korean women at the Monkey House during the Korean War. You asked me what happened to them when I burned the place down. The truth is, I don't know. I've heard nothing from or of them since. But one thing I can say for sure is that I did try to save all of them. The day I laid waste to the House was the day of the girls' monthly medical check-up, when they were taken to the big military hospital in the city. On that morning, when I put them into a truck, I slipped a gun, which I'd stolen from the warden, into the pocket of one of the girls. I made slip knots under the girls' wrists, which could easily come undone at one long, gentle tug. I told them to free their hands when the military truck slowed down along the winding mountain path, to shoot the driver in the head, then jump out of the truck, run away through the woods. I don't know if they succeeded or not. I could only hope they did. At least some of them.

"What I'm trying to do now is not that different. I'm trying to save myself by giving a second chance to me and my daughter together. I deserve one. I went through a shitstorm, and then some more. You must know by now I don't give a damn about the ideology, and neither does my daughter. I've just made the best out of all that drivel thrown in my way.

"Only this time I can use some help. But I'm not a crook so I don't beg you to give it to me for free. You help me and I'll help you. From me and my daughter you'll learn more about the inner workings of RGB than you've ever learned from anybody else, especially all those fake spies you guys have framed here at KCIA.

"All I want is full acceptance of me and my daughter, full immunity to what we have done so far, in exchange for the invaluable information concerning RGB that we've accumulated. It should be done in full secrecy, of course, no media, for if RGB learns of our change of heart, they will certainly change every secret code, every secret manner of operation we know, as fast as they can.

"As soon as you and your bosses agree on my terms and guarantee our safety, I'll bring my daughter in. She's even more valuable than I am. The one with a fresh memory, with the most up-to-date intel."

The silence settles again between us. The longest yet. But this one is neither cold nor sharp. It's warm and jittery, like vertigo. He needs time to digest. So I let him. I've already handed him the hilt that he can't refuse to grab.

"I don't understand."

I can see millions of question marks flash through his blinking eyes.

He turns toward the wide gray mirror, as if asking for back-up, or an agreement.

"To begin with, how did you stay in touch with your daughter, Ms Choi? As you said, there's always surveillance, some other party in the service that censors any form of correspondence between agents. You're not supposed to reveal anything about a mission to another agent unless she's on it with you."

I repress another grin.

"We used the simplest method, Mr Park. It was Mihee's idea. As I said, she's good at finding a little crack others tend to overlook. In the midst of all the novel technologies achieved over the Cold War, we turned to the most archaic form of communication there was.

"Letters. Handwritten. She loved composing them. As a rule there was always a hidden third-party agent who caught them in between and censored every word that might implicate RGB in any way. Mihee was careful, but by the time each of her letters fell into my hands, it had occasionally a couple of words cut or crossed out.

"But, of course, Mihee made those small mistakes on purpose. Little decoys. Like she'd made up those minor offenses for the life-purification class, just to keep the canaries occupied and happy. Then she filled the pages with harmless, humdrum accounts of her life that she wanted to share with me. I loved reading about them.

"She wrote the forbidden details, mostly about her mission and her plan for the future, on the inside of the envelope. A mustard-color manila envelope. The commonest kind you'll find in any office. She opened, unfolded it and wrote her secret message on the inner side of the envelope, with an old candle. The taper one that's easy to grab and write with. We used to have a lot of them hanging around the house all the time, since power outage was very frequent in North Korea. Those candles were initially white but after a long time in storage, they went stale, turning slightly yellow. That color blended perfectly with the natural hue of a manila envelope. Even if you held it right in front of you, you wouldn't notice anything.

"All I needed to do was wet it, brush it with any dark watercolor paint, for the waxy, treacherous text to stand out and speak for itself."

Now it's my turn to let out a deep sigh – half exhaustion, half satisfaction.

Then I notice my heart beating a little faster. An old clock that chimes more and more out of tune.

Luckily I know how to calm it, to cheat it to feel at home.

I grab the only object I'm allowed to grab in this tiny room: the yellow peel-off wax pencil. A hybrid between a crayon and pencil. I place it between my index and middle finger, and rub it gently against the bony bump on the latter – a *writer's knob*, they call it – as if I'm writing. The familiar weight of calm presses me down pleasantly, and I feel anchored and whole again, like words on a page.

The 7th Life

Confessions of an
Ordinary Marriage

2006

ROUSSEAU

Aimé Adel once said that marriage is a trip from the extraordinary to the ordinary.

An ongoing process of discovering, drop by drop, that what you once believed to be so special is nothing but mediocre. It sounds a lot like how my mother described the end of her relationship with my father – how all the things she had once found original and exciting about him turned out to be just the run-of-the-mill flags of a womanizer. *A sad, pathetic cliché*, she said.

The confident way he asked for her hand on their first date. The bold way he got her nickname tattooed on his inner biceps on their third date. The suave way he made her slow-dance with him, barefoot, on the hood of his second-hand Cadillac, to "Earth Angel (Will You Be Mine)," on their fifth.

All those special moments, however, were never solely hers. It turned out Father had acted out the same script with quite a few other women as well – he had even recycled the tattooed sobriquet *Mon Petit Chardonneret*, My Little Goldfinch, for at least four. The latest of those girls was a local stripper named Angela Diabola. When I was nine, Father left us for the strange-named girl.

Not long after my father left us, God left me as well.

I grew up in a religious family. My grandparents had been missionaries in their youth and my mother brought me to church every Sunday. As a little child I had a literal faith in the Bible, as did most kids raised in a firm Christian environment. One of my favorite passages from the Bible was Matthew 17:20: *For verily I say unto you, if ye have faith as a grain of mustard seed, ye shall say unto this mountain, Remove hence to yonder place; and it shall remove; and nothing shall be impossible unto you.* Like Philip in *Of Human Bondage* by Somerset Maugham, who had absolute faith in God that He would fix his club foot, I believed He would return my father to my mother and me if I prayed with all my sincerity. So just as little Philip did, I set the date for receiving God's miracle, and I prayed. The waiting was exhilarating. I had no doubt God would grant my wish for I knew having absolute faith in His power was the sole qualification for His miracle. Harboring even a sliver of doubt was to butcher my own blessing in the making. And since my faith was absolute, just as Philip's was, the dejection I felt a month later on the morning of the planned miracle was also absolute. In the story Philip's club foot is never cured, and in my childhood my father never returned to us.

Quickly my literal faith in God unraveled. My faith in the Church as a community, however, continued. People from my grandparents' church helped us through the difficult time: they visited our house frequently to make sure we had enough food while my depressed mother spent most of her days in bed. Once she was back on her feet and began to work double shifts to support us, they often invited me to their homes for dinner, so that I wouldn't be alone for too long with sad thoughts in my head. Growing up in the comforting companionship of the church community, I felt heavily indebted to them for their kindness. And I also felt it was my natural duty to pay it forward in the future when I would be in a position to help others. My passion for the Bible continued too: when I stopped seeing it as the source of truth, it began to fascinate me as a great work of fiction, so rich in enchanting, swashbuckling tales and poignant lessons about human folly. Although I no longer believed in the omnipotence of God, I went on to play the role of a good Christian when I was with people from church. Playing along with them came naturally to me. I knew how to speak their tongue already, the words of the Bible and the melodies of Gospel hymns. And despite my secret loss of faith, I still enjoyed praying, a force of habit that offered me consolation when all other means failed.

I wondered if marriage to ordinary people was what religion was to me after my father's departure: a companionship they abided by, out of habit and loyalty, which, even after the absolute faith and passion had long gone, would continue to offer support and consolation. A constant that was satisfactory, if not thrilling. *Not a bad thing at all to live by*, I used to think.

But I hate to think of us, my wife and me, as ordinary people.

I sift through my memory to find the first fine fissure of my marriage. I wonder when we began to see ourselves as just another ordinary married couple, like the ones we used to pity. The kind that stares into the void over each other's shoulders rather than each other's faces in a restaurant. The kind whose strained attempt at a conversation ends only in a string of sighs. The kind so drained of mutual interest that they don't even care to fight anymore. The kind that can no longer recall the last time they had sex. The kind in which the only thing that holds them together is their child.

It seemed that the world around us was filled with those unhappy couples, and whenever we spotted a particularly gloomy one Seong-mi and I would make a sad-puppy face, silently mouthing *I love you* at each other. Our way of basking in our romantic superiority – guilt-smudged and yet (or *and thus*) potent. "If one day I turn into one of those sad, repressed wives, you'd better *shoot me in the head*," she whispered to me, in her exaggerated North Korean accent, then feigned death in my arms. I would place a gentle kiss on her forehead and she would wake up to return a long, proper one on the mouth. Seong-mi could surprise you in that way: normally a quiet, brooding soul, in unexpected moments she can be the embodiment of boldness, if you're really close to her.

If you really get her, know her.

I thought I was the person on earth who knew her best – until I discovered the simple, cruelly short note she left on my computer desk, in my study room.

The study is the only room in the house Aram can't barge into; the summer humidity has blossomed around the upper corner of its wooden door, making it nearly impossible to budge unless pushed with the full force of a grown-up. So the room has occasionally served as our secret venue for sex when we felt like a change, where we could be playful without worrying about our little son walking in on us.

I need some time away from everything. Alone.

Please take care of Aram.

The note is in my wife's handwriting – neat and tight, terse as a cliff – no doubt.

Given the tidiness of the writing, she wasn't in a hurry, so I don't reckon she was in physical danger when writing it – *thank God.*

If she had to vanish like this, though, there must have been a kind of crisis – if not physical, emotional.

My own emotions shift throughout the day: pure shock at first, then the daze, a brain-numbing kind, which with time has escalated into anger, before finally molding itself into an amalgam of bewilderment and anxiety.

If Seong-mi had been depressed, I should have noticed it long ago.

How could I be so blind? I ask myself. But I still am. I do not know the reason for my wife's disappearance.

I look at Aram, our mixed-race cherub, one year old. His wide, carefree smile reminds me that there's at least a small mercy out of all this: Aram is too young to carve this moment into his long-lasting memory, this baffling incident of his mother gone one morning, leaving merely a note of thirteen words.

I feel ashamed to admit that I didn't notice anything unusual last night. And nothing even this very morning when she asked me to take Aram to the playground, saying she was feeling a little under the weather. When I got home our helper, Ms Kwon, was there but I saw no sign of Seong-mi. I put Aram to bed for a nap. I went into the study to turn on the computer and found Seong-mi's note next to the keyboard. I ran into our bedroom and discovered her suitcase was gone.

Seong-mi has disappeared. Like an illusion. *Alone*, she said. *I need some time away from everything.*

I never imagined I would be included in the category of *everything* – whatever is ailing her. I thought I would be the first and the only person she would turn to and confide in when she faced hardship. I never thought I would be the part of mundane, stifling reality she wanted to run away from.

An illusion. The thought that you really know someone. That your spouse is an open book to you, every page, every word. You could be blind to what exists between the lines. So many old scars and sorrows scribbled in invisible ink.

Who is this woman, this stranger?

Bae Seong-mi. I slowly whisper her name, like I've never heard it before, like I need to memorize it.

Both Seong-mi and I are special, but not in the banal romantic sense of *unlike any other*. We each had formative years that were an antithesis of ordinary, though I consider hers much more astonishing than mine.

I was born in Durham, Maine, to a French father and a Korean mother. My father was an ex-soldier who had immigrated to America in his mid-twenties, and my mother was a war orphan adopted by an American missionary couple. My mother was about thirteen when she came to the US, but my grandparents never knew her exact age. I inherited my father's sharp, high-bridged nose and deep-set eyes; and my mother's dark-brown irises, jet-black hair, and ochre skin that can turn chocolate after forty minutes in strong sun. In a small rural town of the American north, where most kids are pale-skinned and sandy-haired, I stood out like a fly on a wedding cake.

My grandparents were smart, loving people who practically raised me alongside my mother. I went to their place in Bangor every weekend and they shared many invaluable things with me: their love for literature, their sophisticated English vocabulary, and stories of the world they had seen as a young missionary couple. They often talked passionately about Korea, the country I barely knew despite my racial heritage. But learning about Korea wasn't my priority back then: I was struggling to avoid any association that would distinguish me from others around me. What I desired was to be ordinary, to be just another kid in class that nobody would ever point a finger at. But things changed a little as I grew older. Although my exotic looks continued to turn the heads of strangers outside Durham and Bangor, I also began to benefit from certain elements of my appearance.

The boy I'd despised so much, who'd stood awkwardly a head taller than other kids in class, matured into a slender and muscular man, with sturdy upper arms just like my father's. I was good at sports, particularly anything that involved throwing balls. Although my body wasn't strong enough to make me a professional athlete, it worked well as a protective armor that warded off school bullies, even without having to engage in an actual fight. And it came to me as a big surprise that certain girls at school had taken a liking to me. Throughout my teenage years, though, I mostly kept to myself: I was anxious about becoming the talk of the town again, attracting unwanted limelight that would pull me out of the ordinary – my eternal comfort zone.

Seong-mi was perhaps the first extraordinary thing that I longed to be around.

I met Seong-mi in Shenyang, China, when I was working as a missionary at the Church of New Life. Just as Grandpa Nolan had, I went to Cornell after high school and double-majored in English and French. I went on to obtain my master's and then a PhD in English literature. After my long studies I decided to spend a year in East Asia to *broaden my horizons*, as Grandpa Nolan had recommended. Through one of his old missionary friends I learned about the Church of New Life, a South Korean Protestant church in China that was secretly helping North Korean refugees escape to South Korea. The church was looking for a young Korean American who could work as an English translator and assistant to the senior pastor, simultaneously teaching an English class at a local school as a cover. Back then I had no idea that what I'd expected to be a year of voluntary work would turn into a half-decade job in harboring and helping North Korean refugees in China.

Seong-mi was a North Korean defector who ended up on our doorstep.

Seong-mi had had quite a life. She was born in Hyesan, one of the northernmost cities of North Korea, which shares a border with China. She's younger than me, but she's had experiences that might take an ordinary person ten lifetimes to catch up with: she had survived the famine that took away half of the lives of her village; survived an abusive marriage that had turned her into a teenage mother; persisted through drug-dealing and forced prostitution. And yet she has never lost her lust for life. In her mid-twenties, she decided to escape alone from her fatherland, the most totalitarian and isolated nation in the world.

What I found most extraordinary about her was her calm. Despite all the turbulence in her life, she's remained a person of stone-cold composure; it reminded me of the Vietnamese monk from the sixties, who sat in the flames of self-immolation unshaken. Although some of the defectors I've met exhibited similar stillness, they all eventually had their moments of eruptions, often triggered by the memories of their loved ones or indelible traumas they'd survived.

When we first met, perhaps a small part of me had already fallen in love with her, despite all the rest that fought hard against it; I was frightened of myself, of the possibility that I might take advantage of a human being in need of my help.

She seemed like an old ghost trapped in a young woman's body, the weary stranger who had just limped into our church. I studied her face while she was telling me her life story. Her eyes, though clear of crow's feet raking the edges, were tired and steady and unapologetic as an old man's – lots of sorrow but no regrets. They never roamed or flitted about as did many of the young ones' when confessing their vulnerability. Even when she was describing the most painful pages of her life – years trapped in violent bondage by her husband, months in a Chinese brothel – her eyes remained calm, undaunted. Her hands weren't squeezed into nervous claws either; they just sat on her lap gently curled, like half-open lotus flowers. I liked that she wasn't effusive in her storytelling. She kept her sentences short and simple, and never gave in to the temptation of exaggeration. I instantly sensed honesty in her speaking. And I loved her no-nonsense attitude. I liked being around her. I was pleasantly humbled by her life and her quiet presence. We provided her with a shelter and a job in our church, and shortly afterwards, she began to work for me as my assistant.

Aimé Adel said that a love blooming in extreme circumstances can't survive the autumn of monotony, of everyday life.

I wonder if our move to South Korea, settling down together to start a family, was the beginning of both our making and our undoing as a married couple.

Since we've been in Seoul, everything has been secure and in place: she was no longer an illegal refugee; our love was confirmed on paper; and together we became parents, the hallmark of adulthood and stable life.

I remember the day it all began, our life as adults, of commitment.

I proposed to Seong-mi when we saw each other for the first time in Seoul. It was nearly four months after her escape to Seoul from Dalian, which I'd arranged with a Chinese broker I'd known for many years. And it was only a day after she'd finished her three-month education in Hanawon, the Settlement Support Center for North Korean Refugees. Though I'd been certain about our love, I waited to propose till she arrived safely in Seoul, till she was legally free to make such a decision; I never wanted her to feel pressured or forced to take my hand only because she needed my help.

It was the first time I saw her cry. As soon as I uttered the words she lunged forward and wrapped her arms around my neck. She locked my head tight in her bosom, as if I needed to take heed of her heartbeats, or, with hindsight, in the way she would hold a year-old Aram in her arms to squeeze the frantic giggle out of him. "You don't want to marry me, you idiot," she whispered in my ear, "not a wretch like me." Her face was smiling but tears kept rolling down her cheeks.

"I won't say the past is just the past, because it isn't true," I whispered back. I saw her smile and sob freeze. "Your past leaves me in awe of you, Seong-mi," I told her, "and no one has made me feel this way before." After my final words her frozen face resumed crying. And then she kissed me. A handful of passersby – mostly diminutive Korean grandpas with frowns etched on their brows – gave us dirty looks. But we couldn't have cared less.

Then I think of another beginning. The moment – the day or the month, hard to tell – her extraordinariness began to shed its dying skin, scale by scale, to morph into its very antithesis: ordinariness.

Mediocrity. An eventual point of arrival in every marriage, according to Aimé Adel.

Her personality. Her signature imperturbability that had made me fall for her.

The enigmatic quiet that had once made all other young women seem insipid and vain by comparison.

At first I thought living in the stability of Seoul would bring out her cheerful side a little more, the expressive Seong-mi I'd seen on the day of my proposal. But she carried her darkness around her like an invisible fog, a little cloak she would retreat into whenever she felt it necessary. And I was the only one who could feel it. Her face went blank, as if somebody had just turned off a switch under her skin, her limbs slack and heavy, as if she was moving underwater. In those moments she sometimes failed to respond to my gentle calling, "Seong-mi, sweetheart." But I tried not to worry too much, for after those seconds of inner blizzard she would always come back to me. She never failed to answer to my calling of her name the second time around. And as though she had a moment of epiphany, she would suddenly become thrilled. She would walk up to me and clasp her arms behind my neck, then purr into my ear, as she often does before she lures me into bed without waking Aram. A couple of times I asked her what she was thinking. "Nothing much," she answered once. "Better off not knowing, dear," she replied another time, with a grimace of false seriousness, like an old prophetess.

Slowly I began to resent her profundity a little – something that had previously charmed me, pulled me toward her presence. Sometimes Seong-mi could make people around her, including me, feel too simple and naïve, even immature, as if she was senior to them, and me, even though she was often the youngest in the crowd. At certain moments I felt she was ready to open up: I caught her gazing at me from a distance, in those pensive, old eyes of hers, her mouth ajar, a millisecond away from uttering the unutterable. But she never did. "I'm here for you, honey, whenever you feel like talking. Remember: whatever you did in the past won't change my love and admiration for you," I told her once, as gently as possible.

What I got in return was a deep sigh, which her hands waved away a little too airily, and then a faux smile. "Thank you, honey," she said, and ran her fingers through my hair as though I was a little boy – the way she often does to Aram to calm him down or help him fall asleep. A gesture sweet and irksome at the same time. I thought I could read her mind, hear it murmur: *Thank you, honey, but there are just things you'll never understand.*

The walks, her solitary hobby. They had once struck me as beautiful. In Shenyang, as soon as she acquired a fake Chinese ID card, she started to take long walks regularly to the local park, always with a book in her hand. When asked where she often disappeared to after her work at the church, she answered that she liked wandering around the old market, or the big public park several kilometers away. "It's something a young woman can't do back in my home country, walking alone, just for the sake of it." I saw her blush and then beam. She said she also loved reading in the sun, whether it was high in the sky, or hung low and orange on the horizon. "After all, it's a hobby that costs nothing," she added. I couldn't help staring at her, as if she was a rare wild creature you didn't know really existed. The book she was holding was a Korean copy of *The Open Ceiling*, a semi-autobiographical novel by Aimé Adel, my favorite French writer. It was a smuggled copy I stored in my office cabinet, to which Seong-mi had access as my assistant. Heart pounding with excitement, I asked her how she liked the author. "Not a fan," she answered straight away – to my surprise and disappointment. "He's a preacher who can't practice what he preaches, isn't he?" said Seong-mi. "You'd know what that means since you're a preacher yourself."

A week later I asked her if I could join her walk to the Dongling Park. After a small moment of hesitation, she said yes. A slight unease had lingered in my thoughts ever since I had had the terse conversation with her about Aimé Adel. Back in my undergraduate French classes at Cornell, and probably in the equivalent of every other Ivy League school, *nobody* had a right to diss Aimé Adel. Adel was a significant European thinker of the late twentieth century: the smasher of European colonialism and the beacon of all civil-rights movements, especially of feminism. All French majors had the black-and-white photo stickers of Adel and his partner Sandrine Mauraux, with whom Adel had enjoyed his famous open marriage. In the photo Adel and Mauraux were in bed, emaciated and half-naked, on a hunger strike to support the anti-Vietnam war movement. Adel was a god and rock star of post-World War II philosophy; nobody, not even the professors, had the guts to disapprove openly of him in class, in the face of his angry young revolutionary students. *Adel and Mauraux liberated women from the conventions of marriage!* Many of the female students were ready to use that line as their bumper stickers.

But this doe-faced refugee girl walking leisurely beside me, with neither degree nor pedigree, said to me: "Plus, that open-marriage thing is bullshit, isn't it?" I felt both hurt by and smitten with love for her. I asked her how come she'd found the greatest philosophical marriage of the century a hoax. She laughed and said that none of the terms of their union were set by Mauraux. "It's Adel's artsy excuse for sleeping around," she said, "without having to face consequences." She summed it up: "You do any women you like and simultaneously possess the giving-tree wife you can always return to. A dream life every king and dictator has lived. The only difference is that Adel gets to be called *feminist* for it," she murmured with faint scorn. North Korean bluntness. I found it mesmerizing that her tone remained quiet and measured as always, although her words were biting. Their little teeth were stuck in my guts, prickling my loins for hours before I could finally give in to sleep that night. In a fitful dream I saw myself with her, my mouth between her thighs. The next morning in the office I felt too ashamed to look her in the eye: I had assumed that a woman like Seong-mi, given where she was from, wouldn't possess many of her own opinions on metaphysical matters – subjects that don't directly involve survival.

I thought her solitary walks would no longer be solitary once we were married. I had no idea that this crepuscular stroll in Shenyang, during which she blithely dismissed Aimé Adel, would be our first *and* last walk together. She said the stroll was something she always preferred to do alone, with a book in her hand. Now that she no longer lived by herself, she explained, it was more important than ever for her to walk alone. "I'm what you Westerners call an *introvert*," she said, her face puckered in mock gloom. After Aram was born, her need for a solitary walk seemed to have grown. "I need that time alone to stay sane," she told me, "to remain a good mother and a good wife." So I made sure she had it, thinking she deserved every second of it. At the same time I felt belittled by the exclusion. I felt lonely, wondering about all the things she might prefer to do in my absence. And I disdained myself for feeling that way. For being the petty, jealous husband I'd never wanted to become.

In my darkest moments of pique, I went so far as to imagine a secret lover on Seong-mi's side – maybe someone from the gathering of North Korean defectors in Seoul, which she attended on occasion. A fellow refugee, born and bred in the ruggedness of North Korea just like Seong-mi. A man who would effortlessly understand her suffering. A man she wouldn't need to talk down to. I felt as though I was in competition for tragedy in life and knew I was losing. That imaginary man made my life, which I'd once considered complicated, seem trivial.

How well do you know the life of your spouse?

How well can you know her or him?

In Korea, people use the concept of *chon* to measure familial intimacy. For instance, I'm only one *chon* away from my parents whereas there are two between my siblings and me. And my parents' siblings are three *chon*s apart from me, while my cousins and I are partitioned by four. Korean words for uncle and cousin, *Sam-chon* and *Sa-chon*, literally come from this *chon* definition; *Sam* and *Sa* respectively signify three and four in Korean. In its razor-sharp poignancy, the Korean definition declares no *chon* between a husband and a wife. This harbors multiple layers of meaning: first, as a pair bonded by physical and psychological love, they're nearly as good as one at the peak of their intimacy; but secondly, a husband and a wife, after all, bear no biological relation to one another; and thus, lastly, having neither *chon* nor biological relation between them, a husband and wife could technically turn into complete strangers, or enemies even, once their flimsy legal tie of marriage is fractured.

Before, I only understood the term's perspicacity theoretically. Now, I understood it viscerally.

MIHEE

Mihee was to pick one from two different identities.

"Both are real," Comrade Cha said, so Mihee asked him why real characters instead of the made-up ones they usually assumed.

He whispered, a glare in his eyes, that this was simply a more efficient way of doing business. "Statistically proven." Agents play their assigned roles better when they are rooted in true lives, even though they're playing false whether their cover stories are fiction or non-fiction.

While Comrade Cha's words were soft, his glare weighed on her mind, reminding her they're never fond of a novice asking questions. "Besides," he continued, "if you prove yourself successful, you'll be eventually sent to South Korea, which requires you to take over a real person's identity anyway."

The first option was a man named Kim Cheol.

"Don't let the sex throw you off," said Comrade Cha. She didn't: she knew the Famine had locked the bodies of many men in forever-delayed puberty. "Kim Cheol is short, slight-built, so you can cover him easily, if you're good at what you do." She wondered if this was a test. Comrade Cha continued about how this, if played well, could come later as a great advantage one day when she needed to escape unnoticed from her lieu of mission. "You can be a girl again, while they fruitlessly look for a boy."

She met Kim Cheol in his cell, a day before his execution. They offered him the last meal of his choice, cold buckwheat noodle with a hardboiled egg, and three cigarettes, and he was more than happy to cooperate. "To tell you the truth, Miss," Cheol mumbled with smile, the burning tip of a cigarette dancing between his scabby lips, "I would have cooperated anyway, with or without the meal." She felt irked by his calling her *Miss* but she let it go, thinking he would be cold meat by tomorrow. She understood what he meant, though. Any life, on the verge of annihilation, would feel the urge to carve a mark. And all Kim Cheol ever wanted was to leave a smudge of existence on this world, through telling the story of his life. This – his right to the final speech – made him seem cocky at times, as if he were a war hero interviewed for his gallantry.

Cheol's life was defined by hunger. He spent hours of his limited time talking about food, things you can and can't eat, as though all the things in the world could fall into those two simple categories. "Dogs and cats and rabbits were already all gone so we turned to smaller things, like mice, rats," Cheol said, "and when even those were done, we went for frogs and tadpoles, then cicadas and grasshoppers." Mouth ajar and eyes empty, Cheol was swimming in nostalgia. Even a slice of Mihee's childhood reminiscence, shiny red dragonflies waltzing in her family's garden of cosmos, couldn't seem to survive Cheol's appetite. "You need to remove the heads, though," he emphasized, "'cause they're too bitter, but without the heads, dragonflies taste just as good and nutty as pan-fried anchovies." She felt both disgust and pity for the man.

Cheol was *kotchebi*, one of too many orphans begotten by the Famine, a period of mass starvation and economic crisis in the nineties that had swept away a quarter of the North Korean population. He had no memory of his mother, who'd run out on him when he was three, and his workman father with low *songbun* had entrusted Cheol and his older brother to an orphanage. His brother had died of typhoid fever in the orphanage, and Cheol escaped from the place shortly afterward. He'd never seen his father again.

Eleven-year-old Cheol scraped by on whatever he could find to eat, train-hopping from one place to another, losing and picking up companions, robbing and being robbed. He'd mastered the art of hunting and gathering by the age of twelve. And bartering by thirteen. At fourteen he made the decision of his life: to cross the frontier. Ever since, he'd been an illicit rag-and-bone man, selling scrap metals and North Korean bric-a-brac to the Chinese across the border. Quickly he became the richest man of his age he'd ever known: pieces of iron and copper, pottery and jewelry North Koreans gave up for a dollar plucked fifteen from a pocket of a Chinese buyer. The business had thrived till Cheol turned sixteen, the age of majority. "I'd already made about ten illegal border crossings by then," said Cheol, chest puffed up with pride. "I know the spots along the Tumen River, where the border guards are pretty lax." Cheol, with an ID stolen from a pile of dead men behind a rail station, acquired a safe house near the river, and there he stashed some of his goods and a last-ditch emergency fund.

In the end it wasn't border-crossing that got him the death penalty. He was arrested by the Secret Police in his safe house while he was taking out some of his emergency fund. He had hidden the cash inside picture frames, behind the portraits of Kim Il-sung and his son, Kim Jong-il. Cheol thought it was an ingenious hiding place that nobody would dare to rummage in: any visual representations of the Father and the Son were regarded as sacred, and damaging them amounted to an act of treason. When the Secret Police barged in, Cheol dropped the half-open picture frame of Kim Jong-il on the floor. The glass shattered and the portrait was ripped in the corner, giving the Supreme Leader an eerie lopsided smile. "You see," Cheol said, "you may get away with border crossing but you can't get away with insulting our Great Commander." *Never*, especially if you're a legal adult, Mihee thought. Looking at Cheol she nodded. Their generation had grown up with stories of small heroes, who had salvaged hallowed portraits of the Father and the Son from a burning building or a sinking ship, righteously risking their lives.

Mihee wondered if she could be as calm as Cheol when faced with death. Like many other North Koreans who had survived the Famine, both Mihee and Cheol were blasé about death: they'd seen too much of it, everywhere. But Mihee could never be indifferent toward her own death. The mere thought of it – knowing that your expiration would take place the following day – seemed impossible, too monstrous to imagine. Cheol scoffed gently when asked if he was scared. "Nothing gets under my skin anymore, Miss," he answered. "Having seen what I've seen, having done what I've done, I feel like I'm a thousand years old already." He said he would rather live if he had a choice. "But I don't have many regrets even if I can't," added Cheol, shrugging his shoulders. What he'd truly dreaded was starving to death – the slow, suffering, delirious kind of demise that robs you of humanity.

"Mine will be quick, gun shots and no pain, so not really a bad one. Besides, I'll die with a full stomach, a proper meal of beef broth and real buckwheat noodle. *Not* the fake one made of cornhusks, or the inner bark of pine trees, you know."

Those last words he swallowed with a smile. And yet a shadow of sorrow hung over his face, like a still curl of cigarette smoke.

The second option was a woman named Bae Seong-mi.

A tall, skinny woman. A paper-pale face. Puppy eyes – slightly drooping at the corners. Thin lips, but a strong jaw.

She was younger than Mihee but looked much older.

Unlike the gushing Kim Cheol, Bae Seong-mi was a cautious speaker. She unraveled her life only a fraction at a time. Like Kim Cheol, however, Bae Seong-mi had crossed the Korean-Chinese border numerous times before she was arrested and sent to a labor camp. She had sold drugs: *bingdu*, crystal meth. "Before all this, I was just an ordinary mother," she said under her breath, accompanied by a bitter grin.

Seong-mi never cried. And yet each time she mentioned her son, a prolonged silence ensued. She spoke slowly, her voice small and tender, nearly devoid of inflection. This captured Mihee's attention. Whenever Seong-mi hung her story in the air in mid-sentence, seemingly consumed by the intensity of her memory, Mihee felt her heart leap, tantalized. This knack gave Seong-mi an additional four days to deliver her life story before her execution, whereas Cheol had only one.

Like Mihee, Seong-mi was from Hyesan, one of the northernmost cities that face China. This was beneficial to Mihee: nothing new to study and memorize about the city where she had grown up. This would save Mihee lots of time. Seong-mi was born into a low *songbun* family and married off to an upper-middle one. Her husband was a propagandist working for the public radio station in Hyesan. "He was a burly, handsome man with a hearty laugh," Seong-mi said. "Raffish but well-spoken, he was loved by both men and women equally." The sweet recollection ended there. "He'd changed literally overnight," Seong-mi murmured, and from the wedding day on there had been booze and abuse. Mihee found it strange that Seong-mi spoke of his violence with such detachment, as though the pain she'd endured belonged to somebody else. The compulsion to run away had struck Seong-mi abruptly one day, another morning after a drunken thrashing, followed by tears, pledges of *it-won't-happen-again*, and the passionate declaration of love, the routine speech she'd grown so used to that she could recite it backward. While she was applying tinted talcum powder to the bruising on her eye and neck, every joint in her hand on slow fire, the simple truth dawned on her: that he would kill her one day. "This will never stop as long as I live," she realized. Seong-mi had two choices. "I kill him before he kills me," she whispered, "or I flee." As if possessed by a ghost, Seong-mi ran out of the house, only a thin layer of nightgown on her skin. She never returned home.

She decided to cross the Yalu River and go to China, which was the only option left to her anyway. She had a vague recollection of Uncle Majo, her great-aunt's son living in Changbai, a Chinese county mainly populated by ethnic Koreans. Uncle Majo's family was neither welcoming nor cold. They just did what they felt obliged to do for a distant relative they hadn't seen for a decade. They fed her and sheltered her till she began to look normal, and all the bruises on her body had faded. "Then I was on my own again, eight dollars in my pocket, with a carpetbag full of Auntie Majo's clothes." An undocumented alien, she hopped from one dangerous low-paid job to another. "The only choice I really had, as an illegal North Korean female, was prostitution, of varying degrees," said Seong-mi, eyes staring into the void. From massage with happy ending to playing a wife to a handicapped Chinese farmer – and then to the classic red-light district as her final destination. The second week into her time in the cathouse, however, she escaped again. When all the female workers were sent to a public bath, its entrance guarded by the pimps, Seong-mi pretended to go for a pee, then jumped out of the toilet window. By the time she began to realize that the path beyond prostitution wasn't a bed of roses either, her mind wandering around the thought of ending her own life, she was approached by what she saw as her second chance.

"I was offered a job smuggling drugs out of North Korea," she said. It was a dangerous job but very lucrative, the scar-faced Chinese gang told her. For decades North Korea had been producing and refining opium on a grand scale – one of few NK-made goods that met international quality standards. Technically, as a means to raise foreign currency, drugs were only for export. Under such a failing economy, however, in which bribes put more food on the table than salaries, drugs found their way into the hands of the general public as well. Due to the dearth of Western medicine and medical supplies, crystal meth became people's panacea. They used it for all kinds of pain, and conditions from herpes to final-stage cancer. Even healthy people resorted to it to distract themselves from hunger, or from reality. "North Korean *bingdu* was in high demand in China for its good quality and relatively cheap price," Seong-mi went on, "and Chinese gangs were bent on finding better ways to get their hands on it." They figured Seong-mi, an ordinary-looking North Korean female, neither young nor old, would make a perfect smuggler. She was insignificant and non-threatening in a crowd, and as a woman, less subject to strip-search. She could move in and out of the country unnoticed.

She was active mostly in winter. Thick winter clothing provided more space for stashing drugs, also some cash and cigarettes to be used as bribes for the border guards. The biting winter cold froze the Yalu River thick and hard, so she walked across it without worrying about damaging the goods. "First time in a while I had a purpose in life," whispered Seong-mi, eyes closed. The business was indeed lucrative – the first crossing landed her a fee equal to a year of her husband's salary – and she began to picture the new future, with her ten-year-old son in it. She'd never worked with such ferocity before. She needed more money to buy her son the safest escape route and a decent domicile in China. The next winter she made several more successful business trips to North Korea. She was caught only once by a border guard, but she bought him off easily with three dollars and a pack of cigarettes.

Her dream was shattered when it seemed just ready to kick off. One wrong yank of a thread that undid the whole weave. One day, passing her old neighborhood in Hyesan, she couldn't resist the urge to walk up to her son's school. "Just to catch a glimpse of him from a distance." Seong-mi's voice trembled. She didn't spot her son but someone spotted *her*, a man named Injae, an old neighbor, and a very close friend of her husband. The police showed up within minutes.

Seong-mi knew her luck was draining. Contrary to most policemen, Comrade Injae refused to be bought. The bribes she offered infuriated him: "*Filthy defector, traitor to the Party and the father of her child!*" Injae shouted at Seong-mi.

"He followed me to the station, to make sure I didn't get away this time." Left alone in a holding cell, with the yapping background noise of Comrade Injae feeding her husband the whole story over the phone, she realized she'd hit a dead end. No more running. She knew too well what was to come: the labor camp, then back to her husband. She had to make the last decision quickly while it was still available. She'd stashed *bingdu* all over her body – she shoved as much of it into her mouth as fast as she could before the guard stopped her.

"The amount I took was enough to knock the life out of a horse, but somehow it couldn't kill me," Seong-mi whispered, head tilted forward. Silence filled the air. Mihee wondered if Seong-mi was crying. "I was tried, and sentenced to death," she said finally, with a little laugh, then a sigh.

"The main reason for my death sentence was neither the border crossing nor drug trafficking." Seong-mi was now staring Mihee straight in the eye. "It was the suicide attempt."

Of course it was, Mihee thought quietly. The state abhors suicide. Suicide is evil, a passive protest against the Party. An inward form of defection. They could not let this happen on their own turf, in their own cell – the place that's supposed to strip you of liberty in its entirety. They could not leave this shame unavenged.

Seong-mi began to sob. Mihee felt lost, appalled. It wasn't a pretty sight to witness: the collapse of someone who'd seemed so impenetrably composed. Mihee wanted to simultaneously slap her and hug her. But she remained seated, silent. As she'd been trained to be.

After drying her tears, Seong-mi said something Mihee hadn't expected to hear: she said she felt lucky despite everything. She was happy to have the opportunity to tell her life story before it evaporated. "Most death-row convicts aren't given this kind of last chance, are they?" she murmured, with a lean smile. She wasn't denying that she would die tomorrow, but knowing that she would continue to exist, even if it was through the charade of somebody else, was comforting. A vicarious happiness, strange as life itself.

"In a way, we're giving each other a new life, aren't we?" said Seong-mi. Tears began to roll down her smiling cheeks.

They said goodbye to each other.

As Mihee was stepping out of the cell, Seong-mi called her back. She said she had forgotten to tell her something important.

Seong-mi grabbed Mihee by the shoulders and whispered in her ear: "If you cross the Yalu River when it isn't frozen, make sure you take off all your clothes before setting foot in the water."

Mihee watched Seong-mi walk away.

What Seong-mi had said reminded Mihee of her own mother.

Mother, her idol. It was because of her Mihee had chosen this profession – much against her mother's will. But as the old Korean saying had it, *There's no parent who wins against its child*. With time Mother acknowledged it too. From then on, Mother had been a staunch teacher.

Mother had once told Mihee that she had had to cross many rivers for her old missions.

"Yalu, Dooman, and even Imjin," she said. "I was some sort of experiment they were running."

Since Mother wasn't a typical agent who'd followed the elite course of training, they used her as a human testing board for a variety of muddy, lowly, and dangerous jobs. They'd thrown her straight into the wilderness to see if she could come out alive.

She told Seong-mi to weather it all. "The first mission is crucial," Mother said, with emphasis. "Only after I had proven myself worthy through the first series of ordeals, was I given stable cover as a businesswoman."

Before wearing the shining armor of businesswoman, Mother had worn a flower in her hair to play a demented war orphan. Posing as a tramp, she had secretly collected information about the US military base in Paju, South Korea. To Seong-mi, a demented mute sounded like a horrid role to play, but Mother said it was a smart and convincing character to assume. Every South Korean town, she said, had its own crazy orphan girl after the war. The grief had turned her blind to reality. Too wretched and detached, she was never considered a threat. So she enjoyed a strange kind of freedom, Mother explained.

Just as Seong-mi had, Mother told her she'd better remove all her clothes before crossing a river. "Especially the Yalu River," Mother said. "At night, even in summer, its water can get cold as death. You don't want to die of hypothermia even before you steal a glance at the outside world." She smiled.

*

Mihee had to make a choice between the two lives, Cheol and Seong-mi.

From the beginning, however, the choice seemed too easy to make. It was Seong-mi, no doubt about it. Then she wondered again: what if this whole thing was just a test? She knew they rarely handed over the power of decision to a new fish. Is this a perk of having a legendary adoptive mother? Mihee pondered. Or do they want to know what kind of gambler I am?

Is she the textbook conformer? Or a gutsy risk-taker?

Within the walls of this uncanny business, the truth was always hard to know.

ROUSSEAU

Seong-mi's carefree dismissal of Aimé Adel. It had once scratched my heart as well as won it.

I marveled at her blunt boldness, at how she didn't get easily swept away by the mainstream opinion. I envied that confidence. I, on the contrary, had spent my childhood and adolescence afraid of how others saw me.

But I began to resent that, too: her easy put-down of what others think.

Although she wasn't a fan of *The Open Ceiling*, she ended up reading all the books of Aimé Adel on my shelves, in our humble nuptial abode in Seoul. And once she was done with Adel she moved on to some of Sandrine Mauraux.

One day I saw her reading *The Greenhouse* by Mauraux, a story of a female botanist who suffers from her lifetime commitment to her philandering poet lover. When Seong-mi finished that semi-autobiographical novel I, hopeful as a lark, asked her if any of the books she'd read had made her change her opinion on Adel. She flashed an enigmatic smile and shrugged her shoulders.

"I like the message of his philosophy. It gave hope and purpose for life to lots of people. I just don't like him as a person."

"How so?" The tail of my brief question rose a little too high in pitch. My heart pounded unpleasantly.

"Many of his actions in real life belied what he wrote. He sold himself as the smasher of white supremacy, calling himself an *outcast* for his mixed race. But the guy was dirty blond with blue eyes. The quarter Afro-Arab in him didn't show. He never suffered racism in real life but profited a lot from his invisible Afro-Arab heritage. He had never set foot in his father's homeland, just wallowed in his comfy white European first-world privilege, which he'd said in his writing he abhorred. What a phony." She laughed.

Although I wasn't the person talking, I felt out of breath.

Seong-mi continued: "And he called himself a *feminist*. With that revolutionary *open marriage* he proposed. Well, he was indeed *open* about one thing. Screwing lots of women, without having to face consequences. What an easy, brilliant term he coined."

Seong-mi was laughing again at her own cynicism. "Sorry," she added, with a snort, "I can't sugarcoat my words the way South Koreans do."

I was mad. I hated that her tone stayed stone-calm throughout the talk, and even playful at times, while my face burned. I felt as if I had suffered an ambush. But my attacker seemed fine, guiltless. In my head the little tower of literature I'd built since I was a boy was teetering on one of its corners. But Seong-mi, who had just caused the storm, had already moved on, sashayed into the kitchen, and was rinsing the rice for dinner, humming.

That brutal calm.

MIHEE

So Mihee was reborn as Seong-mi the moment she set her bare foot in the Yalu River. Baptized from chest down in freezing water, Mihee thanked both Mother and Seong-mi for their indispensable advice: that she take off her clothes before crossing the river. Everything she'd put into the large waterproof plastic bag – clothes, a small towel, a coin purse, a pair of socks and rubber shoes – remained soft and dry as the inside of a newborn's cradle. Getting into her dry clothes after the cold water felt like sinking into a deep sleep after a white night. She let out a little cry of fatigue and relief.

Truth be told, Mihee thought, the crossing itself was easy to the point of disappointment – for her the only adversity came from the cold of the water, not from a shout or the flying bullets of a border guard. Such a small distance, not even fifty meters wide. A few dozen, slow steps through water, which most young women could manage without help, were all it took to get you out of the most secluded nation on earth. But Mihee had already learned from Seong-mi that border-crossing wasn't the heart of the hardship: that was surviving undocumented.

Such a strange sight, Mihee thought. Born and raised in Hyesan, she was already familiar with the sight of the other side of the border. Looking back at her hometown, however, from the opposite side, was something she had never experienced before. The low and gray skyline of Hyesan in darkness felt so intimate yet so foreign. It was like an out-of-body experience of watching yourself sleep, hovering weightless over your own face, suspended in torpor. The small physical distance she had covered to cross the border began to weigh heavily on her mind.

Unlike most North Korean runaways in China, Mihee

knew where to go. As a reincarnated Seong-mi, she was to infiltrate Saesaengmyeong Gyohwe, the Church of New Life. This Korean Protestant church in Shenyang was rumored to have helped hundreds of North Koreans defect to foreign countries, mostly to South Korea. The church had been founded by a South Korean businessman, and was run now by an American pastor, Adrien Rousseau.

"He was born in America," Comrade Cha explained, "to a French immigrant father and a Korean adoptee mother. His main language is English but he's also fluent in French, Korean, *and* Chinese." Comrade Cha stuck out his lower lip and raised his eyebrows – acknowledgement of the enemy's accomplishment. He described the pastor as a cold man, a distant man, the kind hard to impress, and thus not easy to fool. Her job for the time being was to keep an eye on Pastor Rousseau, reporting on all of his activities and talks that might concern the Party. In due course, she would enter South Korea under her North Korean defector identity, through the help of Pastor Rousseau. "This mongrel is rumored to be a CIA informant," Comrade Cha emphasized.

Mihee felt peeved by Cha's choice of word. *Mongrel.* It brought images of Western monsters to her mind: like the Minotaur, or Frankenstein. It wouldn't be such a pretty thing to keep an eye on all day long, six days a week, she thought.

She first stopped at Changbai to receive the fake travel document she needed to head for Shenyang. She showed up at the door of the address that Comrade Cha had made her memorize. It was the back door to a hot-pot restaurant in the middle of a crowded spice market, which faced a narrow, dim-lit back alley, dense with the smell of stale lard and red-pepper powder. She gave the door the arranged knocks – fast four then slow two – and a slight old woman appeared imme-diately. The woman, dressed in a rubber apron stained with blood, told Mihee to wait, then returned inside. Through the half-shut door Mihee saw a row of little bodies hung upside down from the ceiling, like a colony of immobile bats, animals that looked like large skinned rabbits, yet Mihee knew were not. The old woman returned with a small backpack. Mihee took it and thanked her. The woman said nothing. Comrade Cha said Mihee wasn't supposed to know the woman's name and what she was doing. Most of the necessary materials would be delivered to her in a similar way in Shenyang, by another nameless agent nearby in the field, with as few words and as little physical contact as possible.

Mihee got off the train one stop earlier than necessary and walked to the Church of New Life. Seven kilometers before arrival, she changed her shoes. She threw away the old pair by the side of the road. The new pair she put on looked old by intent, a chunk of the left sole missing. Upon arrival, she was in real pain, limping on her left foot.

She saw two people at the entrance: a janitor with a thick Chinese-Korean accent and a middle-aged woman the janitor had addressed as Deaconess Kang. They looked at her foot, and took her in right away; Mihee knew those God-believers couldn't cast away an injured woman in need of God's help. She found the exterior of the church unremarkable; it would have been entirely indistinguishable from other blocky brutalist buildings around, insipid and gray as boiled meat, had it not been for the red neon cross hung above the gate. Seeing the cross brought tears to Mihee's eyes, real ones pumped by pain and relief. Without a word they shepherded her into their underground prayer hall, a cavernous chamber with no windows, which smelled of lacquered wood and mold. There they tended her injured foot, then told her to wait. She knew they were fetching the pastor, the church's decision-maker when it came to refugees. She looked down at her foot: significantly swollen, yet with only superficial cuts and bruises, it would serve as a perfect excuse for her stay inside the church, till she could start walking again properly. She found herself grinning, and soon began to feel faintly fearful of herself, wondering how far Agent Mihee would go, even in hurting herself, compromising her body, if it were required for the job.

Then Mihee decided to wonder about something else – the question at hand, much more important and urgent than her bloody foot, of course. Who was Pastor Rousseau? she asked herself. What kind of person was this strange man, a mixed-blood American and a taciturn polyglot? Mihee thought of the archetype of Americans she had grown up learning about in school: a pale-eyed monster with a long, pointy nose that resembled a Japanese soldier's bayonet. Jackals, teachers called them. Sly predators hungry for little Korean children's blood. But, even as a child, Mihee was too smart to buy those images wholesale.

Pastor Rousseau, of course, ticked none of the boxes of her imagination. He was young, tall, and darkly handsome. A honey-skinned, raven-haired man, a face like a clean-cut gem. A strange beauty, Mihee thought. It was her first time seeing a biracial person, and she wondered if all mixed-race men would be so pleasing to the eye. The pastor's Korean was nearly impeccable, except for the tiny American drawl after every *uh* sound, and the random stress he put on some con-junctive particles that should have remained flat. The manner of his speech in general, however, curt and straightforward, reminded her of her North Korean boss's. *This man's up for no bullshit*, she felt, *so don't beat around the bush and stick to the point.* And that was exactly what she did when he asked her to tell him about her journey, how she had ended up on their doorstep.

As Mihee unspooled a pithy version of Seong-mi's life story with composure, Pastor Rousseau seemed to be merely observing and listening, his face immobile. A laconic man – the last thing Mihee would normally have expected from an American Protestant pastor. None of the smarming condescension, Mihee noticed too, that many evangelists showed toward the poor third-world subjects they targeted for conversion. Could this be evidence that the man was here not on a religious mission but a political one?

He was a hard nut to crack but Mihee knew where to strike. Earning trust from a man like Pastor Rousseau was like getting to know a strange dog. Take time – you should never rush into approaching to caress him: you should let him approach you. Do not look him directly in the eye, for this may anger or scare him away. You may walk closer and sit down near him very slowly, and yet again the key is for him to think that *he* is approaching *you*, not the other way around. All you can do in the final moment is to extend your hand in front of him, eyes still downcast, but it should be him who brings his head close, sniffs, then licks your fingers.

So for a while, unlike other North Korean refugees at the church, she never went to bother the pastor in his office. She limited her spoken words to a minimum but kept her hands busy. She volunteered to clean around the prayer hall, and wiped all the pews and Bibles and hymn books, removed mold stains from the walls, polished the pulpit, emptied the flower vase and filled it with clean water regularly. Every Friday she cleaned toilets on every floor. "The least I can do with my uninjured hands, Deaconess Kang," Mihee told the female superintendent of the church, when Pastor Rousseau just happened to be within earshot, walking out of his office. Though Mihee said hello politely to the pastor every time she ran into him, she never initiated a conversation.

The chance came before Mihee began to walk normally again. It was a few days after the tenth anniversary of the Church of New Life. Thousands of people gathered to celebrate the Korean church's birthday. South Korean businessmen, owners of furniture and canning factories in Shenyang, came with their workers, bearing exotic fruits and money in red envelopes. And various ethnic Koreans from surrounding regions, Dandong, Changbai, and even Yanbian, travelled with their families to Shenyang, to enjoy the festivity and free flow of Korean food. After three days of the feast, shouting the same greetings to thousands of bright faces and shaking thousands of hands, Pastor Rousseau lost his voice and the grip of his right hand temporarily.

"You said you can type?" Pastor Rousseau asked her that morning, abruptly, his voice cracking, when Mihee was straining to remove a coffee stain from his office door. She found his casual tone baffling: he hadn't spoken to her at all for the last month. Though thrilled by the opportunity, Mihee hesitated: she'd never mentioned that she could type.

"Yes, I can type. Sir," answered Mihee, finally, keeping her voice small and wary.

Pastor Rousseau smiled. "Good. Would you help me? I can barely type with my left hand." He briefly raised his right hand, which was covered with pain-relief patches. The piquant smell of the mint camphor made her eyes water a little.

She followed the pastor into his office. He pulled up his chair and gestured to her to sit. Then he started to dictate what seemed to be his sermon for the following Sunday. Though baffled all the more, Mihee kept her mouth shut and moved her fingers across the keyboard as fast as she could. Beads of sweat appeared above her upper lip. She focused fiercely. She felt as though asking him to slow down or to repeat what he'd just said was equivalent to losing a game.

By the end of his dictation, his mouth and her fingers were dancing in near-perfect unison, as if they'd been partners of this *pas de deux* for years.

Pastor Rousseau took the papers from Mihee's hand and began to read them. Mihee found herself studying his face desperately for a sign of approval. "Good," said Rousseau, and Mihee felt a surge of joy, like a nervous child pampered by her normally aloof mother. "Too good, actually," added Rousseau, with a small crinkle in his brow.

Mihee's stomach lurched. "What do you mean by *too* good, may I ask?"

This was Mihee's first question to the pastor.

"*Methuselah*," he answered, under his breath. "You spelled the word correctly. I just said it once and you typed it fast, without a mistake."

He asked her if she was already familiar with the biblical figure. She answered that Methuselah, Noah's grandfather, was the oldest man in the Bible, who lived nearly a thousand years. To cover her lies Mihee decided to throw him a little bone of truth: "My mother was a Christian, educated and baptized by Canadian missionaries before the wars. She was my Bible teacher."

Mihee saw surprise on the usually expressionless face.

Fingers leafing through the papers again, he nodded. Mihee saw a faint smile spread across his face.

"North Korean defectors come here claiming they want to learn about the Bible, that they want to be Christians," he said, "but, of course, their true goal is elsewhere. I don't blame them, though. They do what they need to do to have a shot at a better life."

He shut his lips tight and stared at Mihee, as though pressuring her to say something. But Mihee stayed silent, only staring back harder at him.

"You're one of the rare ones, who *do* know about the Bible, Miss Bae Seong-mi."

He wore the smile again. But Mihee didn't reciprocate. "I'm no different from the rest, Pastor," she said instead. "What I want eventually is the same. Maybe the only difference is I don't like to be in debt."

Mihee kept her words brief and left the room shortly. She knew her month-long drudgery of wiping, washing and polishing had spoken a better message already.

In the evening, Pastor Rousseau summoned her back into his office.

He told her that what she wanted could not be done right away. She might need to wait, even up to a year. "The North Korean government's just begun their largest crackdown yet on North Korean defectors hiding in China." He heaved a sigh and confessed he'd had to turn down several defectors already, those who had arrived last month, just before Seong-mi.

She told him she was in no hurry. "My goal is to save enough money to pay for my own escape, no matter how long it takes," she said patiently. "I've been in debt before, to people I wish I'd never been involved with. And I promised myself I won't let that happen again."

After the conversation Pastor Rousseau appointed her as his assistant. Early next morning Mihee was back in his office, typing his post-anniversary thank-you letters to the church's benefactors. Deaconess Kang, previously fond of Mihee for sharing the burden of manual chores, now threw her a dirty side-eye every time she passed by, infusing the air with hostile silence. "So what kind of *skills* did you show off, girl?" asked the deaconess a few days later, when she ran into Mihee in the ladies' room.

Skills you know nothing about, answered Mihee, in her mind.

Mihee liked working in the pastor's underground office. It reminded her of her father's tiny study in Hyesan, a room full of old books and illegal vinyl records. She was secretly in love with its smell; just like her father's, the room breathed out slightly moldy air – *the gray smell*, little Mihee used to call it. The soothing odor you could sniff from only two places: a stack of time-stained hardcover books and the entrance to Hyesan airfield in the rain. Little Mihee used to run to it whenever she saw the dark clouds gather in the sky, just to inhale the ashen beauty of a smell: the vast, smooth pavement of milky concrete soaked in rain.

Mihee, a helpless bookworm, went through every book in the pastor's bookshelves and cabinets. She was disappointed to find little of the American literature she'd hoped to read again. The world thought North Korea had banned all cultural influences of America, but that wasn't quite true. Mihee had grown up watching *Tom and Jerry* on TV. The Party had recognized the metaphor of a small entity outfoxing its behemoth enemy with its cleverness, and used it to their own advantage: as an allegory of North Korea's victory against the big bully of America. And as a top student at the country's elite university, Mihee had had the privilege of reading some of the forbidden literature of America – to *know thy enemy*, as Sun Tzu advised. As an agent in training, she'd had nearly unlimited access to American, European, and even South Korean literature, to learn how to pose as an insider of Westernized Asia.

She thought of the Yankee novels she'd loved as a college student – *Gone with the Wind*, *The Great Gatsby*, *East of Eden* and so many more. But the pastor owned none. He instead had countless books on philosophy, and several novels, mostly written by European scholars. She was shocked to find two shelves full of Aimé Adel and Sandrine Mauraux. They were the two best-known *useful idiots* from the West. The naïve left-wing intellectuals who declared their sympathy toward Communism. They had been invited to the Soviet Union and North Korea. They toured the staged sites of Communist stability, while real citizens were starving and abused behind the scenes. Once back in their rich Western countries, those canaries sang, loud and clear, the beauty of Communism. Two decades later they recanted what they'd said – but only partially.

An irony, Mihee thought. An American Protestant pastor, blacklisted by a Communist government, was a fan of Communist sympathizers. She picked up the copy of *The Open Ceiling*, a famous novel by Adel, although she had read it. Her curiosity and fondness for the pastor convinced her to give it a second chance. But again she failed to appreciate it, and again the book's naïveté made her scoff. People who know Communism only by the book, Mihee thought. To them poverty was words on a page, never woe in the guts. They were often the loudest soap-boxers on such subjects. Mihee clicked her tongue and smiled bitterly.

In the office, Mihee and the pastor worked mostly in silence.

But when they started talking, their conversation went quickly into great depth on personal topics. This seemed to be one of Rousseau's particular skills – pulling others naturally into his web of conversation, where they would spill their guts.

"Did you ever wonder how I knew you could type, Miss Bae?" said the pastor one day. He said she had told him on her first day. But she didn't remember saying it. "You said you'd been a secretary for a propagandist in a local radio station before you got married. The main job of a secretary there is proofreading and typing, am I right?" said Rousseau.

Mihee nodded.

She wasn't going to give him the satisfaction of divulging her secret thoughts. Of course not. Her goal was to gain his trust first with her actions, then gain some more by staying reticent. She was to reverse the common roles of confessor and confessant – at the end of the day every psychiatrist needs his or her own listener.

A week later, Mihee was typing the pastor's Sunday sermon on the topic of trust. It was based on the story of Lot's wife in the Book of Genesis. While describing the notorious scene in which Lot's wife looks back at Sodom and turns into a pillar of salt, he stopped. Then he asked Mihee another strange question: "Do you know when I first thought you might be trustworthy?" he asked, smiling.

Mihee evaded his gaze; guilt tugged at her stomach.

He said it was when they first met, when she told him a brief version of her life story.

"You were the first defector here who confessed in the first meeting that she had turned to prostitution." He said he knew prostitution was one of the few means of survival available to female North Korean defectors in China. He didn't judge those who were driven to it: he would probably have done the same under the circumstances. But he said he admired her honesty, her bold refusal to apologize or regret what she'd had to do. He had rarely seen it from others with similar experiences.

"It's really a brave thing, isn't it? To live unashamed of your past, of who you are," Rousseau intoned.

"God's love is for everyone," she answered. "Mary Magdalene was no exception."

With his arms crossed, the pastor turned his back on her. He sighed deeply, shoulders drooping a little. Mihee felt uncomfortable, like the time Seong-mi had broken down in tears in front of her. That evening, before leaving the office, the pastor said goodbye with a big smile, and a tight squeeze on her shoulder.

Mihee remained frozen in her seat long after he had left.

There were many thoughts stuttering in her mind.

First she wasn't sure how to interpret what had just happened. She had gained some sort of trust from Pastor Rousseau, for sure. But what does he expect from me now by telling me all this? Mihee wondered.

Could I be so candid about my past in a bawdy house even if it were my real body to compromise? This thought brought Mihee back to her beginning at the Church of New Life. The question she had asked herself, looking down at her injured foot. *How far would Agent Mihee go, even in hurting herself, compromising her body, if it were required for the job?* She felt the pressure of the pastor's squeeze again on her skin. The scent of mildewy papers in the air, the familiar odor she'd been so fond of, suddenly made her stomach churn. Mihee left the pastor's office.

The next day was Tuesday, her day off. She headed for the Shenyang Dongling Park, nearly an hour's walk away. Dongling was one of the biggest parks in Shenyang and the least crowded one, and thus there was little risk of running into people she knew from the church. During the day there were only a few groups of little children on bicycles or old couples practicing their tai chi. "At night, the north-western corner of the park gets busy with a handful of fairies," Comrade Cha had told her, "Pansies who gather in the pine grove behind the public toilet for their little party." So there she was in the evening, the time between day and night, when the park was usually empty, to pick up her first package.

Behind the pine grove, there was a narrow leafy pathway along the north-western stone wall, quite removed from the public eye. She sat on the fifth bench from its northern end, her signal site. She extended her hand to feel the underside of the bench, and grabbed the little package wrapped in manila paper – her first dead-drop collection. Comrade Cha had told her to get herself fully acquainted with the park as it was where most of their secret communication would take place. He added that the park was ironically the safest one there was for her at night, if one day she needed to make an emergency contact. "Fairies would leave you alone," Comrade Cha muttered bluntly. Mihee knew that a nighttime contact was the last resort an illegal agent would turn to: an act of desperation that could put both parties in danger. Mihee prayed she would never have to bank on that.

She expected no written instructions. She was supposed to know instantly what to do with the dead-dropped object when she saw it. Inside the beige paper were a face mask and a small metal can. Pastor Rousseau would leave in three days for Yanbian to visit other nascent Protestant churches that the Church of New Life was in partnership with. And the night before his departure, Mihee, wearing the face mask, was to sprinkle the contents of the metal phial onto the pastor's clothes, briefcase, and shoes. "Radioactive dust," Comrade Cha had taught her, "Low in concentration to avoid poisoning but strong enough to get RGB's Geiger counters working." They're going to tail him to Yanbian, or wherever he's going, Mihee thought.

She spent the three following nights sleepless, gazing at her door. In the office the pastor's behavior wasn't different from before. But she began noticing little things on his body that she hadn't previously: his awkwardly large, sinewy wrist; the back of his neck, which grew firmer and wider like that of a Rottweiler whenever he stretched his arms, yawning. Uncouth bodily details of a grown-up male, both revolting and riveting.

Like most other North Korean women of her age without experience of marriage, she knew little about sex. The only experience she'd had was with the bottle Comrade Cha had given her. Though an imperturbable man as a rule, Comrade Cha had turned red to the roots of his hair when he handed it to her. A long object that looked like a small wine bottle, its neck and mouth covered with smooth rubber. He told her to practice. "First use it to lose your hymen, then to get the feel of it," he muttered, his head slightly turned away from the object, as if holding a disease. Mihee asked no questions. She just did as she was told.

Each evening he said goodnight to her, still sitting at his desk littered with piles of papers. "I have more work to finish before my trip," he said tersely.

Lying in bed she stared at her door. Haphazardly repurposed from a small storeroom, her bedroom was at the end of the corridor, only twenty steps away from Pastor Rousseau's office. Whenever she heard the slightest noise, she thought she saw a lumpy shadow looming over her door, the ungainly monster that would flush down the toilet whatever private admiration she'd felt for the pastor. But in reality it soon dissipated into thin air, leaving her small door alone and silent as always. On the third and last night before the pastor's trip, when Mihee finally realized that what she had expected to happen wouldn't, her body melted into deep sleep. Though a sense of relief dominated her sleep, beneath it was the faint hue of disappointment, too subtle for her consciousness to grasp.

She woke up before dawn and let herself into Pastor Rousseau's office to carry out her first assigned mission. She wore the face mask provided and a pair of rubber gloves she'd pinched from Deaconess Kang's cabinet. Though she hesitated for a second before opening the lid of the phial, she carried out her job as required. As usual, however, she played it by ear: instead of sprinkling the radioactive dust all over the coat, she allowed it to fall only on the lower back so that its owner wouldn't accidentally breathe in the dust or touch it with his hands. For the same reason she also left the handles of the briefcase and the shoelaces clean of the dust.

In Pastor Rousseau's absence Mihee had lots of free time. She read many books she'd borrowed from the pastor's cabinet. She visited Dongling Park three times a week. She also frequented nearby Chinese markets with her fake travel document, sweeping the rust off her spoken Mandarin. Strolling through the park, she revisited the long list of communication codes she'd had to learn by heart: leaving a mandarin-orange peel on the signal site meant *I'm in danger*; an empty lychee shell *I'm leaving the country tomorrow*; a Y-shaped bough *In need of emergency contact tonight*, among others. She always kept a sharp eye on her signal site, the fifth bench from the northern end of the north-western stone-wall pathway, not only to look for a possible signal or a dead drop but also to shoo away unwelcome visitors, like squirrels, which might obfuscate communication by littering the site with their own food waste.

Strolling through the park she also thought about Pastor Rousseau. How little I know him, Mihee realized. She knew nearly nothing about his private life. She wondered what kinds of people he would see in his free time. Some random others in RGB would know that by now, by tailing him closely with their mini Geiger counter. She felt odd jealousy toward those faceless agents. Though every day she worked face to face with Adrien Rousseau, she would know only a fraction of him. RGB kept every agent in his or her own shell of secrecy, allowing each to feel only one part of the elephant – the wide fan of an ear here, the serpentine tube of a nose there, the colossal column of a leg farther down. The whole picture was entrusted only to the higher-ups. *A trustworthy spy is a spy in a cemetery*, an RGB joke Comrade Cha had once told her. "Because only a dead spy is sure not to sell out," he said, with a cold chuckle.

Mihee had once asked Mother if she'd ever been involved with someone forbidden to her. She nodded. "First mission, of course. It usually happens in the beginning, dear," she said. It was in Paju, a South Korean county near the 38th parallel, where she was gathering intelligence about the US Army stationed along the southern side of the border. "I was disguised as a demented waif, a war orphan, so I could come and go freely and be left alone most of the time," she said. Some of the young boys in the village, however, didn't leave her alone. They were cruel to her as only boys of that age could be. Those poor souls, Mother described them, their childhood taken away by their war-ravaged parents. "But there was this one child, his father as brutal as my own, who had still kept his innocence uncompromised somehow," Mother whispered. Although unsuccessful, that little boy strove to protect her from pelting stones; he brought fish he'd caught from the Imjin River to her doorstep so she wouldn't go hungry; he even brought her a bouquet of wild flowers. "One day, after the end of the rainy season, I saw that boy again near my doorstep, bleeding freely and unconscious." Although she knew her involvement might blow her cover, she held him in her arms and ran to the nearest hospital in town, her *hanbok* soaked red with his blood. "The boy lived, to my greatest joy, and I had to leave the town soon after." What injured the little boy was an antipersonnel mine, Mother said, planted by the US military during the Korean War. It had been washed up on the riverbank by heavy rain.

Mihee interpreted Mother's story as a subtle yes to taking

matters into her own hands, as long as they stayed small and unnoticeable. "Neither you nor I work for the glory of the Party exactly." Mother had lowered her voice to a whisper.

Mother was right, Mihee thought. Mihee wasn't the young revolutionary warrior the Party had assumed her to be. On the surface, Mihee didn't pursue RGB, for it wasn't a company you simply applied to: it pursued you. It was Mihee, however, who had made them turn their heads toward her. She was a perfect elite candidate they would covet: at the top of her class in Pyongyang University of Foreign Studies, twenty-year-old Mihee already excelled in three foreign languages. Her moral record was spotless. Her mother was an important *business-woman*, her father a former tailor for key Party officials. She knew she was an opportunity they couldn't pass.

To Mihee, a career in espionage was her legitimate ticket to a defiance she had long desired. Secrets and deception, two crucial elements of espionage, were already in her blood. Everyone around her had lived with secrets, deceiving one another for better or worse. She realized at an early age her parents weren't the people she had once assumed them to be. Little Mihee discovered one day, behind the old walnut bookshelf in her father's study, a wall safe. Over the years she had witnessed numerous little items come and go out of that wall safe: banned American novels, their covers switched with those of Russian; illegally duplicated cassette tapes of South Korean pop songs; and the real vinyl records of British bands that Mother had procured from her business trips, one each year for Dad's birthday. Just like her parents, Mihee was a quiet dissenter. And Mother recognized it first: she saw through Mihee's little mind and knew her curiosity would grow irrepressible. So Mother taught her how to control it, rather than kill it.

A career in espionage promised you travel or even a

life abroad, which other North Koreans had no access to. It was also a gateway to uncharted power – an influence that required no witness, no critic, and thus relatively little responsibility. It was perfect for someone like Mihee: a double-dealing snob quietly proud of her intellectual superiority, a furtive sense of knowing things of grave importance that ordinary others around you were completely blind to. And deception was seductive, although guilt followed as its inevitable shadow.

ROUSSEAU

But how much does she know about me?

How much truth did I let her know?

Rousseau. My family name.

One of our early days in Shenyang. Seong-mi, out of the blue, asked me if by any chance I was related to Jean-Jacques Rousseau. At first I almost burst out laughing at her naïveté. A cute misunderstanding, which rendered her even more likable. Then I soon realized something else and I was impressed: she knew a Western philosopher that most North Koreans probably didn't. In fact I was slightly tempted to impress her, too, and I imagined myself confirming her conjecture proudly – *Yes, I am* – basking in the vicarious glory of somebody bigger than myself. But in the end, of course, I gave her the answer I felt the truest: Rousseau is a very common French surname. If she lived in France, I told her, she would naturally meet quite a few other Rousseaus. She shrugged her shoulders, and said under her breath she wouldn't want to meet another Rousseau. Shortly she left the room, without meeting my surprised gaze.

Pastor. My title. Everyone at the church in Shenyang called me Pastor.

But I wasn't technically a pastor.

This confusion began with the Korean term *jeondosa-nim*. *Jeondosa* was an umbrella term that only existed in the dictionary of the Korean Protestant church, which could mean an evangelist, a missionary, and a preacher, depending on the context. Although in theory *jeondosa* refers to a person training to be a pastor with a degree in theology, in reality many leaders of church youth groups earned that title through their hard work in the community or sometimes by gaining favor with powerful elders. Due to my involvement in the youth group and the North Korean refugee community, people at church referred to me as *jeondosa-nim*. I was good at my job: I helped North Korean defectors find temporary refuges and learn about the Bible. The news spread quickly, and more and more people showed up at the church, some out of curiosity, others desperately bent on the hope of escape and new life. A couple of years later people naturally began to call me Pastor, as most *jeondosa* did become pastors after some time in a Korean church. But I refused the term since I wasn't ordained as a pastor and I hadn't even gone to a theological seminary. At first I tried to correct the misunderstanding each time the misnomer was thrown at me. But the interesting thing about a byname was that you didn't really have control over it: it was chosen and defined by others. Despite my disapproval, people stuck to that term, and thus, to them, I was *Rooso Moksanim*, Pastor Rousseau.

To Seong-mi, however, I confessed the plain truth early on. "I'm not technically a pastor," I said to her, probably in our second day of working together in my office, when she was typing and proofreading my sermon in Korean. "So you can call me Mr Rousseau. Or just Rou – short and sweet, Korean-style. Since nearly all Korean surnames are just one syllable, right?" I told her. To my surprise Seong-mi did call me Rou from time to time, mostly when we were alone in the office, working. In front of the others, however, she always stuck to Pastor Rousseau. Later, when we were properly dating, she began to call me by my first name, Adrien. She rarely called me Rou afterward. I recall only once when that term of endearment was resurrected on her lips: in bed, after we made love in our first Seoul apartment. We were lying down in each other's arms in a stupor. Slowly she began to comb my wet hair with her fingers, then stroked a tickly line from my forehead, over my nose, to the tip of my chin. "Rouuuuuuu," she purred, drawing out the single syllable like delicious caramel. "You're beautiful," she told me, with a wan smile. It was one of the few moments in my life that made me feel *I could die right now.*

Hoyeon. My regret.

My biggest regret. And the final question that I've been too afraid to ask.

I've never told Seong-mi the truth about Hoyeon. It is the only secret I'm keeping from her.

Or so I thought.

Did Seong-mi discover what had happened between Hoyeon and me?

Could this be the reason for her disappearance?

MIHEE

Walking to the Dongling Park she wondered how far she might go for the job. She envisioned another small parcel taped under the fifth bench, the signal site. And inside the envelope would be an M1911, a.k.a. the Colt Government, a 45-caliber six-shooter with a silencer. That's the farthest they could push you, Mihee thought. But can I really put a bullet in Pastor Rousseau's head? She couldn't answer. She could only wish that that piece of ammunition would never find its way to her bench.

She found something else instead, under her bench that evening. Two wooden toothpicks, one superimposed onto another in the shape of X. A message she hadn't expected to see – particularly that day, with Pastor Rousseau still away on his business trip. *Meeting tomorrow night*, she remembered the code clearly. Her heart quickened. Dead-drop or brush contact was always favored. Meeting, face to face, only took place when absolutely necessary. Dozens of possibilities were already stirring in her mind – some good, some bad, and one in particular horrifying. An inauspicious feeling of *déjà vu*, as if her imagination might make the fear into a reality. Comrade Cha had told her a meeting would be rare, reserved for top-secret briefing or delivery of crucial objects: "Big wads of cash, or an expensive weapon we can't afford to lose."

What did you do in Yanbian? Mihee began to wonder. Something treacherous enough to get yourself harmed? The rest of her day passed in a fever of anxiety, her own vivid imagining of the Colt revolver squatting in the corner of her eye, like a stye. Although she knew it didn't help with her apprehension, she couldn't stop herself thinking ahead, combing through her limited options. If their final plan for Pastor Rousseau was indeed termination, she was likely to be summoned back to Pyongyang after the job, the last scenario she wanted. This meant no help from the Church of New Life, no life in South Korea in the near future. Despite the lack of evidence, she trusted Pastor Rousseau's promise that he would support her escape. She wondered if she was capable of persuading Comrade Cha to change his mind, to rethink the costs and ramifications of what they were planning to do. It seemed impossible.

Mihee showed up at the signal site at ten p.m. sharp. Contrary to her expectation the fifth bench was empty. When she walked closer to check its underside, two black arms grabbed her waist. "Walk toward the other end of the path," said a voice, low-pitched and female. Mihee and the stranger walked in silence, arm in arm, as though they were sisters or close friends, till they reached the southern end of the stone-wall trail. The woman gestured Mihee to sit down on a bench. Even dressed entirely in black, she looked wide and short, like a teapot. Her physique, unattractive and unimportant, deceives you, thought Mihee. If Mihee sat next to the woman on a bus or in a pew during the Sunday service, she would never have suspected that she was in the presence of another RGB agent.

Without a word of introduction the woman got down to business: she took out a photograph, shot in grainy black-and-white, and put it on Mihee's lap. "Have you seen this face?" she asked, shining a flashlight on the photo briefly. A smiling face of a young man with straight dark hair.

"No," she answered.

"His hair might have been different. Lighter color and curly?" asked the agent again. Mihee still had no recollection of the man. "Then memorize the face, and take note of everything he says and does if you see him."

"Who is this man?"

The agent shot her an icy glare.

"I can do my job better if I know who he is, what he does, and what he has to do with Pastor Rousseau," continued Mihee.

Eyes still acid and cold, the woman moved her lips slowly, in exaggerated vexation. "Whether you ask or not, I can only tell you what I'm supposed to tell you. And now this is what I can tell you: this man is a journalist, he used to work for the *Washington Post* and now works for the *New York Times*. Nathan Zuckerman is his name."

"He's American?" Confused, Mihee brought the photo near her face.

"His father is an American Jew, mother a Chinese immigrant," said the woman. "In this photo he looks more Asian since he's straightened his hair and dyed it black. His natural hair is mousy and curly."

Journalist – one of the classic covers of legal agents sent abroad, Mihee thought, just like diplomat or businessman. A mixed-race American journalist, who changes his hair to pass as a Chinese. "So we're suspecting this man to be Pastor Rousseau's handler, Pastor Rousseau his asset?"

"Pastor Rousseau saw the man three times during his business trip," the woman went on. "We tried to get close to them in a café, to listen to their conversation, but they sensed something and left. They were very cautious, alert. Then they went into a hotel room, so we failed to follow them farther. Each time, similar pattern. They get together in a café, a restaurant, but when we try to approach them, they always leave, and go somewhere private we can't tail them.

"This is where you come in," said the woman, handing Mihee a small white plastic box. Mihee opened it. Inside the box was a tiny piece of silver metal, rectangular with smooth edges, as small as her thumbnail. Mihee saw it and understood she was to insert this microphone into Pastor Rousseau's telephone mouthpiece.

"What shall I call you?" shot Mihee, to the back of the woman, who was already leaving.

She turned her head slowly toward Mihee. "He told me you ask a lot of questions," muttered the woman. "You'd better grow out of that habit. There will be a point when your mama's name can no longer save you."

Mihee watched the woman's wide back. As she walked away, her black coattail rustled against the edge of the bench. Her short, meaty body waddled into the night like a penguin, both comic and eerie.

The next day, Pastor Rousseau was back in the office.

Mihee was surprised by how excited she was to have him back in the church. His return meant she no longer had to share his secrets with strangers from RGB. She would once again be the main witness of his daily life. Staring at his face, Mihee imagined how stunned he would be if he happened to hear her spit out flawless American English. This strange thought put a sly smile on her face.

Pastor Rousseau offered her a big red paper box. A souvenir, he said. "They're not real, by the way," he added shyly. "It's impossible to find real ones, these days, in this country."

It was a pair of Nike sneakers. The classic white one with a red swoosh on the side, white soles with tapering blue lines in the middle. Mihee remembered seeing them in the underground training camp in Pyongyang. They were shiny and new on the feet of a bit player posing as a South Korean passer by on the replica of Myongdong Street. Mihee's father, too, owned a pair of Nikes: jet-black with a white swoosh. It was an authentic pair Mama had smuggled through from one of her business trips.

"I've noticed your shoes are *overworked*, Seong-mi," Rousseau said quietly, eyeing her feet. Mihee looked down and realized for the first time that her shoes were indeed worn out. Initially a white pair, the sneakers were now earthen-yellow. The rubber bumpers and toecaps had thinned like used erasers – she could make out the shapes of her toenails squeezed under them. They were the covert witness to her hard work, to all of her trips to Dongling Park and back. This recognition was alarming as well as touching.

"I don't understand," Mihee whispered, face flushed.

"What?" Rousseau gave her a hard stare.

Mihee returned it as intensely. "People said you're good at helping defectors, getting them out of the country, but they all said you're a cold man." Mihee narrowed her eyes and pressed her lips together. "But you're not."

"You think I'm this talkative with everyone?" asked Rousseau, with a quiet edge to his voice.

Guess not, Mihee thought. Even Deaconess Kang had once asked her how she got him to talk.

"Have I told you I used to work with dogs?" blurted out Rousseau.

Mihee shook her head slowly.

A thick silence enveloped them. Each time she exhaled, she heard her breath whistle through her nose.

Rousseau curled his index finger, brought it close to his upper lip, and he took a deep breath, as if smoking. Mihee felt surprised and wondered if he'd been a smoker before. Another piece of him she'd been blind to.

"When I was a teenager," whispered Rousseau, with half-closed eyes, "I was always short of money so I began to work at this animal shelter in Lewiston – back then it was the only place in the region that was willing to hire a foreign-looking adolescent as a part-timer. Most of the abandoned animals they kept at the shelter were dogs. My job was cleaning their cages and feeding them."

His voice had shed its usual pastor characteristics. The slight edge of authority was gone, the tone was soft and unassuming, like a lullaby. She felt like balling her body into the fetal position.

"At that animal shelter I learned so many invaluable things about life. I met Jason there, my boss, who ran the place. An Irish American. Carrot-haired, stout as a pick-up truck. He smelled like a pig farmer, and always had a wet, meaty handshake. At work he barely looked at you, barely even spoke to you. *Nothing* like I'd imagined. I'd pictured the place with a blond woman in her early forties, puppies in her arms, with that warm, all-teeth American smile – the kind of face you would see on a cereal box or on the cover of an insurance booklet."

He laughed tenderly.

"When Jason asked me why I wanted to work there, I told him I loved dogs. Jason said, stone cold, there was no place for love in his shelter."

Rousseau's voice tapered off. Mihee could hear the whirring of the electric fan above them. Its soft complaints and groans rose and fell. Mihee wanted to lie down, her head in his lap.

"According to Jason, the demonstration of love is a luxury bestowed only to the owners. When you've got a hundred dogs in your care to feed, clean out, and walk every day, there's no space for love."

Rousseau's voice now seemed to come from a long way off. Mihee imagined running her fingers through his hair, caressing it like a large dog's. His soft eyes, drooping just a little in the corners, always reminded her of a Golden Retriever's.

"Jason said warm tears and angelic smiles, those images we see in the advertisement for rescue centers or UNICEF, are saved for Hollywood actors, for people whose visit to an African orphanage would only be a once-a-year thing. Real workers and rescuers, those who have to see death, abuse and sickness every single day, they can't afford to lose time and energy over *shedding tears*. Each day you have hundreds of little eyes poring over you, wanting food, a hug, wanting survival. You have to be robotic, mechanical to save and attend to as many lives as possible. You can't show emotions, can't show love for all of them, 'cause *love for everyone is as good as love for no one*," Jason said. "And love for a handful means abandonment for the rest of them."

He sat silent for a while. The rims of his eyes and tip of his nose turned a little ruddy. His voice went gruff, and then it swooped to a lush baritone, a pleasure to listen to.

She watched his Adam's apple go up and down, his fingers brushing his hair up from his brow.

Cinnamon. That French aftershave in the dark green bottle he used. It made his skin smell faintly of cinnamon and tangerine, she thought.

"And yet he was human, too. I knew he had a favorite."

What would it taste like?

"A Golden Retriever that Jason eventually named Moxie. Friendliest dog to a fault – even after years of abuse by his owner. Jason adopted him. And ended up adopting five more."

She wanted to grab his collar, rub her face all over him. She wanted her smell on him, his on her.

"Why only five?" she asked, her mind busy switching between two paths of thoughts.

"Jason thought seven was the maximum number of dogs you can own simultaneously, to love and take care of them properly. Anything more, and you'd end up being a negligent hoarder, or you should be running a proper dog shelter."

"So he already had a dog before Moxie?" she asked him, feigning calm.

"Yes," Rousseau said, smiling. *You really listened*, he seemed to be thinking.

Her temples ticked like a clock. She wished she could turn off her thoughts.

"You know what the funny thing is?" asked Rousseau.

She wasn't keen on hearing the answer. Her hands were wrapped around his face. She wanted to lock lips with him but wasn't sure how – and afraid he might laugh. The two locked eyes instead. Liquid-limbed, Mihee would have collapsed onto the floor, had it not been for the arms of the pastor. She was caught halfway through the plunge but still felt like she was falling. She was breathing hard. Rousseau's shoulders had folded her body into a tiny hug. Her heart was beating below her navel.

"Take me to the prayer room, Pastor. Nobody's there."

Now she could feel his heart beating too.

ROUSSEAU

Hoyeon. My regret.

I met Hoyeon at Cornell, in my first French philosophy class.

We became close right away. We were both French majors, we had similar taste in literature and music and, above all, we were the only mixed-race students in class.

Hoyeon was short and skinny, with long brown curly hair. I was tall and broad-shouldered. So when we walked on campus side by side, our heads tilted toward each other in conversation, people often mistook us for a couple. He was born to a Chinese immigrant mother and a Polish Jewish father who ran a garment factory in California. He was as gifted with languages as I was. When I first met him he was already fluent in Chinese and Hebrew, and while in college he mastered French as well. Later, when we saw each other again in China, he was perfecting his Korean, and mentioned his new girlfriend was Korean. Hoyeon was one of the few people in my life who never asked me that wide-eyed question: *How do you speak foreign languages so well?*

Hoyeon was unlike any other man I'd met, the only biracial

boy I'd known who seemed to be comfortable in the double skin he had inherited. More than comfortable, in fact: he seemed to rejoice in his heterogeneity, always ready to make the most of it. Though his real name was the very Jewish-American Nathan Zuckerman, bestowed by his father, he introduced himself to me as Wang Hoyeon. "That's how you Koreans pronounce it, right?" he said, winking. "I learned it from a cute Korean chick I met at the KSA party." He went by Wang Haoran among Chinese students; Haoran was the Chinese name his mother used to call him by, Wang her maiden name. To Jewish students he always gave his full official name, Nathan Zuckerman, while to everyone else, he was simply Nate.

He was the human chameleon. His manners and mood changed quite dramatically according to the group of people he was with, and according to the language he spoke with them. Around white boys he talked slowly yet much more loudly, often used large hand gestures, and gave those belly laughs that were sonorous as a honk in a tunnel. In Chinese he talked much more hurriedly, his pitch higher and his tone sing-songy, but his hands relatively idle. When switching to Hebrew he seemed suddenly sullen, somewhat secretive and a little sad; I thought maybe this impression came from the fact that Hebrew, among the languages he spoke, was the only one I didn't understand at all. With each group, he made mild jokes about the other groups that were not present, putting a temporary distance between them and himself. "Exchanging witty racial jokes is a good way of becoming buddies with a stranger in America," Hoyeon used to tell me.

He was a member of three different student groups – the white fraternity, whose name began with Phi, the Chinese Student Association, and Hillel, the Jewish one – and he seemed at home in all of them. He seemed to fit in wherever he was. At first Hoyeon's ever-shifting identity made me feel uncomfortable. Then, with time, I began to recognize a liberating quality to it: being riven and being happy with it. I had always thought being biracial meant having to choose one side and stick to it for good – otherwise you would never attain membership to any group in its entirety. So in my childhood I made the obvious choice of sticking to my Americanness, and avoided any kind of display of my Korean or French heritage. But for Hoyeon duality wasn't something to hide: it was something to be fully exploited. He embraced and enjoyed it as an advantage. He could be anything he wanted depending on his need at the moment, and he felt neither shame nor confusion about it. I assumed this easy and unapologetic confidence was what always pulled women toward him; though he was far from the best-looking man in the room, he never had difficulty finding a date.

Hoyeon had introduced me to the world of Aimé Adel. He was already a big fan of Adel when I had just begun to read his first novel for a class assignment. Hoyeon said Adel had opened the door for him to a new possibility. "Aimé Adel was one of the first intellectuals of his generation who made it big in his field in Europe despite his mixed heritage, who made people listen to him and respect him," Hoyeon said. "He made outsiders and mongrels, people like me and you, Adrien, feel they matter."

Looking at a photo of Adel, however, I felt puzzled. "Well, he doesn't *look* like me and you," I told Hoyeon, and asked him out of curiosity how Afro-Arab Adel really was.

Hoyeon laughed the resonant belly laugh he often pulled off with his white friends from the fraternity, and told me the degree of Adel's exoticism wasn't the point at all. "It's Adel's willingness and ingenuity to use his identity as he saw fit. *That's* what matters, kiddo."

When I saw Hoyeon again after college, years later in China, I didn't recognize his face. His signature hair, the long, tobacco-colored curly locks that had bobbed around his collar bones, was cut short above his ears. It was now straight and spiky and ink-black, like the hair of many East Asian men. Hoyeon said he'd had his hair straightened and dyed right before moving to China, in order to blend in better with the Asian crowd. "Now I'm a journalist in a Communist country," he whispered with a furtive grin, "and the last thing I want would be to draw more attention than I already am." Although people still recognized the foreignness in his face at a close distance, he could easily glide through a throng of people on the street unnoticed, he said. "Something I could never have done with my old Jewfro." Hoyeon clicked his tongue and sniggered.

It wasn't only ethnic identities he'd switch.

Near the end of our freshman year, I smoked pot for the first time. Hoyeon brought it to my dorm room on a Friday night, after learning that I'd never tried it. The suite was mostly empty: all the students were invited to various year-end parties around the campus. I enjoyed the rare quiet of my dorm. It was pleasing to hear the languorous echo of my own laughter. We exchanged meaningless banter and snickered till we had runny noses. Sipping at his vodka in the Big Gulp mug, Hoyeon brought up questions about Brenda again, my then on-and-off girlfriend. He asked me how far I'd gone with her, what she was like in bed. "You act like you don't know you're good-looking. Why is that?" muttered Hoyeon. "You act like it doesn't matter and that's fucking annoying." Hungry, we were munching the ice cubes he took out of the fridge for the vodka. His elbow jabbed me a little too violently in the ribs and I coughed the laugh that triggered both of us into another round of soundless, gut-wrenching laughter. Then I felt his ice-cold tongue on mine, between my lips, and teeth. I did nothing for a while. My thoughts were slow and cloudy. I guess it didn't take too long for him to realize I wasn't reciprocating. I remember his sudden stop and withdrawal. I was afraid that he might look ashamed and embarrassed, but visibly he was fine. He said he needed to run to the toilet and he did. When he came back, he was the Hoyeon I'd always known, bouncy and sarcastic, and he acted as if what had just happened never did. I played along and never mentioned it again.

The nature and intention of Hoyeon's job are still unknown to me and they'll always remain so.

When I asked him for an answer, he asked me if I knew Michael Foot.

"Sadly that's everything I can tell you about it," he said, and he hung up the phone.

Michael Foot, a British journalist and a politician who served as the leader of the Labor Party, was an alleged KGB spy. According to the former chief of the KGB's London Station, KGB agents met up with Foot many times; Foot gave them information while they paid him money occasionally. Until 1986, the KGB had regarded him as their *agent of influence.*

But the perception of the same situation by Michael Foot was very different. Foot was not aware that the KGB had once classified him as one of their own. Foot did have meetings with KGB agents but they never took place in secret for he had no intention of hiding them. He thought he was promoting the cause of progressive politics and world peace by talking with them and kindly accepting their donations. Foot didn't break the law. He gave away no *arcana imperii.* He was no spy.

The meaning of espionage depends on where your own definition stands.

There never have been clear lines.

The degree to which Hoyeon got involved with the Agency is a mystery. Was he the full-blown agent, picked and trained by the CIA from the beginning, who took the journalist job as a cover? Or was he a journalist who chose to cooperate with the Agency for mutual gain, exchanging useful stories and information? Although I'll never know the true answer, my guess would stay closer to the latter.

If the question was whether I knew about his involvement, the answer is yes. I knew he was involved.

But when did I realize the truth? I do not know.

I know I did learn it but I can't pinpoint the exact moment of discovery. Maybe I knew it all along on some level. Maybe I'd picked it up so gradually that there's no recollection of the tragic epiphany, like the way I'd learned that Santa is fiction. Maybe I just wanted to keep the truth solely in the back of my mind.

Indeed, those lines have never been clear. Contrary to common belief, espionage isn't far removed from mundanity. Most information traded in espionage is not the result of cut-throat covert actions but of seemingly prosaic conversations in cafés or restaurants. Most information is not procured by full-time James Bonds but by bored two-timers in office cubicles, nameless and pot-bellied. The information itself isn't always of a secretive nature: it's rather a gleaned medley of hearsays, newspaper and magazine articles. An agent's job is at times simply sorting out and editing those public pieces of puzzles, to read the private connections hidden behind them.

All I know for sure is that I was happy to see my old friend again. Living in the north-eastern corner of China as an American, far removed from other people like you, can get very lonely. Though I appreciated the company of all the diligent members of the church, I was hungry for secular conversations. I missed having those pensive strolls around the campus, philosophizing on girls, sex, race, and everything that had rushed into our minds. I missed having someone with whom I could share my raw thoughts and feelings in the tongue I felt most comfortable with, someone who understood my back story and old demons. Someone to whom I owed neither justification nor apology.

So when Hoyeon contacted me in China, I was ecstatic. Whenever we had a chance we met up and we talked.

They say a therapist needs a therapist. A father confessor needs his own confessor. Hearing life stories of traumas from North Korean refugees was an invaluable, humbling experience but it didn't come without a price. And Hoyeon miraculously showed up, materialized amid the desolate monotony of north-east China, as if he had come to my rescue. He was my friend, my therapist and my confessor.

He took my sorrows and my stories. Stories of the defectors I could and couldn't save, certain faces that invaded my dreams at random and so vividly. In the seedy hotel rooms of Shenyang, Yanbian, and Changbai, I had my time with him, long overdue. A shameless sinner, I cried in his arms, as if mourning a death of a loved one. I had no specific death in mind, though. There had been simply too many. Hoyeon saw and took in everything without passing judgment. At a certain point I knew some of my stories made their way into the articles he wrote for *The Times*. Yet I hadn't felt alarmed: I trusted our friendship and his discernment.

At first I didn't quite understand the importance of the information he'd got from me. But time enlightened me: I was one of the very first people in the world to receive first-hand testimonies of North Koreans who had just escaped from their country. I held information that could paint the most up-to-date picture of the most closed society in the world. It was information that many powerful countries would covet.

But by the time Seong-mi came knocking on our gate I was experiencing exhaustion. And the execution of the job was becoming more and more complicated. The North Korean government's crackdown on the refugees in China became severe, and as a result few decent Chinese brokers were now willing to work with us. I turned several defectors away who had come seeking our help; I wasn't sure if we could be useful for them under the new circumstances, and above all I couldn't stand the death or disappearance of someone under my protection again. I felt I'd done enough. I was in desperate need of a break. I thought about going back to America, probably resuming my path to professorship in literature.

Then Seong-mi hurtled into my life, by the most beautiful chance of luck. And we fell in love. Moving to South Korea with her seemed like a beginning of the dream life I'd yearned for.

I wanted her escape route to be the shortest and the safest. Seong-mi was to fly Korean Air to South Korea from Dalian. She posed as a South Korean tourist returning home after a weekend in a popular seaside resort in Dalian. The broker's fee was ten times higher than usual. Blame the volatile political circumstances, they said, and furthermore, the job required stealing and modifying a real South Korean passport. To pass as a middle-class South Korean woman, Seong-mi followed the broker's advice and had her hair permed and dyed, her nails painted. She took a lesson from the broker on how to fake a South Korean accent, which fortunately she picked up fast. To minimize suspicion, another broker with a South Korean passport posed as Seong-mi's husband and accompanied her on the journey till she got off the plane at the airport in Seoul. If there was a hierarchy in their service, those brokers said, grinning, Seong-mi was getting the bona-fide royalty service. Seong-mi deserved every bit of it, for she was my love.

MIHEE

Mihee never thought that her major life decisions would be defined by such mundane things – the birth of her child and the death of her parent. It was as if she were no different from most other women she knew.

Aram was born a month early. Her gynecologist said the baby would be fine. "Thirty-six weeks is not full but long enough," he said, patting her shoulder. So she felt betrayed by Dr Go later when she learned that the nurse had had to run downstairs with the newborn, to the NICU, only ten minutes after Dr Go and the pediatrician had left the hospital, exchanging jokes and hearty laughs. Mihee felt horrible. She had been kept in the dark, her body still petrified waist down by the epidural, lying alone in the delivery bed, useless and helpless in her first post-partum torpor. A killer whale washed up on the shore, sure never to kill again.

Adrien was with the baby the whole time. He carried him with the nurse to the newborn nursery, and he stayed with him while the nurse weighed him again and got his footprint taken. It was Adrien who noticed first that the baby's finger-tips and feet were turning purple. He followed the baby to the Neonatal Intensive Care Unit. He was there when the nurses put an oxygen mask over the baby's face, strapped the heart monitor to the foot, only as big as his own thumb, and jabbed needles into those lipstick-thin arms. He was there till Dr Go came running in and asked him breathlessly to leave the room.

Then Adrien waited just outside the opaque glass gate, alert and numb at the same time. When he heard the burst of the baby's cry from the NICU he was ecstatic: the cry meant he had regained consciousness. When the cry lasted, however, ripening into a ripping wail, Adrien's heart sank back into the dark pit where he had first seen those tiny curled fingers turn violet. Adrien prayed as he'd never prayed before.

Mihee saw the baby much later in the NICU, once he was stable. Mihee didn't cry: tears just ran from her eyes like they were breaking out of her body. The tears were not hers to control, just like the helpless creature in front of her in an incubator, his brow creased in pain even in his sleep, like he was carrying the biggest woe of the world. The little body that everyone called hers. *Your baby, Mrs Bae*, they kept saying it, as if she was about to forget. If he's really mine, why can't I protect him? Why can't I make him well? Mihee asked herself. Dull drips of her tears hit the linoleum floor, one after another.

Mihee found herself engaging in negotiation, even though there was no kidnapper. *If You let him live and grow, just like other ordinary kids, I will do anything, You can take anything from my body or give me any other tragedy you want, You can take my legs away, You can take my eyes, You can even take my life if You guarantee he'll live a normal life after I'm gone, I'd rather be asleep for good than be awake and know there's nothing I can do for that little suffering flesh of mine.*

Mihee intoned in her head, fingers clenched into one fist. *Or do You want me to come clean? Is that what You ask of me? That's nothing! I can do that in the blink of an eye, I can turn myself in tomorrow first thing in the morning, if You guarantee he'll live, just healthy and normal.*

Two weeks later, when the baby left the NICU and finally came home with them, Mihee realized one thing about herself she hadn't known before: that she could pray. What she had found herself reciting that night in the NICU was her first prayer. Though a primitive and selfish kind, it was still a heartfelt prayer. And, like the tears, the prayer had broken out of her body as though it had a mind of its own.

Putting the sleeping baby to bed, Mihee cried again. She was stunned by the beauty of the little creature, which she hadn't had the breadth of mind to appreciate before. The smallest, the prettiest, and the most terrifying human being she had ever known – a person who was yet to speak but had the biggest say in her life already.

Adrien pulled her into his arms and held her tight.

"I'm so sorry," whispered Adrien, his voice gravelly, "about what happened to Seung-ho."

A long, pained sigh escaped his mouth.

Her chin resting on his shoulder, Mihee stared down at his back.

Who? she was about to ask, stroking his back with her fingers. Adrien sighed again and tightened his hold of her. Then Mihee remembered the name.

Seung-ho. The name of Seong-mi's son. Mihee had nearly forgotten about him.

While Seong-mi's real son was likely to be alive somewhere in North Korea, Mihee had killed him in her storytelling to Adrien, in the concise life narrative of Seong-mi that Mihee had edited and fed to Adrien when they had first met each other at the Church of New Life. Mihee had told him Seung-ho didn't live long after his birth. Mihee had killed the baby in her fiction to keep matters simple. To Mihee, to anyone, the experience of having raised a child was hard to fake. She didn't want her ineptness as a mother to betray her lie.

Adrien remembered the name of her fake child, which she had told him only once when they had first met.

Adrien thought her tears had come from the memory of her lost child. Adrien thought the sight of her new child brought back the death of her first.

Adrien had taken her feigned tragedy to heart.

Right then and there, she nearly told him the truth.

I'm not Seong-mi, I'm Mihee.

She felt the phrase between her jaws like a retch of truth. She had to swallow it back, choke on it for a split second. Her eyes and mouth watered. Sewer-sour.

But my love for you is real. She thought it, and once she even practiced it, whispered it looking at herself in the bathroom mirror when she was alone. Though those were words of truth, as soon as they left her lips and shot through the air, they ended up sounding cheap, fake.

She needed to do something she had never done before: she needed to make her truth sound true.

"But my love for you is real." She practiced it again to the mirror.

"Don't you think it's time?" said Mother, without looking at Mihee.

Here they were again, perched on each corner of the same bench, a meter away from one another like empty bookends. Their old bench sat behind an abandoned tennis court in the Sohn Kee-chung Memorial Park, their regular meeting place. The first time Mother had asked this question was right after the birth of her grandson. *Don't you think it's time, Mihee?* she had asked, but Mihee ignored it. Mihee didn't want to give a yes-or-no answer. The act of answering felt already like a betrayal, even if it was *no. Don't you think Aram and you deserve a clean start?* Mother had persisted calmly. Mihee had stood up and left. Mother asked the same question again now. "Don't you think it's time?"

They looked ahead instead of at each other, and they spoke quietly without moving their lips much, like a depressed ventriloquist and dummy. Though exchange of encrypted letters was their main mode of communication, they also had been conducting face-to-face meetings, their bimonthly rendezvous, ever since Mihee moved to Seoul. Mihee always made sure she had her lone stroll to the Sohn Kee-chung Memorial, a desolate public park in a shady neighborhood of Joongnim-dong. The park was an attraction for only a handful of adolescents playing hookey during the day. And its many lush sycamore trees and overgrown boxwood hedges provided a good shelter from any leering eyes, plenty of little dark-green nooks where they could hide in case of emergency.

The second Mother had walked into her line of sight an hour before, Mihee had known what had happened. Mother was nine minutes late though normally she was never tardy. Mother looked haggard: two-thirds of her hair had turned pewter-silver as though she had aged a decade within a month. They sat in silence for a while, with the usual one-square-meter void between them. Neither cried but both knew they would later – separately, each in her own bathroom, shower running to kill the sound.

Mother said it was peaceful. *A sleep death*, what people say as a gesture of comfort. The kind of passing most people dream of: no pain, no scream, just a night's slumber that segues into serene expiration. Dad deserved that kind of death, thought Mihee, but she never said it. She was afraid it might trigger her rock-steady mother to break down in front of her. Mihee didn't want that to happen, not today.

Did he ever know who you were? Mihee wanted to ask Mother instead. But she knew the answer already: of course he knew. He had the heart of a dove but that didn't mean he had the brain of one. The relevant question was: when did he know?

The biggest deception of all is to be deceived.

When Mihee was little her dad had told her this, making full moons of his already deer-like round eyes.

Mihee had come home from school feeling puzzled that day. She showed him a little red eraser she had been holding.

"Yeonjoo gave me one of these *again*, saying her father sent them to her from Cuba. Do you think she's really taking me for a fool?" she asked.

"No, dear," Dad answered. "She just wants to be friends with you. It's her own peculiar way of making friends, expressing her interest."

Her own peculiar way. Mihee ruminated on her dad's words. It was true that Yeonjoo was a peculiar child. The kind of girl most kids wanted to ignore with polite indifference. She wasn't stupid, though, Mihee thought. Yeonjoo never failed to answer the teacher's questions correctly, and she could read and write better than most kids in class. Yeonjoo was the odd one out who spent way too much time looking out of the window – too dreamy and too tall for her age. Too skinny as well: her wrists were so thin that Mihee thought they might snap like a rabbit bone if grabbed too tightly. Yeonjoo was poor; she wore hand-me-downs with threadbare patches at the elbows and knees. Her complexion was urine yellow. And she always smelled like wilted cabbage.

"This isn't even Spanish," said Mihee, looking intently at the tiny black foreign characters imprinted on the eraser. "This isn't from Cuba. I know that for sure." Mihee crinkled her brow and pouted her lips in mock distress.

"It's Cyrillic," Dad answered quietly.

It was a day of presentation on family at school. Each child had five minutes to talk about his or her family members in front of the whole class. When it was Yeonjoo's turn she stood behind the teacher's podium, her back ramrod straight, and declared that she was tremendously proud of her father. "My father is an intelligent man, an educated man," said Yeonjoo, oozing confidence, "A successful diplomat, currently working in Cuba."

First Mihee felt stunned, then angry. Mihee looked at her teacher, Ms Bong – a kind-hearted woman in her mid-forties who was also a stickler for the rules – expecting to find the same emotional reaction in the teacher's face as in hers. Ms Bong seemed neither shocked nor cross, however. She looked sad instead. She remained quiet and let Yeonjoo return to her seat unscathed – no questioning, no reproach.

Ms Bong of all people knew Yeonjoo was lying. Yeonjoo's father wasn't in Cuba: he was in a gulag. Most people in town knew Yeonjoo's father had been caught stealing medical supplies from the public hospital where he'd worked as a janitor. Any sensible people in town, including Mihee, of course, knew Yeonjoo's family was from a very low *songbun*, and thus hardly eligible for a prestigious job such as a diplomat. Rumor had it that Yeonjoo's mother, to make ends meet, had begun to wear red lipstick and bring strange men to her house while Yeonjoo was at school. And those men paid her in food and various goods, such as rice, barley, coal, and clothes. Certain goods that were neither edible nor wearable ended up in Yeonjoo's hands and Yeonjoo sometimes brought them to school, handed them out to kids she liked, saying those were gifts her father had sent from Cuba. Mihee was apparently one of the few kids Yeonjoo wanted to be friends with.

Mihee told her dad she didn't want to be friends with such a bare-faced liar. Yeonjoo's impudence shocked Mihee. She hadn't thought it was possible for a child her age to lie through her teeth in front of an entire class, in front of a teacher, accompanied by no sign of remorse. Mihee was angry that no adult had punished the girl.

"You're a smart girl, Mihee," said Dad.

Mihee caught the peculiar tone in her father's voice, lower and grittier than usual: *His scolding voice*, she recognized. Dad never yelled. He had his own way of instilling discipline through slow words, calming, yet intense, like a sunset.

Mihee observed, eyes and ears wide open.

Dad said that, although what he was about to say might sound a little confusing, she would be able to understand it eventually. "Not all lies are bad, Mihee. Sometimes a lie isn't a tool to hurt others but just one's effort at survival. One's effort to stay sane."

Mihee knitted her brows in confusion but kept on listening.

"Yeonjoo's deception wasn't to fool you so she could steal what was yours. It was her way of hiding her own painful past. Like a bandage that protects her wound."

After a few seconds of silence Dad kneeled in front of Mihee, and gently held her arms with both hands. Dad looked so big and so small at the same time.

"Sometimes, Mihee, the biggest deception of all, and the kindest there is, is to be deceived. That could mean invaluable comfort to the other, sweetheart."

Mihee saw grief in his eyes, a misty gleam that made him bite his lip a little. But soon he effaced it with his usual smile, sweet and silky, like butterscotch. He placed a tender kiss on Mihee's forehead and held her tight in his arms. The astringent aroma of Dad's hair tonic rushed into Mihee's nostrils. Mihee tasted it a little in her mouth as well, raw ginger and aniseed. It always made her feel heady, then sleepy. She smiled.

As only a child could, Mihee understood what Dad had told her without realizing she did. The next day after school Mihee went up to Yeonjoo and thanked her. Mihee told her that she was grateful Yeonjoo had shared a meaningful family gift with her, that Yeonjoo must be truly proud to be the daughter of her father. Mihee asked Yeonjoo to tell her more about Cuba, all the fascinating things Yeonjoo had heard from her father about the world outside. Though she could feel little beads of sweat on her forehead betraying her qualms, Mihee still did her best to appear earnest.

Mihee would never forget the look on Yeonjoo's face.

She knows I know. Mihee sensed it right away.

Yeonjoo stared into Mihee's face in silence, her mouth ajar and eyes aflame. Mihee wasn't sure if Yeonjoo was going to break into tears, like a baby, or fly into a rage, like a bruiser.

Yeonjoo's face curved into a smile, the purest and saddest kind there was. It reminded Mihee of her dad's after he'd spoken of deception. Yeonjoo's eyes, with the small downward lag at the corners, brimmed with tears, while a pair of deeply etched dimples tugged at her cheeks. Mihee could see almost all of Yeonjoo's teeth behind her wide-open mouth, awash with delight.

Walking homeward side by side, the girls were in conversation. Mostly Yeonjoo talked and Mihee listened. Yeonjoo talked about her father's flight to Cuba, how the airplane shook and its engine growled; talked about how women in Cuba were notoriously under clothed, often baring their thighs and their cleavage; how the Cubans ate their meat, smothered in garlic butter then char-grilled, table legs quivering under the weighty platters of pork sausage, veal and lamb chops. Mihee's mouth watered even though she knew Yeonjoo's stories weren't real. That Yeonjoo knew Mihee knew the truth changed nothing. It couldn't diminish at all the meaning and pleasure of what they had shared that day on their walk home. The tearful smile on Yeonjoo's face told Mihee that as long as

Yeonjoo's story lasted, and Mihee listened with all her heart, Yeonjoo was the happiest person on earth.

They were intimate in their shared fiction.

Yeonjoo and Mihee became best friends, and they remained so until they parted ways for high school.

Dad knew.

Dad might never have needed hard evidence.

Sometimes things like this, one doesn't guess or reason. One just knows.

Mother might have thought she had always tricked everyone, but in the end the only person she couldn't, and the only person who tricked her effortlessly, was her beloved husband.

He deceived her by letting her deceive him. She didn't know he knew.

That could mean invaluable comfort to the other, Dad had told Mihee.

"Don't you think it's time?" said Mother, without looking at Mihee.

Fitful drops of rain pinged off Mihee's forehead.

"There's nothing holding us back there now."

Mother sank her gray head onto her chest. That signified she knew the weight of what she'd just uttered. Mihee was supposed to bark in anger at her mother but couldn't. Her chest tightened. She couldn't afford to be a hypocrite now, not today.

Mother continued: "I'll turn myself in first and then deal with what follows. It will take a few months. You may need to disappear for a while, too. But not for long, I promise."

Mihee listened to the rain patter against the leaves of sycamore trees. Through the fat blankets of arching branches she heard the first rattle of the cicadas. Summer had seeped into the trees already. Soon the harsher pounding of rain drowned the bleating of the summer creatures.

Neither moved. The air felt lush and thick around them, like velvet.

Mihee opened her mouth. "But they may come after you, Mother. Do you really want this? It means living a life of running and hiding, assuming a false name for the rest of your days."

Speaking through the tumbling rain, Mihee realized her words came out as a shrill cry. She wasn't sure if she was bawling at Mother, or at herself.

"My dear," said Mother, quietly, "aren't we already?"

Mihee had never thought that her major life decision would be defined by such mundane things – the birth of her child and the death of her parent – as if she was no different from ordinary women she knew.

Maybe it's about time I deserved something ordinary in life, she thought, but not without guilt.

The hammering rain had dwindled to drizzle, which tapped languidly against the show-windows, their Monday lights lonely as the emptiness of the road. Though soaked, Mihee didn't really feel cold.

As she often did in the rain, she walked to the Chungjeongno subway station. But she wasn't going to take the train home. Chungjeongno was her favorite subway station in Seoul. Though located in the very center of Seoul, the CJR station was never crowded, even during peak traffic hours. It was in stark contrast to its famous neighbor, the City Hall station, which was buried in crowds from morning to night, haunted by the constant noise of hurried footsteps. CJR was also the most barren and colorless station in Seoul. While the inside of City Hall station was covered with burgundy bricks, its central passage punctuated by the genteel white marble colonnade, CJR's interior was a monotonous stream of gray tiles, a coarse and shallow cover for massive blocks of concrete that formed the backbone of the station.

But those brutalist hunks of concrete were exactly what had been bringing her to the place again and again – in the rain, especially. *The gray smell*, little Mihee used to call it. The scent of the entrance of the Hyesan airfield. Little Mihee used to run to the airfield whenever she saw the dark clouds gather in the sky, just to inhale the ashen beauty of a smell: the vast, smooth pavement of concrete soaked in rain.

Musty and musky – an olfactory crossbreed of wet earth and ancient paper, with a note of sweaty embrace.

Mihee was back to her dad's tiny study in Hyesan, a room full of old books and semi-illegal vinyl records. Stacks of time-stained hardcover books exhaled the familiar sigh, thick with mildew and ink. The smell of her childhood.

Mihee knew she would never go back home again. She would never smell the Hyesan airfield again. It was sadly comforting, however, to know that whenever the memories of her father grabbed hold of her, whenever she yearned for the smell of her childhood, she would come back here, to the Chungjeongno subway station in the rain.

ROUSSEAU

"How's Aram?"

Her first words. After a long absence, her voice now rings uncannily in my ear, like a celebrity's dubbed on a cartoon bunny's mouth.

"Aram is okay," I tell her, swallowing a cry. "He just misses his mother. Like I miss my wife."

I feel as if I were a child again, vulnerable, prone to tears, and constantly afraid of abandonment. When Aram was born I made a promise to myself and Aram that he would never grow up knowing such anxiety.

Around the time Aram was born, I heard the news of Hoyeon's death.

Opioid overdose. His body was found four days after he had died in his duplex apartment in LA, by his Ukrainian girlfriend. The girlfriend testified he had been taking an increasing amount of drugs for the last few months of his life. Heroin especially. They couldn't be sure if it was an accident or a suicide.

Hoyeon's death would have consumed my thoughts had it not been for the birth of Aram.

Newborn Aram was a black hole that we were all happily sucked into. A perfect storm whose cries and short-fuse naps and frequent bursts of appetite lost us sleep and upended all of our daily routines. Simultaneously, he filled our every waking hour with wonder. He reminded us of the forgotten marvel of our childhood: how we perceived the world around us as newcomers, letting every ordinary object or person ignite our infinite reserve of curiosity. Being with someone so full of love for life is such an uplifting experience.

My wife didn't like Jean-Jacques Rousseau because he abandoned all of his children upon birth. Given the dire lack of hygiene in eighteenth-century Parisian orphanages, it is unlikely that any of his five babies lived long after their abandonment. She said it was a horrific irony that a man known for his advocacy for justice and equality, a man who preached love of childhood and the childlike mind, left all of his five children to certain death as soon as they were born.

Jacquelin Rousseau, my father, abandoned my mother and

me when I was nine. Though I grew up in love and stability, thanks to my mother and grandparents, the absence of a father had left a little hole in my life that couldn't be filled. A question mark stuck in the limbo of the unanswerable. Then Aimé Adel came my way. A philosopher who had all the answers. Of course I liked Adel for the same reason Hoyeon did: Adel was a symbol of hope and a role model for all the hidden underdogs of the Western world. But to me Adel's words meant more than a good success story. It was Adel's point of view on marriage that catapulted the young me, Adrien Rousseau in college, into his world of literature. Aimé Adel saw traditional marriage as a doomed convention. *A trip from the extraordinary to the ordinary.* A slow process of disillusionment. Though brutal and pessimistic, his fatalism on marriage provided a philosophical answer to the mystery of my life; a sort of justification that I'd sought subconsciously throughout my childhood. Why my father was as he was, why he suddenly left us for good. Adel's idea that marriage is an archaic convention bound to fail made my father's giving up much more bearable, even understandable, to me. It conjured up a secondhand forgiveness that I hadn't been able to muster as a boy. It made the scar that I'd kept looking back on seem less repulsive. It saved me from living the rest of my life hating my father. Expecting less from men made it less difficult to swallow the sadness of the world. Expecting less from men made me less critical of men. A man like Adel, faulty and even double-dealing as he was, still managed to achieve greatness in the world, doing great things for the people. Maybe that was how I wanted to imagine my father, too. A flawed man, but who might have been great in his own way.

Maybe that was why I was so mad at her for what she'd said about Adel.

She saw through the facile justification and was brave – or blunt – enough to point it out to me.

"First, I want you to know that I love you, I love Aram. Now the only thing I truly want is to be with you and Aram. I need you to know that."

Seong-mi clenches her jaw as though she's angry, or as though she's containing herself from crying. To know that I'm not the only one with jitters relieves me. Her voice is gruff and taut, like a rubber band about to snap. It reminds me of the first time we met in the Church of New Life, in Shenyang, when she told me her life story. She seems different now. She looks younger, and more vulnerable. Her fingers are locked into a fist, as if in prayer, her grip so tight that the knuckles turn white. Her eyelashes flutter fretfully.

My stomach coils in on itself. I'm terrified of what she may say.

According to my favorite writer, my own marriage, this love story between two unusual human beings under such unusual circumstances, is surely ill-fated.

Aimé Adel said a love that blooms under extreme circumstances can't survive the autumn of monotony, of everyday life.

But I'm no longer the pessimistic teenager inexperienced in love and parenthood. Although Adel was an eloquent writer, he was a man-child when it came to marriage and commitment in a relationship. He had no first-hand knowledge of responsibility as a parent. He never knew what it meant to cherish another human body more than your own. What he might have comprehended was limited to his head as an academic. He died never knowing how it makes you feel in your guts.

Besides, what's so horrible about banality anyway?

In her absence, the things I missed most about our marriage were mundane ones.

A strand of her charcoal hair on the shoulder of my suit. The theme song of that corny soap opera she always hummed in the kitchen *à la* bossa nova. The fluffy touch of the beige woolen vest she wore at home on chilly nights; *A human shag carpet*, I called her in it teasingly, or *A teddy bear I'd love to shag*. The smell of that cheap bar of soap she used to wash her face, the whiff of cucumber and lemon from her pillow. Muffled giggles of Aram and her behind our apartment door – sometimes I stood there for a minute in silence, just to absorb the sound of guileless happiness a little more, before I opened the door and returned home to them. I miss those small pieces of our daily life together. Insignificant details that matter only to me, to us.

Mouth unhinged, she stares at the ground. My chest tightens. A silence follows again, louder and thicker than a shout.

While she collects her thoughts I look around the bench we're sitting on, in the Sohn Kee-chung Memorial Park. The tall sycamore trees cast shadows everywhere, leaving only a few gently quivering patches of light here and there on the ground. I lift my head and look up. An orange dusk is spilling across the sky. The air once choked with the loud summer cry of cicadas is now occupied by the lonely *chirr* of crickets. Autumn is here.

So this is where you take your lonely walks, I think.

"Why did you want to meet up here?" I ask her.

"Because the beacon doesn't shine on its base," she murmurs, as if she's talking to herself in sleep, eyes still fixed on the ground. "This is the last place where they expect to find me."

Her odd answer hits me with a feeling of *déjà vu*. Something chimes in my head, a metallic ping. I want to put it into words but I swallow it: I'd rather hear it in her words, at her pace. Besides, strangely enough, I feel as if I know half of the answer already. Hope and angst, two butterflies at war with one another, tug at the inside of my stomach.

She finally looks up at my face and opens her mouth. "I have a confession to make, Rou." She utters the sentence like a long-practiced line in a script. And yet her voice still quivers.

"I have mine to make, Seong-mi," I tell her, looking into her eyes.

I see the drawn-out anxiety recede from them. Surprise claims the stage briefly, till the familiar curiosity materializes, with a dash of dread. Now she understands how I feel. We feel newly intimate in our mutual secrets.

Then Mihee introduces herself – first a foe, but then a friend.

The 8th Life

8 Lives of a
Century-Old Trickster

The prospect of death endows most people with veracity, but it can drive a small number of others in the opposite direction. Throughout the obituary project I've met a few good old flim-flammers. When asked to tell a brief story of their lives, they made up legends instead, an amalgam of their sufferings and their fantasies. Three months before his death, Grandpa Park Myeong-yi claimed he was once a highly trained assassin, who was sent to North Korea and nearly killed Kim Il-sung. But when I called the Association of HID Veterans, a black ops unit of ROK Army, with the information Mr Park had given me, they confirmed there was no such soldier under the name and description. Another nonagenarian, Grandpa Gaam Boo-yong, confessed he was once a secret right-hand man to Chun Doo-hwan, the worst military dictator in South Korean history – and he claimed it proudly. I didn't even bother to check this one since I sensed the bluff right away: Mr Gaam was the kind of old man who jabbered about politics with the faux air of an expert, calling every liberal either a Commie or a carpetbagger. When he died, four months after this confession of his, no funeral wreath showed up under the name of Mr Chun. No wreath came at all in fact – and no weeping visitors either.

A question I always harbored about those old men was: who did they want to impress with their self-made legends? Me, an insignificant obituarist? Or themselves? Maybe they believed that a lie told so convincingly can take on a life of its own and become a private truth in itself. Maybe that was how they wanted to remember themselves before their minds dissipated. And I tried my best to honor their last decisions, by listening to their narratives with full attention and without judgment, regardless of how I felt about them personally. Sometimes the only and the best thing you can give to others suffering is your ears.

Mook Miran was different. She wasn't like those typical desperate characters. First of all, she was the first female blowhard I'd met at Golden Sunset. Grandmas sometimes engaged in boastful blather, but their harmless exaggerations were reserved for the achievement of their children and grandchildren, rarely for their own.

When I asked her how one could possibly live all these lives of the characters she'd mentioned, she said, with such easy confidence and steady eyes, that it was possible in her time. What a generic answer for an old soul, I thought.

The most unflinching liar I've ever seen.

She claimed she was not just a murderer but a *serial* one. "They say from number three you earn the prefix. Another fan of number three right there," said Ms Mook, slippery sarcasm in her voice. I asked how many she had killed and she answered four.

"Then how come you aren't in jail now? Serial murderer *and* a spy, according to your own words." I was incredulous.

"Is Kim Hyon-hui in jail now?" she asked me. No expression on her face.

Ms Mook was right: Kim Hyon-hui, a former North Korean agent responsible for the Korean Air Flight 858 bombing in 1987, which killed 115 people, wasn't in jail. She married the former South Korean intelligence agent who had handled her case, and they had two kids. She had been alive and well in South Korea as a free woman, ever since President Roh Tae-woo had pardoned her.

"I killed no one in my spy missions," said Ms Mook.

"Then who were they? The four victims," I asked, with renewed humility.

"Three were soldiers. One, a family member." She dithered a little at the word *family*.

"Your husband?" Only after those words flew from my tongue did I realize I had said them too quickly, too loudly.

I saw her eyes light with curiosity.

"Problem with your husband?" She was teasing me. The tip of her right canine tooth shone behind her lips.

"*Ex*-husband."

And there, I had said it. The dreaded word. It was my first time to say *ex-husband* out loud, hear that term in my own voice. Once uttered, it sounded not so sad, not so terrifying anymore. My confidence pumped up a tad, I uttered the word again. I needed to get used to it.

"My ex-husband and I, we aren't friends anymore."

She puffed a gentle snort. "There's no such thing as a happy break-up," she murmured softly, like it was an aside meant for a secret audience.

"And I killed my father, not my husband. My husband was a wonderful man." Her voice tapered off from the word *husband*.

"Why did you kill your father?" I asked.

"Self-defense," she answered swiftly, as though on cue. "He was going to kill my mother and me." Her dry matter-of-fact voice came back, the robotic spokesperson.

I asked her if the three other murders were also acts of self-defense. "*Of course*," she replied, then shot me a bitter scowl. *How could they be otherwise, halfwit?* it seemed to say.

"It was all during the wars," she said. Empty stare frozen on her face. A silence ensued but I didn't dare to fill it with any sound.

"The Pacific War, then the Korean War," she continued. "Those men were war criminals. They lied. They took girls and enslaved them. Too many young girls died. I killed only three soldiers, trying to save some of the girls and myself."

Comfort women. She was claiming to have been a victim of wartime sex slavery.

"Grandma Song Jae-soon wasn't a stranger to me, in fact."

She stopped to take a deep breath. "We'd met each other during the Korean War, when her name wasn't Jae-soon, but Jenny. A nickname given by the American soldiers."

Jenny. The name elicited a pained sigh from Ms Mook.

"I nearly cried when I saw her here at Golden Sunset. But she didn't recognize me at all. Her memory had receded too much already. But I still remembered everything she'd told me. Stories of her childhood, of her little sisters. Talking with her was what got me through that time."

Her red eyes nearly closed as a soft smile returned to her face. But gradually it made way for a different kind of smile: the wicked one, with a flash of her canine tooth.

"Before running away to the North, I set those poor girls free. And then I set fire to the house near Busan where they'd been keeping them. I watched it go down in flames. I had no idea that act would turn me into a wanted *guerrilla terrorist* in the South."

Ms Mook laughed in a low key, an eerie flare of joy. But soon it turned into something else, a sound that walked the line between an infantile gurgle and a muffled animal growl. Then the growl became a cackle, soon a cough that shook her thin chest violently up and down. I ran to her side but she pushed me away, with a force I hadn't expected from such brittle wrists. "Leave me alone," she whispered, out of breath. "Don't touch me."

I wanted to call the nurse but she firmly refused, telling me there was nothing the nurse could do to help her. "I need time to calm down, that's all," she said, in a low voice, fingers clasping the push rims of her wheelchair.

Maybe I should have stopped right then and returned her to the ward.

I didn't. Just as much as Ms Mook did, I wanted our conversation to continue. I couldn't wait to hear more of what she had to say about her killings. Out of courtesy I asked her if she wanted to change the subject and she threw a gruff *no* in my direction without looking at me.

"How did you kill them?" I asked.

Though not short for her age, Ms Mook didn't strike me as someone built for fistfights, especially not against trained military men.

She stretched both arms toward me, palms flat open. Under the thick white sleeves of her padded jacket showed her bony wrists. A pair of trembling twigs, they seemed to belong to a fawn rather than a fully grown human being.

"What do you think? Hand-to-hand combat?" she said.

She laughed, and I burst out laughing as well.

"Poison," she said sharply.

As soon as she uttered the word the look on her face flipped. The cheeky smile vanished, all soft curves on her cheeks gone. The deadpan eyes came back as if on cue.

"Poison is everywhere, because anything can be poison," whispered Ms Mook. "Any substance can kill a man, depending on how much, how fast it enters the body."

She said one can discover poison in the home. "Also in prison, in school. And places like a hospital and a nursing home, *jackpot*. Even here," she murmured, and turned her head toward the long, empty strip of land that formed a half-circle around the garden. It was where the cosmos flowers had flourished in the fall. The sun had begun its descent and the air grew colder. I zipped my duck-down jacket all the way up. I noticed the tip of Ms Mook's nose had turned pink so I unfolded the wool blanket lying on her lap and wrapped it around her body.

Ms Mook didn't react to my touch. Her gaze was fixed on the empty flowerbed. She slowly raised her arm and pointed a scraggy finger at the tall metal fence behind the flowerbed. "It's over there, the poison," she said, "I can smell them each time the wind blows from that direction."

Eyes closed, she breathed in the cold air drifting from the north, then breathed it slowly out again.

"Behind the fence, there's the abandoned land that leads to the woods. That wild place choked with tall weeds. There, there are *sanak*, the snake's peanut. A load of them. They have this peculiar smell, which is nutty and rotten at the same time."

She gestured for me to sniff the air and I did, my eyes closed. But I didn't notice anything, except for the earthy green odor you get in any given patch of wild land in Paju.

"That means the earth over there is good," she continued. "*Sanak* isn't a herb you can find easily. It needs specific soil to flourish. The soil should be about half loam, half sand, with just a dash of clay. Neither too dry nor too soggy. The smell means that the earth over there is good and rich."

Once again she inhaled deeply the icy breeze. Then she opened her mouth wide and swallowed the wind. A chill crawled down my spine as I watched her smack her lips.

"*Sanak* is medicinal *and* poisonous. If you chew three leaves – if you can, despite its smell – you'll get a nice dreamless sleep. If you drink one cup of the first brew steeped from its roots, however, you'll never wake up from that sleep. The roots are much less odorous, and much more poisonous.

"Poison, however, isn't the heart of the job. *How* and *when* to give the poison. That's the part that requires your wit."

Her eyes squeezed into slits.

"The easiest way with the soldiers was through their drink. Their whiskey and rum, cheap *sake* and *soju*," she whispered, her gnarled fingers clasped into a fist. "They drank themselves numb, those soldiers. Toward the end of the war, especially. Maybe they wanted to wipe their sins and memories clean with alcohol, sterilize themselves into immunity."

A snigger escaped through her parted lips.

"When they're drunk already, simply looking for more liquor to stay wasted, that's when you hit. When they're too drunk to notice the strange taste or smell from their bottles. That's how I killed them."

Shoulders relaxing into a small arch, she sat back in her wheelchair. She rested each hand on an armrest, palm facing the sky. Like a queen – quiet and satisfied.

I read no guilt.

Ms Writer, Ms Mook called me playfully, the next time we saw one another.

The New Year holidays were long over and the cosmos garden had regained its popularity. A dozen patients were either strolling along the small cobblestoned promenade or sunbathing in their wheelchairs near the garden fences.

Ms Mook and I preferred to talk in more privacy, so I took her to the Counseling Room. "I've never been here before," said Ms Mook in surprise, arching an eyebrow. I told her that on a weekday afternoon the place usually remained empty. "So we've got plenty of time to chat here today till your dinner call," I told her excitedly.

"Is this where you write?" she asked me, looking around the tight room. The walls were painted in light Green Tea Latte, the shade that's supposedly good for your eyes, that helps you relax. And yet, filling the slim space with Ms Mook, face to face, I felt rather keyed up.

I told her this wasn't my workspace and I wasn't even really a writer.

She shrugged her shoulders brusquely. "You write about people's lives and the readers love you for that. That makes you a writer."

What she said pleased me, and I felt myself blush. An unguarded smile broke on my face, the one with full teeth and gums. The kind of smile I wasn't fond of. I knew it made me look like an imbecile. I withdrew it as quickly as I could, but Ms Mook would never have missed a chink in armor like that. I was waiting for her to tease me.

But she didn't. In her gaze there was no sign of scorn.

"Was it your childhood dream? To be a writer?" she asked, rather seriously.

I realized I'd never been so close to Ms Mook before. Sitting opposite to her in a four-square-meter room, only minimally furnished with a desk, two chairs and a tiny pot of golden pothos, revealed a few features I hadn't noticed before. Two little specks on her cheeks, which I had interpreted as dimples, now emerged as scars – pockmarks, possibly. The skin around her long neck and collarbones was punctuated with similar scars of various sizes. A particularly eye-catching one began from the tip of her right collarbone and descended diagonally toward her heart.

She recognized my stare and sighed softly. "Wondering how I got them?" she said.

I didn't answer but she knew I was.

"Cigarette burns, an army knife and whatnot," she muttered, and exhaled a deeper sigh. "Look, sorry, but today I don't feel up to heavy talks."

It had just begun to drizzle outside, a sign of the transition to spring. The weather had grown much warmer, but increased humidity in the air made many patients complain of back and joint pains. Ms Mook was more quiet and pensive than usual. Fatigue sat on her slumped shoulders.

"Yes, it was my childhood dream, to become a writer," I told her, with a shy smile. "Along with ... becoming a mother."

I felt the smile on my face recede and I knew what had triggered it: *mother*. Another word I needed to work on after *ex-husband*. I forced myself to say it again after a deep breath.

"Mother. I always wanted to become one. I know it's no longer in fashion to say this out loud as a woman, these days, but I always had this fantasy of being a soccer mom." I chuckled lightly.

"What stopped you?" she asked.

"My ex-husband. The doctor said he had a low sperm count. I wanted to try IVF but he wouldn't."

I told her about my husband: he was never a violent man, he had never even yelled at me throughout our time together, but he could get incredibly stubborn in his own quiet way. I thought his firm cold no meant always no. I was afraid of losing him. I was afraid of ending up old and alone, so I acquiesced to the childless life he'd wanted. In the end, I found myself in that dreaded place all the same: old and alone. But the upside was that the dread had shed its initial aura. Only after I was seated in the feared nightmare was I able to realize it wasn't actually all that terrifying. The reality of living alone wasn't as bad as it had been in my imagination, where my fear of it had fermented into something out of all proportion. There were, of course, the shock and grief but they were subsiding with time. Little bouts of loneliness still haunted me now and again but they weren't anything I couldn't handle. Life alone was pretty doable, and it was becoming more and more so with each passing day.

"I still feel angry, though," I confessed to her. "I'm angry at him for having taken away my opportunity to be a mom. It's too late now. Menopause already – *zip*." I drew an invisible cut across my neck with my thumb, as if humor would hide my sorrow. I felt a sob writhing right under my diaphragm and I repressed it. This was how I dealt with anger usually: since erupting anger outward made me feel lousy all the more, I turned it into sadness and sobbed over it. But now, in the presence of Ms Mook, I didn't want to cry – not on her precious, ticking time. So I held back my tears.

Still, I told her how mad I was when I heard he'd been to the fertility clinic, with his new girlfriend only five years older than his niece. I observed Ms Mook's expression closely, thinking it would fit her character to shoot a caustic invective against my ex-husband. But she remained quiet. She was just nodding slowly, her eyes downcast.

"How does it feel to be a mother?" I asked her.

"It's wonderful," she whispered. "And hard."

She stared into the distance even though there was nothing but a green wall in front of her. Then she beamed, blushing like a little girl. I knew she was seeing her child in her mind's eye. And I felt deeply envious of her.

"My girl, as she was growing up, was so beautiful, and so *difficult*," she said, her face creased with bittersweet reminiscence. "What can I say? Like mother, like daughter," she simpered.

"They say smart ones are more difficult to raise, and that was quite true in my experience," she continued. "My daughter went to Kim Il-sung University in Pyongyang. The very best in North Korea," she said.

Boasting about her child seemed to have lifted the weight from her shoulders; her back and neck straightened, giving her a silent look of triumph – the same bizarre vibe I'd picked up from her in the cosmos garden, as she'd confessed to poisoning her abusers.

But this change made her seem more relatable as well – more approachable as a human being. I had seen that expression many times before, the pride and pleasure grandmothers had shown when talking about the success of their children and grandchildren. Finding the same in Ms Mook was both surprising and reassuring. Ms Mook, after all, knew one of the common languages of ordinary women: being a proud mother. Once again I felt jealous of her, and I was also deeply happy for her.

Ms Mook said she had wanted her daughter to become a diplomat but she'd been more into the field of intelligence. "And I couldn't stop her," she murmured. "She was as pigheaded as her mother." A little groan escaped her, then nervous laughter.

I thought it wasn't a bad time to question her about her second most interesting character: the spy. But my question brought the cold, flat stare back to her eyes. Then came the reply that sounded as rehearsed as the recorded message on an answering machine: "There are certain matters of national security I'm not allowed to talk about," said Ms Mook. "It was a part of the deal with KCIA, the South Korean intelligence agency," she added, in a lowered voice.

"Is this an if-I-tell-you-I-have-to-kill-you kind of thing?" I asked playfully, expecting her to chime in with her customary sarcasm.

But her answer was dead serious, which made me feel uncouth. "I'm too old to be hurt, but it could be detrimental for my daughter, her husband, and my grandson, who are living in the US now." Her expression had turned stern and distant, as though she was talking to a stranger.

Nevertheless, when I told her I hadn't known she had a grandchild, a wide smile bloomed across her face, and the volume of her voice bounced back to normal. "I do. A beautiful one. My daughter married an American and they're living near his hometown. They're professors at a good university." Vicarious pride returned in her neck and back – a snob in her I couldn't hate.

I found Ms Mook's reticence on her espionage convincing. The tall-talkers I'd met before at Golden Sunset, such as Mr Park Myeong-yi and Mr Gaam Boo-yong, were eager to enumerate perilous missions they'd engaged in as an assassin and a dictator's henchman respectively. Their lack of immediate families seemed to encourage them to confabulate further; there were no visiting sons and daughters with whom I could verify their stories. I thought that if Ms Mook was a true-blue mythomaniac, she would rather happily spill out her cock-and-bull spy stories and get a kick from it, the way those old men had.

Or would she?

The parrot of doubt on my shoulder croaked an uncomfortable truth. Ms Mook might have clammed up simply because she had nothing to say. How could she illuminate me on the job she'd never done? How could she engage in shop talk when its jargon was Greek to her? The best way to protect her false identity would be just shutting up. People always slip up when they talk too much, as cops often say.

And that her daughter and son-in-law were professors at an American university sparked the skepticism in me again.

They're living in the US.

This was a familiar line in Golden Sunset. Many elderly residents, especially the ones without immediate families or with few visitors, claimed that their children and siblings were living abroad, mostly in America. According to them, those family members were usually doctors and lawyers, professors and businessmen. Some of the claims were true, others either difficult to prove or blatantly false. Certain patients lied to save face, others to protect their families from criticism – so their kids wouldn't be thought of as ungrateful offspring who never came to see their parents.

Whatever their reasons might be, their lies seemed to share one fundamental belief: that America is the land of opportunity, of the greatest wealth and power. Today the average living conditions of Americans and South Koreans aren't much different but the minds of those old folks weren't in tune with the times. With age, memories of their youth seemed to take a larger role in their thoughts: their witnessing and survival of the Korean War, and the potent hand of America beneath it all. After all, Ms Mook, despite her striking singularities as a woman of her generation, might have dreamed of – or at least desired the pretense of – power and success, just like many others of her day, whose goal in life was not to be poor and downtrodden.

Then I realized how difficult it was to remain non-judgmental. I remembered I had made up my mind to be an audience who would appreciate Ms Mook's stories, whether they were fiction or true. I had believed that to give my full attention to her life, just as she presented it in her own words, was the most valuable gift I could provide in the last stage of her life. In reality, though, I found myself constantly parsing her comments into digestible morsels, trying to dredge up signs of truth or falsehood. The more I got to know her, the stronger my urge to detect facts. The more invested I felt in her life, the more I wanted her stories to be true.

I snapped back to the present and gazed at the old woman in front of me.

Her eyes were roaming around the small room. She stared at the low ceiling for a while, then moved on to observe the golden pothos in an earthy-red flowerpot that sat in the corner of the room. The glossy, heart-shaped green leaves were piled on top of each other, shouting for more space.

"They need to find a bigger pot for this poor creature," Ms Mook mumbled softly, leaning toward the golden pothos. She caressed the lush leaves with her twiggy fingers, lowered her head and sniffed. "You know what Westerners call it?" Ms Mook asked, but she didn't give me time to think and went swiftly on to answer her own question. "Devil's ivy," she whispered. "When I was little I heard a Canadian missionary call it that, and I thought the plant must contain wicked poison, just like *sanak*. But it didn't. Westerners called it devil's ivy because it grew so well anywhere and stayed green even when kept in the dark."

I told her I also had golden pothos at home for the same reason it had earned its nickname: its vitality and low maintenance needs.

Her smile dissipated as her gaze left the verdant leaves and moved back to the low ceiling.

"You know what I miss most, living here in Golden Sunset?" she asked, without looking at me. "Not that I complain about the place. This is as good as a public nursing home can be," she added quickly, shooting me a sidelong glance.

I asked her to tell me what she missed most. Sleeping outdoors, she answered. "How crazy is that?" She laughed off-key, eyes still locked on the ceiling. "I hated it. I absolutely hated it when I was forced to do it during the Korean War. Nearly all the houses and buildings were destroyed by incessant bombing. I can't count how many nights I had to sleep without a roof over my head."

Her voice grew tight. She stopped to catch her breath.

"It gets so cold at night outside. If it rains, you're sure to catch cold. Some refugees died like that – not from bombing or shooting, but from hypothermia, pneumonia, from the wet cold of night. But sometimes, when it wasn't so cold, with no cloud in the sky, you could see the beauty. The most breath-taking sky you'll ever see. I saw my first shooting star on a night like that, sleeping in the open. Sometimes the night was so devoid of human noise you could hear the moon breathe down on you, crisp and minty and so loud," she whispered, then chuckled softly like a tickled baby, "though my husband said that might just have been crickets chirping far away. The moon so ripe, round, so radiant you could count every damn pockmark on it."

She shivered slightly, as if cold tingles shot through her limbs. The look of euphoria on her face was eerily charming.

"Every now and then I forced myself to stay awake, to take it all in, from start to finish."

She described how the soft night wind sighed and whistled against the dark sky, and the stars, their brightness so forceful they seemed like a million fireworks frozen in time. How she loved witnessing the subtle transition of the sky from night to dawn, the pale blue glimmer of morning spilling languidly across the horizon.

"I wish I could be outside at night," she said, looking up at the ceiling. "At my age, days feel so short but nights are long. Sleep becomes restless."

She said the old clearing near the woods, behind the tall garden fence, would be the best place to lie down and observe the night sky.

"I could also collect a few leaves of *sanak* there, and save them for my sleepless nights. One leaf would do for a shrunken, ancient body like mine." A smirk tugged at her mouth. "A night of deep baby slumber."

I began to feel uncomfortable. I wasn't sure if she was still talking out of nostalgia, or if she was subtly pressuring me to break a rule for her – to arrange an escapade.

"*Sanak* might do you good, too," she said casually.

I asked her what she meant.

"Aging also comes with an unexpected upside, you know. With age, you lose your fear of things that once terrified you." Ms Mook kept talking, ignoring my question.

"How can that herb help me? My sleeping is fine," I asked.

"You know what I'm *not* afraid of at this stage of life?" she asked, her chin on her hand – like a child with innocent curiosity. A tantalizing moment of silence followed.

"Life sentence. Death sentence," she murmured.

I stopped asking questions. I just glared at her, slightly irritated and intrigued.

"What would happen to that irresponsible man, that lying man who was once yours? If someone could let me loose for a night or two."

I was speechless.

"Tell me," she said, an empty look on her face, "will he disappear?"

First I heard the high-pitched ringing in my ear, the sound that drew out thinner, sharper. Then all at once the noises from outside came at me: the automobiles purring; Ms Docgo's raspy voice shouting at a patient; the lazy footsteps of old people trudging along the corridor.

"What the *fuck* are you ... "

Ms Mook gave a strangled laugh. Like hiccups it shook her torso up and down. Blood rushed to her face. "I got you," she said, out of breath. "I really got you, didn't I?" She kept on chortling till her giggles turned into dry coughs.

"You really scared me there," I told her, with a sigh that was both miffed and relieved. I massaged her back to calm the coughing.

Later in the evening, on my way home, a little afterthought popped into my head, like a sneeze.

What if I'd stayed calm, and seemed intrigued? Would she still have burst out laughing?

I had my own answer. I left it at that.

The following week I went to the administration office.

Nobody there gave me a suspicious look since I had been a frequent visitor, running errands and picking up documents for Director Haam.

I was looking through patient files to find documents on Mook Miran. When I found her file, I opened it and took quick photos of the contents, which weren't even three pages long. I read them during my coffee break, feeling disappointed that there wasn't much information about her in the file that I hadn't already known.

But when I looked at it more thoroughly the second time, I discovered something quite strange. In the photocopy of her Korean identification card was the date of her birth. I calculated it in my head and came up with ninety-eight. In disbelief I used the calculator on my desk and it gave out the same number.

Ms Mook's age, on the official document, was ninety-eight.

I'm turning one hundred the day after tomorrow, she'd told me. And, of course, I hadn't believed it. Now I realized there were things I'd completely misunderstood. First of all, I didn't pick up the metaphor: *the day after tomorrow*. People, especially old folks, sometimes use that figure of speech to mean *the year after next* – a witty way of expressing how fast time seems to pass for the elderly. Despite her sharp mind and wits, and her octogenarian-looking body, Ms Mook was indeed what she had claimed to be. She was only two years away from a century-old life.

With a strange surge of energy I trotted to Director Haam's office. Her office was a little museum of her motherhood. Her bookshelves were inundated with her children's achievements. I saw hundreds of trophies and award certificates bearing the names of her three kids, from taekwondo tournaments and English-speaking contests and piano competitions. Photos were everywhere. The smiling faces of her children decorated her desk and walls, some in brightly colored frames made of wooden popsicle sticks.

In contrast, the smell of her office was thick with seduction. The sultry odor of a French perfume she sprayed on her coat dominated the room. Whether you liked that musky rose scent often depended on the weather and your mood: on relaxing days, with fresh weather, the smell was invigorating; on hot, humid, tiring summer afternoons it could be nauseating.

That day, the smell seemed to invigorate me, although the weather was warm. Director Haam stared at me with her startled-rabbit eyes, unmoving in her chair, and listened carefully to my effusive talk on Ms Mook: the truth about her age, how smart she was, somebody's terrible mistake in moving her to Section A, and so forth. When my jabbering was over, I was slightly out of breath.

Director Haam sighed. "I meant to talk to you about this," she said. "I should have done it earlier."

She stooped down and opened the gray metal cabinet wedged between the wall and her desk, mostly hidden from my view. She took out an orange paper file and dropped it onto the desk with a thwack.

"The head caretaker and Nurse Docgo have been telling me you spend a little too much time with Grandma Mook. They're worried about it. And so am I."

My chest tightened. I wondered if it was worry or pity.

"What I learned through two divorces, and raising three kids from two different fathers, is that keeping a healthy distance is key to a good relationship. Whether it's with a man or a woman, even with your own child. With anyone, essentially."

Suddenly she stood up and began to walk in circles, her hands planted deep in the pockets of her velvety sweatshirt. Her attire distracted me from focusing on her speech – where on earth do you buy a tight burgundy training top made of velvet? I wondered this out of genuine curiosity, not sarcasm.

"Look, I know you're a wonderful girl and you've been through a lot recently. I'm just afraid you might be seeking comfort in the wrong place."

I thought it was inappropriate for her to call me a girl. I was forty-seven. But it was kind of sweet, too: Director Haam always showed strong motherly sentiment toward anyone slightly younger than her, and she cared for them as best she could.

"You should be more careful about Ms Mook. She isn't exactly who you think she is," she said.

I asked her what she meant.

"I know I told you this isn't exactly my dream job but that

doesn't mean I don't care about it. I've always kept this place nice and clean. All the patients here have proper meals, a proper bath twice a week, and I've never, not once, played false with the public funding. That's why there are always so many people on the waiting list. Some even offer a bribe under the table to secure their parents' space at Golden Sunset. But every time I refuse it point-blank. I play by the rules.

"Grandma Mook won her place here because she is a North Korean defector. North Korean defectors, like families of war heroes or National Independence fighters, have priority to enter public educational institutions and nursing facilities. That she's a North Korean defector is probably the only thing proven true about her, among all the things she's been claiming to be."

Again Director Haam sighed. Then she shook her head and crossed her arms, her gaze turned away from me.

"North Korean defectors often lie about their age in South Korea. Young ones claim to be younger to be eligible for free university education, old ones even older to receive social welfare benefits for the elderly. Frequently they change their names, too. We can't check their original records over the border, can we? So their fiction becomes reality here in the South, with their new ID cards," she said, with a bitter smile. "Not that I blame them. They have the right to start afresh," she added reluctantly.

She opened the orange file lying on her desk.

"Mook Miran. Rather a strange name, isn't it? Mook is not a common family name in South Korea, and Miran too modern a first name for a nearly century-old woman."

She turned the open file around and placed it right under my nose. "I'm supposed to share this with no one other than the medical staff but I'm breaking a rule just this once for you," she said, after a little hemming and hawing.

The page was a medical chart, filled with the illegible hand-writing of a doctor. I began to feel irritated and very tired. Haam's heavy perfume, along with the increased humidity in the room, was now taking its toll on me. I asked her what this all meant.

Wordless, Director Haam turned to the next page of the file. I saw more than a dozen tiny black-and-white images of what appeared to be an MRI scan of a head.

"Grandma Mook has a brain tumor. Inoperable. Size of a tennis ball . . . " Haam's voice trailed off.

I couldn't find anything to say, though my mouth was open.

"Grandma Mook has always been *special*. Quite a talker when she's in the right mood, as you already know. A biting joker, too. Some people find it refreshing, fun. Others find it arrogant and rude. She often corrects the grammar and misused vocabulary of the nursing staff she doesn't like, just to annoy them."

She stopped to laugh. And now I understood the reason for Nurse Docgo's undisguised hostility toward Ms Mook. Director Haam put on a sad face again and continued her talk.

"But her facial expressions – the way the look on her face sometimes changes from one second to the next, like it's sud-denly jerked away from her face, you know? And the way she stares into space in the middle of a talk. Those are new. We assume it's the tumor."

My hands grew clammy with sweat.

"We roomed her with Grandma Song partially because they got along well. Grandma Song seemed to do a lot better with Mook than any other patient she'd roomed with before. But the main reason was that they both had pica."

Pica. I felt as though I knew what that word meant even before learning it.

"They both eat things that are not food, largely non-nutritive and harmful stuff. Grandma Song is notorious for occasionally trying her own number two, and Grandma Mook, well, she eats *dirt*," whispered Haam.

Dirt. Director Haam pronounced the word with such embarrassment, as if she were talking about Grandma Mook's sexual promiscuity. Her face was brick-red.

"Early last year Nurse Docgo caught Grandma Mook gorging on soil in the cosmos garden. She was banned from the garden stroll for a week. Then we spotted her again the following week, stealing soil from the flowerpot of a Christmas cactus in the lobby."

I was puzzled. Dirt was the last thing I would associate with keen, haughty Ms Mook. The idea of her on her knees, scooping soil into her mouth, was as unlikely as an image of Director Haam in a nun's habit.

She pulled the orange file toward her and flipped a few more pages. Then she pushed it back to me. Massaging her temples with her fingers, she told me to look at the photo.

It took me a while to make out what the image was.

Texture of over-fermented dough, whipped and battered in disorder.

I looked more closely. Then I saw the long curved scars, over which the edges of rough, flaccid human skin drooped like misshapen curtains – as though she was carrying giant gills on her belly.

I felt a little dizzy.

"Dr Koo told me, after Grandma Mook's first ultrasound check-up here, that she had no uterus," Haam said. Her fingers moved desperately around her temples. She looked sad and angry.

"He said the scars were ancient. He said no sane doctor performs a hysterectomy like that anymore. It must have happened to her when she was very young. She could never carry a baby, poor woman. She wrote so herself in the admission form, that she has no child."

My mouth was dust-dry. It had hung open too long, barren of words.

"I hear her wild stories get wilder these days, especially when she's around you. I can't be sure if it's the tumor or just her, but that doesn't really matter. Because what I'm concerned about is you, your wellbeing."

I couldn't look Director Haam in the eye. I felt as though I was complicit in the chain of mythomania.

"If Grandma Mook's magical thinking is what makes her happy at the end of her life, *fine*. Good for her. She'll pass away soon and nobody will tell her to eat her words. But you, honey . . . " Her sigh again. A long, gruff one. "You seem way too invested in what she says. Don't forget you're recovering from deceits that devastated your marriage. I can't watch you get hurt again by lies, not when you're so vulnerable, reeling from your divorce."

My heart was a clock. I heard it ticking loud and clear.

I took a vacation from work. Almost two weeks. Director Haam was very understanding. She said travel might do me some good. But I mostly stayed home. I watched old cable-channel films at night. During the day I read novels and took lots of catnaps. I still forced myself to go to the gym three times a week; it was the only time I stepped outside my apartment.

I was licking my wounds. I thought about many things: my marriage, my ex, and my boss. But mostly I thought about Ms Mook. And her tales. And my relationship to them. Although I'd always been half in doubt about the validity of her stories, and I'd even sworn to myself I would remain their faithful fan regardless of their truth, discovering their blithe falsehood from another person, a person of authority with evidence, left me in shock. It reminded me of the ironic jolt I'd felt on learning the truth of my ex: I knew most men cheat but I was still astounded to know my own husband had. I felt angry at Ms Mook.

But I pitied her as well. I felt sad that, just like the handful of tall-talking grandpas, she had had to fabricate her life for redemption. The last happiness she'd planned for herself was a delusional kind. I was sad because she'd seemed better than that, because I thought she deserved so much more. She could have used her unusual intelligence for much more constructive purposes.

And her tumor. The size of a tennis ball and growing. It was what made me go to see her again, at least for one last time. Even though I still felt betrayed, I knew I needed to see her for my own sake: I would feel tremendous guilt if I didn't complete the job I'd started. I needed to say a proper goodbye to her. I needed to see her face before she died or lost her senses. I was afraid that this inoperable tumor, a ticking bomb in her head, would rob me of the chance for one last talk with her.

I saw her in the cosmos garden. I couldn't take her out at night, as she'd wanted me to, but at least I could let her enjoy the perfect sunny afternoon in the garden, where spring had arrived. All the tree branches were covered with tiny mint-green buds, and all the dry and sandy-colored grass had been replaced by firm verdant shoots. The air was as crisp as ice chips, but the breeze that lapped against my cheeks was refreshing rather than chilly. Birds chirped loudly from all sides.

She appeared in a wheelchair as usual. This time she was with Ms Hwang, the youngest nursing assistant of Section

A. The bubbliest one, too. "Have a nice talk," she told us, in her mezzo-soprano voice. Her chubby cheeks rose high as she smiled. Ms Hwang's warmth seemed to have rubbed off on Grandma Mook. She looked more content and relaxed than usual. Despite the balmy spring weather, she still had the extra layer of thick winter blanket over her lap. I asked her if she was feeling cold and she said she was fine.

I swore to myself that I would first let her enjoy the weather for a while, but my patience frayed fast.

"Is Mook Miran your real name?" I asked her, after a short silence.

"No," she answered slowly, but without a moment of hesitation. Her eyes were still and steady. No sign of guilt.

I was surprised. I had shot her the question without even saying hello, thinking it would throw her off-guard.

"What is your name then?"

"Depends on what you mean by my name," she said, her tone unchanged.

"The name your daughter and husband knew you by," I said flatly.

She looked me squarely in the face, with a scowl. Tut. She clicked her tongue.

"Do you think the South Korean intelligence agency would have let me keep my North Korean name here? I told you I made a secret deal with them. Do you remember the things I've told you? I've got people to protect."

Her voice grew taut and dry. She grunted sharply.

I felt the sudden strong urge to bite my nail but I fought it off.

"You want to know the name my husband and daughter knew me by? It's Yongmal. But that isn't my real name either. What do you want to know? I have a list of names I've lived by. English name, Deborah. Japanese name, Kaiyo. What did you expect?"

She was angry. Although I was the one who should have been angry.

"Why didn't you tell me about the brain tumor?"

"Did I have to?" She glared at me, then shook her head.

Her anger was subsiding. But the irritation was still there.

"What difference does it make? If I'd told you, you would have looked at me with pity right from the beginning. Don't get sentimental on me, dear. I've already lived the average lifespan of a woman. Does it make any difference now, to die of a brain tumor or angina or cancer? How about heart attack or flu? Death is death. I'm dying anyway, with it or without it."

"How about your child? Your daughter in America?" I heard my voice tremble.

Ms Mook didn't look mad. Any sign of emotion seemed to have drained out of her face. Only the empty eyes and closed lips remained. They were somehow worse than her frown and swearing.

"If you want to play a game of truth or lie, I'm out," she muttered, like a synthesized voice message. Purple and blue veins jumped in her brittle arms as she turned the wheelchair slowly away from me.

I grabbed the handles. She turned her head and stared at me, with the same icy look. I lowered my voice and said I was sorry, which was what I truly felt. I said it again as she turned her head away from me to face the entrance to the garden. Without looking at me she asked me what I was sorry for.

"I didn't mean to pry. About your family."

She sat still in her wheelchair without making a sound.

"If you don't want to talk about family, fine, I respect that. But I think I'm entitled to some more explanations on other things. After all, *you* chose *me* to write about your life. *You* reached out to *me*."

Though I couldn't observe her face I could feel her mind shifting. Her hands were still on the push-rims of her wheel-chair but it hadn't made any forward movement yet.

"Can you tell me why you eat earth? I'm not being judgmental. I just want to understand."

I heard her snort. That brief and crunchy noise. I'd missed it.

I asked her if geophagia was a new habit caused by the brain tumor.

This question made her turn back to face me. I felt a deep relief.

"No. I ate earth when I was little. Quite often. And a lot. I stopped for a while, then began to do it again, like a hopeless alcoholic who keeps bouncing back to the bad habit. But in my thirties I lost the urge altogether, just like that, like magic."

Click. She snapped her long, skeletal fingers. An odd little grin materialized on her face.

"I'd never relapsed for more than half a century. Then, one day, out of nowhere, it reappeared. As if it'd never quit me."

Her grin bloomed into a full smile, unreserved as a happy child's.

She used the language of disease to describe the condition, *relapse* and *alcoholic*, but thinking about it made her face light up with euphoria, like somebody who'd just regained her long-lost sense of taste.

She said, as they get older, people seem to go back in time. Grandma Song had returned to her early teens; many others with Alzheimer's in Golden Sunset had forgotten the faces of their daughters and begun to call their sons by their husbands' names. But people without Alzheimer's also travel back in time in their own way, she said. They fall back on old habits that they've nearly pushed out of their memories. Many turn baby-like: their bodies shrink; they can't walk alone; they wear diapers; and they lose their teeth. Their gummy smiles resemble more and more those of newborns: guileless and innocent. They become helpless. They're in need of others' eyes and arms around the clock, just like babies. But the crucial difference between them and babies is that they have no future, she said. And that is why their return to their old bad habits can be justified. They don't have much of a future left to destroy, only the little moments of happiness to pursue that may not come again tomorrow. If you're a ninety-year-old weary body and crave cigarettes, you smoke them, she said.

"If I crave earth like I've never craved it before, I eat it. It's not like I strive to keep my body pristine and live till I'm a hundred and ten." Ms Mook chuckled. She said *carpe diem* shouldn't be preached to teenagers who were reckless enough already: it was meant for shrinking old bodies like hers. "Seize the day. There might not be tomorrow, literally," she whispered, and chuckled again.

She said old people are like salmon: their minds keep swimming against the streams of time and memories. They don't know why they do this – they're just programmed that way. Old folks often talk about *gohyang*: their hometown and birthplace, where the memories of their childhood are rooted. Even many refugees from North Korea she'd met in China and South Korea, people who had risked their lives to escape from their totalitarian fatherland, often have dreams of returning to their *gohyang*. They said these dreams mostly end up as nightmares, in which they break their necks to run away from the North Korean Secret Police. They wake up, their faces and armpits clammy with sweat, a scream trapped under their tongues. Every now and again, however, they find themselves looking forward to these nightmares: they're the only way they can see their *gohyang* again.

She recognized the puzzlement on my face and asked me where my *gohyang* was, probably in an effort to help my understanding. "I'm from Ulsan, Gyeongsang-do," I told her. But I added that I didn't feel much longing for Ulsan, that I didn't even think about it very often. I had no desire to go back there to live. I preferred Seoul or Incheon for that matter. "Does this mean I'm still too young?" I jested.

She uttered a flat no. She said I didn't miss my *gohyang* because I knew I could go there anytime I wanted; all I needed to do was purchase a ticket and hop on the next fast train to Ulsan at Seoul station. When you know you can never go back, however, everything changes, she said. She told me to imagine my *gohyang* forever forbidden from me. "The nest of your earliest memories, where your ideas of family and friendship were formed. You know it's right there, where it has always been, but somehow it's become sealed off from you for good. Imagine that," she murmured.

I asked her what she missed most about her *gohyang*. She answered that she missed its earth.

"Isn't that funny?" she said. "I'm hopeless, aren't I?" She wrinkled her nose in feigned disgust.

"I had my first intelligence mission here in Paju," she whispered, eyes hazy. "It's so close to North Korea that even now, on windless days, you can hear the North Korean radio propaganda.

"Long time ago, when they had the big US military base just down the road, farther north, I was made to collect information. I was trained to draw the detailed plan of the base inside my head and memorize it. I could still see it clearly in my head with my eyes closed."

Eyes shut, she lifted her right hand. A blind music conductor, swinging an invisible baton. Or a ballerina: her fingers danced briskly in the air, one pirouette after another.

"But that map is useless now. The base is empty, obsolete."

Her voice dropped as she opened her eyes slowly. Her narrow shoulders sloped forward.

"But the earth is still the same. The earth of Paju is quite similar to the earth I ate as a child in the North, in my *gohyang*."

A nostalgic smile returned to her face.

Speaking of returning home, she said, she had a formal suggestion to make to Golden Sunset through me. I told her I was curious to hear it. She cleared her throat and said we should build a bus stop in front of the main building. A proper one with a big wooden bench, the shelter made with strong metal columns, glass walls and a glass roof, so that patients could enjoy the sunlight when the weather is nice, but also be protected from rain and strong wind during storms.

She stopped to laugh a little when she saw my surprised face. She reassured me it would be a fake one, not a real stop where patients could make their escape freely. She said it would serve the opposite purpose in fact: to make them stay, safely, in Golden Sunset.

In the Reading Room, flipping through newspapers, she came across an article about a nursing home for the elderly with Alzheimer's in Germany. "You aren't the only one who reads magazines and newspapers here," she said, with a wink. After numerous incidents of their patients going regularly missing, the article said, the nursing home had decided to build a small bus stop near their main gate. Like salmon, led by their homing instinct, patients who wandered out of the facility began to take shelter at the bus stop, thinking they were waiting for a bus to take them home. There had been a couple of car accidents caused by male patients, who had escaped from the facility and had been wandering on the nearby highway; in winter patients had been found in various places in the vast gardens, mostly in the bushes and behind large sycamore trees, in a state of near hypothermia. The bus stop had put an end to those dangerous escapades.

While waiting for the bus on the bench the old folks had occasion to talk to each other, seeking and finding comfort in their company. A bus would pick them up, and take them for a ten-minute drive around the neighborhood. And then it would return them to the facility, telling them they had arrived, that they were home. This way, feeling they'd returned to where they should be, nobody resisted going back to their rooms. They did so voluntarily and happily.

"Grandma Song will be a lot safer and happier with a bus stop at Golden Sunset," Ms Mook said. "No more midnight chases with a syringe full of Haldol for you guys."

I told her it was an excellent idea, and she beamed. I thanked her and promised her I would do whatever I could to make it happen. My approval made her blush. Tears hung in the corners of her eyes, and she mouthed a quiet "Thank you." It felt good to watch her soften.

"Today is your lucky day," she said, dabbing at her eyes with the sleeve of her white patient gown.

She pulled a corner of the thick blanket covering her lap and revealed what was nestling underneath. On her bony thighs, propped up by her tiptoeing feet, sat a small stack of notebooks. She gestured to me to take them. "Go on," she said impatiently.

There were seven in total. They were all soft-covered and made of thin beige paper, slightly transparent like *hanji* – traditional Korean paper made from mulberry trees. Each page was sleek and lightly glossy, pleasant to the fingertips.

Each notebook cover bore the same title: *8 Lives*. Below the title, however, each cover had a different number, from two to eight. Each notebook was filled with Grandma Mook's large and uneven handwriting.

"They're all in block letters. I had only thick wax crayons to write with," she said. "I told you I had nothing that's forbidden in the drawer, didn't I?" She eyed me triumphantly, as if she'd just won a bet.

I remembered the wooden dresser in her room and its bottom drawer, where I had caught a glimpse of a pile of papers and a jumble of little colorful objects. Now I understood what they were and what she meant: any sharp objects, including pens and pencils, were forbidden in the patient rooms of Section A, so Grandma Mook had turned to writing with crayons.

She said those notebooks contained her life. "Only truth there," she whispered, "but, of course, my version of the truth."

I asked her why she had chosen me for this.

"You agreed to write my obituary. Think of it as a longer version of that," she answered.

I asked her why the title was *8 Lives*. She shrugged her shoulders and stuck out her lower lip. *Not much meaning*, her body language said.

"We promised, right? Eight words. Good enough reason?" she said, and then she raised her shoulders again. "Plus, I like the number, just like you like the number three." She shot me a naughty grin.

She explained it was also a favorite number for people in China, a symbol of wealth and fortune. "But above all," she murmured, "I love the shape of it. The beautiful, curvy loops you can draw in one continuous stroke. When drawn perfectly, you can't see where it begins and where it ends."

Her finger painted the number in the air in the measured cadence of a poet; when drawing the half circles at top and bottom it slowed down gracefully, and accelerated as it neared the slender waist, the intersection of lines.

"Where is notebook number one?" I asked. "I can only see from two to eight. So only *Seven Lives* in total. Not eight."

She puckered her lips and raised her open palms toward me, as though what I had just said was nonsensical. "Yeah – Where is it? Is it ready yet?" She turned the question back at me.

She said what I was writing as her obituary would serve as the opening chapter of *8 Lives*. She was certain it would illuminate nicely how her life had transmuted itself into a book.

"I entrust you with full powers over the book," she said, in her mock solemnity, like a priest absolving a sinner. Her hands trembled as it made the sign of the cross toward me.

I still had many questions about the seven notebooks but I figured most of them would be answered naturally when I sat down and read them. But one question lingered.

I asked her how she had found the time to write. It would have taken quite a while: several uninterrupted hours a day for at least six months, I would say. In Section A, patients were monitored around the clock. And to make the monitoring easy, patients' schedules revolved around group activities. I thought Grandma Mook used the tiny crack of daily free time she had for browsing newspapers in the Reading Room.

"I wrote at night," she said. "It's the quietest time. Best for thinking." A lean smile tugged at her mouth. "I didn't choose to room with Grandma Song only because I wanted to help her. It was also because she could be a help to me too.

"Most evenings they give Grandma Song sleeping pills, or sometimes Haldol injections for her night restlessness. Then she sleeps so deeply even an earthquake couldn't wake her up.

They turn off all the lights in the patients' rooms, but I turn on the light of my cellphone and write."

"You have a cellphone?" My voice squawked. "You said you have nothing that's forbidden!"

She said that question of mine was only regarding the bottom drawer of her wooden dresser. "Hair-splitting? Maybe. But not lying."

"How did you get the cellphone?" I asked.

She dropped her head and puffed a little sigh. "Let's just say you aren't my only fan here," she answered, raising her head languidly. Her narrowed eyes seemed to beseech me: *Ask me no questions and I'll tell you no lies.*

I thought of the bubbly Ms Hwang, the youngest nursing assistant of Section A. I said nothing, though. I didn't want anyone to name names.

A long silence divided us.

My head bustled with conflicting thoughts. But Ms Mook's seemed to be in its own world of peace. Her eyes, drowsy with reminiscences, were half shut already. I watched the crows' feet around her eyes settle deeper into her skin as a dreamy contentment spread slowly across her face.

I crouched to take a better look at her. I brought my nose close to her bone-white hair and sucked in the air that surrounded her. There was the faint smell of puppy on a rainy day, something I'd always associated with very old people. The sweet and sulfuric scent comforted me.

We were both looking at a giant zelkova tree over the garden fence, standing curt and lonely, dozens of meters away from Golden Sunset. Its branches were already so thick with leaves that from afar the tree looked like a massive head of broccoli. But if you looked at it closely, you could see its thousand tiny green leaves shimmer as the syrupy light of late afternoon spilled onto them. They rippled ruefully as the wind teased their edges.

I looked at Ms Mook, feeling the northern wind on my face again.

I saw her breathe in deeply, her nostrils flare wide, like those of an excited bull. I knew what she was drinking through the air.

Looking into those old vulpine eyes, I asked her the question I couldn't have dared to ask before, for which I had felt nearly a moral obligation, like a priest facing a death-row convict.

I asked her if she felt any regrets about the killings she'd committed.

She snorted. "Would that make *you* feel better?" she said. "Because if I said I regret it, I must feel a little guilt?"

She closed her eyes and opened her mouth. She took another deep breath, and a smile, guileless and innocent, appeared on her face. "I don't dare to pity, dear, and I don't dare to forgive."

Early next morning the call from Director Haam woke me up. She asked me, with chilly aplomb in her voice, if I had known about this already by any chance. The unusual gravity of her tone would have intimidated me under normal circumstances, but it was six in the morning, on a Saturday, and I was in bed, still punch-drunk from the sleep I'd been chasing till four a.m.

"What in the world— Did I know *what*?" I mumbled curtly.

I heard Haam exhale a long sigh. "*Okaaay,*" she said.

Whatever the accusation was, my genuine perplexity seemed to have made her exonerate me.

She went on, "I was terrified, wondering if you'd had any hand in this. If you did, I would have been *very* disappointed."

I sensed the lingering hypothetical anger in her voice, which irritated me further. "What are you talking about?" I barked.

Haam explained briefly what had happened overnight.

I got up and dressed. I didn't bother to take a shower. I needed no coffee. What I'd just heard was already pumping sour adrenaline all through my body. Driving to Golden Sunset, I thought of Ms Mook's imploring eyes of the day before. They were pleading with me not to question her further on what she'd kept up her sleeve. *Ask me no questions and I'll tell you no lies.* I simply thought she wanted to protect herself by guarding her secret, but the protection was meant for me, I realized. She knew my ignorance would prove my innocence. If I had become aware, even in the slightest degree, of what she was going to do, my anxiety and guilt would have shown through my thin skin, inviting misplaced suspicion from others at Golden Sunset.

Grandma Song had woken too early and begun to laugh aloud, then sing. They didn't want her to wake the whole floor, so they had gone to her room to calm her down with a sedative injection. When they got inside the room, however, they realized Ms Mook's bed was empty. They called the security guards and searched the floor to no avail. They quickly expanded the search to every room and dark corner of Golden Sunset, which included two buildings, two large gardens and a parking lot. They still couldn't find her. There was not a clue: no sign of breaking in or out – all windows and doors of the Golden Sunset property remained shut and locked. Ms Mook had vanished, they said. They decided to call the police. Director Haam called me as well.

Hours later, as the police moved farther away from Golden Sunset, past the abandoned land behind the cosmos garden, and began to walk the narrow passage that led into the dark woods thick with tall birch trees, they found the first sign of her: her white night robe. Four staff members from Golden Sunset, including Haam and me, joined the trail and we continued to walk deeper into the woods. We reached the small clearing near the northern end of the woods, and we found her there.

They still don't know how she escaped from Golden Sunset at night, without anyone noticing. One security camera facing the corridor was malfunctioning; the rest had failed to catch any glimpse of her. The security guard on duty claimed he had been awake the whole night but had noticed nothing. The police said there would be no investigation, given that she was an old patient from an Alzheimer's ward, suffering additionally from an inoperable brain tumor. No family members were asking for an autopsy. They assumed she had died of hypothermia: at night the outdoor temperature could drop as low as two degrees Celsius. She had on only a thin white patient gown, and a pair of rubber sandals, no socks. They closed the case as an unfortunate accident.

When we found her body in the clearing I was in shock, but I didn't show it as much as I normally would because, surprisingly, Director Haam seemed to be in a much worse state. It was the first time I'd seen her showing up at work with no makeup. A couple of her red nails were chipped. Her eyes were swollen. I had never seen her cry before; her body shook and so did her voice. I came to her and whispered in her ear she shouldn't feel guilty for any of it. It was inevitable, and there was nothing we could have done differently. "You knew Ms Mook," I told her. "She always had her way, one way or another."

Holding Haam in my arms, I turned around to find Ms Hwang.

She was standing behind the group of police officers, crying, leaning against Nurse Docgo. Her sobs were higher pitched than her usual mezzo-soprano voice, and Nurse

Docgo had to hug her and rock her like a baby to calm her down. Ms Hwang's shock and grief didn't seem feigned, so I put my initial suspicion aside: that she might have helped Ms Mook with this last plan of hers.

Another surprise arrived that very afternoon.

Around four p.m. a young couple showed up at Golden Sunset. A Korean woman and a foreign man. The man caught the attention of everyone: a public nursing home in the Korean countryside isn't a place where you normally expect to see a Caucasian. The man was very tall and darkly handsome. His attire couldn't have been more generic – a pair of dark beige cotton pants, black leather shoes, and a slim black bubble jacket – but he stood out like a black swan among its white siblings. The two young female receptionists at Golden Sunset, craning their necks, murmured to each other how tall and good-looking the foreigner was.

The woman next to him invited only a belated glance. *She's rather ordinary-looking.* The disappointed whispers of the receptionists were tinged with jealousy. Standing beside her man she seemed short and plain. As the couple walked slowly toward me, however, I realized the woman wasn't small: she was at least a dozen centimeters taller than I. She was wearing dark blue jeans, a black trench coat and a gray scarf. Undyed black hair bobbed around her earlobes. No makeup. They were people who weren't fond of drawing attention, I could tell, but who inevitably did in the end.

She had overwhelming cheekbones and a nose too small to be considered pretty. Not a typical beauty by Korean standards. Still, I was charmed by her – it must have been the way she carried her slender body, swift and graceful, like a greyhound. Briskly she extended her hand toward me and told me that her name was Mihee, the way Americans would introduce themselves in a movie. And yet her voice was soft and her Seoul accent flawless, so I didn't think she was Korean American. But I wondered why she chose to come to me among all of the six staff members lingering in the lobby. I happened to be the highest in rank (the others were young receptionists and middle-aged nursing assistants) but I was usually the last person who gave off the ambience of authority. Regardless of my bafflement, the young woman continued to speak: "I came for Ms Mook Miran. I'm her daughter."

The air of Golden Sunset froze for a few breaths.

The buoyant smile on the young woman's face was telling me that she hadn't come ready for the funeral.

The couple was kept waiting in the office of Director Haam.

I had never seen Director Haam so frazzled. Although a big woman with wide shoulders, Haam looked small that day. The series of unexpected discoveries had beaten her down. On the verge of crying, Haam told me she hadn't known about this at all – this daughter of Ms Mook sitting in her office with her American husband – and I believed her: she seemed more stunned than I was.

Haam begged me to help her. She wanted me to go into the office and talk to the couple. I was the closest to Ms Mook, she said, and the last person who'd talked to her before she died. To my surprise I found myself walking into the room without much hesitation, even though I knew agreeing to be the spokesperson meant having to break the sad news to them. Scared as I was, though, I was burning to know the daughter of Ms Mook.

Delicate fingers, such a fine-boned woman. I was at first afraid the news might cause this brittle lady to break down in front of me, rupturing my dam of emotion as well, which I'd been holding up so well for the entire day. But she took it better than most of us at Golden Sunset. For the first few seconds she seemed petrified. Not a sound or movement escaped her. When her hands began to stir, I anticipated the outburst, but she shut her eyes tightly, as though in prayer. The big dark eyes of her husband grew moist instead. He put one hand on the small of her back, the other grabbed her fingers. The sight made me feel lonely. And relieved. I knew Ms Mook would have felt the same, watching her daughter and her man in their quiet togetherness.

Mihee's soft chuckles broke the silence. "This is typical of her," she murmured to herself, shaking her head mildly from side to side. A sad smile broke on her lips. "You're Ms Lee Sae-ri, aren't you? Her biographer." Mihee narrowed her eyes at me. Her arm propped up on the table, she briefly lifted her index and middle finger, as if holding an invisible cigarette. She wasn't exactly a spitting image of Ms Mook, but they shared the same mannerisms. Quick movements of hands, the quiet tone of her voice, the subdued laughs and sighs. The same offbeat charm.

I wanted to confess I wasn't really a biographer but an unknown obituarist, yet I didn't feel it was the right moment to contradict her, so I stayed silent.

"By now you must know as much about her as I do," said Mihee, "Don't you, Ms Lee?"

"Apparently no," I answered truthfully. But I couldn't bring myself to tell her that I hadn't even fully believed in Mihee's existence till now. I told her instead I hadn't known she was coming.

"Did Ms Mook know you're coming?" I asked her.

Mihee snorted – the exact sound of her mother. "What do you think?" She raised her fingers again, arching her eyebrows. "Of course she knew."

I told her about the seven notebooks Ms Mook had given me the day before.

"Did she tell you to change all the names of the characters?" Mihee asked.

I answered no.

"See?" said Mihee, shutting her eyes. "She would have asked you to change the names first, if she'd been intending to stay put. She knew what she was doing."

Her voice trailed off. She covered her face with both hands. She took a few deep breaths and put her hands back on the table. No tears, but her eyes had turned quite red. She then whispered to her husband in Korean that she would like to talk to me in private. "Of course you should," answered her husband, to my surprise in faultless Korean. Before exiting he pulled her close to him and kissed her temple for long seconds.

"I came here today for the purpose of bringing my mother home with us, to America," Mihee confessed, with a small groan. "And she knew about it. I couldn't come to see her here before, due to our unusual circumstances, as you know, but we've been talking to each other regularly."

With her cellphone, I thought, which the police couldn't retrieve. I silently searched her body and then the whole clearing site, but I too had failed to find it.

"After we made our decision in South Korea to turn ourselves in, we stayed underground. After the turn-in, even lower. I moved to America with my American husband. We waited till I got my citizenship and I would be able to invite my mother legally to live with us in the US. That was how we wanted things now, *clean and legal*, because we were so sick of living under the radar for so long. When she told me about the tumor, I said it didn't matter. I said she would be with us anyhow, as long as she was alive, breathing."

Mihee jerked her head away from me and faced the side wall of the office, which was covered with paintings of Director Haam's children.

"Mom loved Aram so much, her grandson." Mihee couldn't keep the quiver from her voice, even though she was still fighting off her tears. "I knew she wasn't very keen to leave Korea. I knew she didn't want to move to another foreign country at her age. She was afraid she would end up being a burden to us. I thought once she was there with us she would feel differently. But the only positive thing she could say when we talked about the plan was 'Well, it will be nice to see Aram every day.'"

Her head sank onto her chest. She brought her hands together and put them between her open knees. As if she was apologizing.

"Mom knew it," she said, under her breath. "She knew. That under my watch she could never have pulled off anything like this."

Mihee stayed quiet, motionless for a moment. Then she summoned a labored smile on her face. Her bloodshot eyes gleamed with the effort. "Having me here, crying all over the place, is the last thing she would have wanted," she said, sniffling. "She couldn't handle sentimentality so well. She didn't like showing it, and couldn't stand witnessing it in others. Including me, even."

A nostalgic laugh escaped her.

"The only exception was Dad. There was no limit to the sentimentality between them. I had never seen a couple so physical and emotional toward one another in North Korea. They even got arrested once, for an offense against public decency. Because they were holding hands in public, in Pyongyang in the sixties." Mihee's eyes welled up but she was smiling.

"Mom mentioned Dad's death only once, when she was breaking the news to me. She never brought it up again. She felt guilty that while we were living here in the South under different names, he had died alone in North Korea."

"You think she chose to do the same, die alone, to punish herself?" I asked her.

Mihee was silent. With the palm of her hand she rubbed teardrops off her cheeks, hiding her eyes for a couple of seconds.

"I don't think so," I said to myself.

Eyes pink, she stared at me without a word.

"That could have been a reason, I'm not sure. But that can't be *the* reason." Of the latter, I was certain.

I asked her if she, too, had geophagy, wondering whether the condition ran in the family.

Her eyes went blank at first, then gave way to a little frown of puzzlement. I realized she didn't know what the word meant. So I explained it to her.

She answered no, and said she was adopted, so she couldn't know if it was hereditary. She whispered that she hadn't known her mother had this condition, that she'd never told her about it.

Mihee wasn't really wrong about one thing: I might have known Ms Mook quite well, even better than I had thought. How strange is human intimacy, I pondered. How we could sometimes confide in strangers and entrust them with secrets we couldn't reveal to those who are closest to us. I felt a sudden ache in my bones, a surge of longing. I would miss Ms Mook.

I asked Mihee if she was ready to go to see her mother's body.

People say that you are what you eat. Ms Mook had tasted and swallowed the earth of various places she had been to. So, not only had she been many different persons, she had also been many different places.

She said the earth of Paju reminded her of her North Korean hometown. Paju is so close to North Korea that on quiet days you can still hear the North Korean propaganda speakers blare their obsolete promises, their bygone glory. A place of the past to which one cannot return.

When I asked Mihee if she was ready to see her mother's body, Mihee said I should first tell her how she'd looked when we found her. She asked me to describe it to her in its entirety, no sugarcoating. "My mama raised me strong," she said. "I can handle the truth."

So I told her the truth, just as I saw it.

We found her in the small clearing within the grove of tall birch trees.

The wind was blowing from the north again, and I thought I smelled a whiff of sunbathing garbage. But then it turned into something else as I stepped closer, as I knelt down beside her body. The smell both strange and familiar. The closest scent I could use to describe it was that of *Yoolmoo-cha*, Korean tea made from Job's tears. That opaque cereal tea, so thick and milky it sometimes feels like porridge slipping down your throat. The consoling aroma of cream and nuts. That was the irony of *sanak, sweet and repulsive.* The scent was wafting up from her mouth and both hands. Under her fingernails there were tiny dark sickles of green.

Her limbs sprawled over the green ground. The big white shock of her hair, nestled around her sleeping head, looked like a pillow made of snow. The peaceful abandonment of a child in her bed, her arms and legs moving over the snow to draw the shape of a butterfly, before she surrendered to sleep.

I crouched lower, then looked up to the sky.

It was cyanide-blue, cloudless and completely open on all sides. The weather had been like this for the past couple of days, so she must have enjoyed a perfect star-studded night sky. Between her slightly parted lips, I saw the tip of her chipped front tooth. The corners of her mouth were subtly lifted, as if in a smile. This trapped the scars on her cheeks in the vertical wrinkles for good – a pair of tattooed dimples.

When nobody was watching, I opened her mouth a little wider as gently as possible.

And there it was – her tongue.

The no-holds-barred trickster that had gotten her through one life after another.

As expected, it was coated with a coarse layer of earth, like sour sanding on a candy.

Acknowledgements

Many of the events in this novel did happen, although I took liberties with chronology and details. *Storytellers* was inspired by stories of Comfort Station survivors, especially those shown in Chung Seo-woon's *Herstory*, *Song of a Butterfly* by Chung Ki-young, and *Spirits' Homecoming* by Cho Jung-rae. For certain details regarding lives in North Korea and espionage, I turned to *Nothing to Envy* by Barbara Demick, *The Girl with Seven Names* by Hyeonseo Lee, *The Spy and the Traitor* by Ben Macintyre, and *Your Republic Is Calling You* by Kim Young-ha. The premise of imposture in *Me, Myself, and Mole* was inspired by the famous true story of Arnaud du Tilh.

Several chapters of this novel have been published in American literary journals as short stories. *Virgin Ghost on North Korean Border* appeared in *Meridian*, Summer 2018. *When I Stopped Eating Earth* appeared in *Black Warrior Review*, Fall/Winter 2019. *Storyteller* appeared in *Pleiades*, Winter 2020. *Bring Down the House* appeared in *Shenandoah*, Fall 2020. *Me, Myself, and Mole* appeared in *the Massachusetts Review*, Fall 2021.

Thank you to my agent Nicki Richesin; my editor

Anna Kelly from Virago, and its amazing team including Zoe Carroll and Hazel Orme; Mary Gaule and Emma Kupor from Harper; Erin Wicks, Jenny Meyer and the great team of Wendy Sherman Associates including Callie Deitrick and Heidi Gall, Page Richards and Brittani Sonnenberg; my North-Korean defector friends from Seoul Church, and Joo-myeong.

Thank you to my daughter and my son, my parents and Jonafe, my uncle Kim Jin-soo and my aunt Lee Jeom-soon, my late grandmother Kim Nam-soon, and my late great-aunt Kim Byeong-nyeo whose journey inspired this novel.

Finally, thank you, as always, to my husband.